KAREN KIRST

The Sheriff's Christmas Twins

HARLEQUIN® LOVE INSPIRED® HISTORICAL

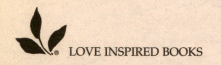 LOVE INSPIRED BOOKS

Recycling programs for this product may not exist in your area.

ISBN-13: 978-0-373-28379-8

The Sheriff's Christmas Twins

Copyright © 2016 by Karen Vyskocil

www.Harlequin.com

Printed in U.S.A.

For I am convinced that neither death nor life, neither angels nor demons, neither the present nor the future, nor any powers, neither height nor depth, nor anything else in all creation will be able to separate us from the love of God that is in Christ Jesus our Lord.
—*Romans* 8:38–39

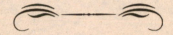

To Teresa Bensch, sweet cousin and friend.

And to editor extraordinaire Emily Rodmell.
Your guidance makes all the difference.

Chapter One

December 1886
Gatlinburg, Tennessee

"We have a situation at the mercantile, Sheriff."

Shane Timmons set the law journal aside and reached for his gun belt.

The banker held up his hand. "You won't be needing that. This matter requires finesse, not force."

"What's happened?" His chair scraped across the uneven floor as he stood and picked up his Stetson. "Did Quinn catch a kid filching penny candy?"

"I suggest you come and see for yourself."

Unaccustomed to seeing Claude Jenkins flustered, Shane's curiosity grew as he shrugged on his coat and followed him outside into the crisp December day. Pedestrians intent on starting their holiday shopping early crowded the boardwalks. Those shopkeepers who hadn't already decorated their storefronts were draping the windows and doors in ivy and holly garlands. On the opposite side of the street, they passed a vendor hawking roasted chestnuts, calling forth memories of bitter Norfolk, Virginia, winters and a young boy's futile longing for a single bag of the toasty treat.

Shane tamped down the unpleasant memories and continued on to the mercantile. Half a dozen trunks were piled beside the entrance. Unease pulled his shoulder blades together as if connected by invisible string. His visitors weren't due for three more days. He did a quick scan of the street, relieved there was no sign of the stagecoach.

Claude held the door and waited for him to enter first. The pungent stench of paint punched him in the chest. The stove-heated air was heavy and made his eyes water. Too many minutes in here and a person could get a headache. The proprietor, Quinn Darling, hadn't mentioned plans to renovate. The first day of December and unofficial kickoff to the holiday fanfare was a terrible time to start.

His gaze swept the deserted sales counter and aisles before landing on a knot of men and women in the far corner.

"Why didn't you watch where you were going? Where are your parents?"

"I—I'm terribly sorry, ma'am," came the subdued reply. "My ma's at the café. She gave me permission to come see the new merchandise."

"This is what happens when children are allowed to roam through the town unsupervised."

Shane rounded the aisle and wove his way through the customers, stopping short at the sight of statuesque, matronly Gertrude Messinger, a longtime Gatlinburg resident and wife of one of the gristmill owners, doused in green liquid. While her upper half remained untouched, her full skirts and boots were streaked with paint. Beside her, ashen and bug-eyed, stood thirteen-year-old Eliza Smith.

"Quinn Darling," Gertrude's voice boomed with outrage. "I expect you to assign the cost of a new dress to the Smiths' account."

At that, Eliza's freckles stood out in stark contrast to her skin.

"One moment, if you will, Mr. Darling," a third person chimed in. "The fault is mine, not Eliza's."

The voice put him in mind of snow angels and piano recitals and cookies swiped from silver platters. But it couldn't belong to Allison Ashworth. She and her brother, George, wouldn't arrive until Friday. Seventy-two more hours until his past collided with his present.

He wasn't ready.

His old friend, George Ashworth, had written months ago expressing the wish to spend Christmas with him. He'd agreed, of course—it had been years since he'd seen George and longer still since he'd clapped eyes on Allison. As tempted as he'd been to deny the siblings, the memory of their father and his generosity had prevented him.

Edging two steps to his left, Shane gained a clear view of the unidentified female. His jaw sagged. Gertrude Messinger should consider herself fortunate because this woman had suffered the brunt of the mishap. The oily green mixture covered her from head to toe. Her face was a monochrome mask. Only her eyes—the color of emeralds and glittering with indignation—and lips were untouched.

Gertrude stared. "That girl was right beneath the ladder when it happened."

She put a protective hand on Eliza's shoulder. "That may be so, but I believe it was my foot that snagged the ladder and caused the can to tip over. I offer you my sincere apology. And of course, I'll make reparations for the damage."

"Your apology doesn't change the fact I'm standing here dripping in paint!"

"See what I mean?" Claude leaned close to murmur in Shane's ear.

As a lawman, his duties ranged from unpleasant to exasperating to downright perilous. This sort of dilemma was far from typical.

Quinn held his hands out in a placating gesture. "I regret this incident ever happened, ladies. It was my hired man who left the unopened can on the ladder unattended. I'll pay for cleaning services, as well as provide enough store credit for replacement fabric and shoes, hats, ribbons. Whatever you need."

The older woman glared down her patrician nose. "This dress is beyond saving. Besides, how am I to be expected to walk the streets looking like this?" Spotting Shane, she summoned him with an imperious flick of her fingers. "It's about time you got here, Sheriff. I want this woman arrested."

Eliza and the stranger gasped in unison. Moving closer to Quinn, Shane was careful to avoid the oozing globs on the gleaming floorboards. Belatedly removing his hat, he addressed Mrs. Messinger.

"And what, exactly, am I to charge her with?"

"Public mischief."

The stranger ripped her gaze from Shane to gape at the older woman. "I am not a criminal."

"Your clumsy disregard for your surroundings is a danger to others."

"I believe that's exaggerating things a bit, Mrs. Messinger," Quinn intervened. To the other woman, he said, "What did you say your name was, ma'am?"

She shrunk back. Even with her features concealed, Shane sensed her distress. His senses sharpened. Years of dealing with those who disregarded the law had nourished his already suspicious nature. Was she hiding something?

A blob of paint dripped from her chin and splattered on the floor. "Introductions can wait, wouldn't you agree? Do you have a place where I can clean up in private?"

"My wife's seamstress shop is in the back. Nicole will

provide you with something suitable to change into," Quinn offered.

Her gaze slid to Shane and then darted to the side. Definitely suspicious. When she started to move away, he clamped a hand on her arm. "You're not going anywhere until you state your name and business here."

"I see you still enjoy being difficult, Shane Timmons," she challenged, eliciting gasps from the spectators.

He released her at once. He should've heeded his initial response. Her voice had been familiar for a reason. The strands of her hair that weren't coated in paint seemed to pulse with the sun's rays. Those distinctive flaxen locks, combined with wide green eyes and crimson lips, reminded him of Christmases past. Bittersweet holidays with a temporary family that had magnified his outsider status.

"Allison. You're early."

A single, green-tinted eyebrow lifted. "After more than a decade apart, that's the only thing you can think of to say?"

The tips of his ears burned. The crowd pressed closer, no doubt delighted by this unexpected turn of events. He hadn't divulged much about his past. Wasn't anything to boast about.

Wesley, one of the new shop assistants and most likely the reason for this debacle, appeared with a damp cloth. She thanked him with a graciousness that attested to her generosity of spirit, one of a dozen admirable traits he'd witnessed during his time at Ashworth House.

He was suddenly tongue-tied, as if he were fourteen again and being introduced to his new sister of sorts for the first time. David Ashworth had brought Shane to live with him and his children—sixteen-year-old George and twelve-year-old Allison—in their grand estate located on exclusive Peyton Avenue. While George had been cautiously welcoming, Allison had greeted him like a long-lost friend. He hadn't known what to make of the effervescent, fair-haired dynamo. Still didn't apparently.

"Um, welcome to Gatlinburg?"

This wasn't how she'd envisioned her first encounter with Shane Timmons.

Allison was supposed to be showing her former infatuation how mature and sophisticated she'd become. Shane was supposed to take one look at her and regret all those times he'd dismissed her as unworthy of his friendship. Nothing in her imaginings had prepared her for this!

A rogue drop rolled to her eyebrow, and she hurriedly swiped at it, refusing to look down to inventory the damage to her person. She might be tempted to cry.

The distinguished, raven-haired store owner looked confused. "You know her?"

Another man peeked around Shane's shoulder. "You're the sheriff's first visitor. Not a single soul has come to see him in all these years."

A third person piped up. "How do you know each other?"

"Is she a special lady friend, Sheriff?"

The skin around his right eye twitched. It used to do that when he was annoyed.

"Go on about your business, folks," he instructed without taking his eyes off her. "Nothing more to see here."

Most everyone shuffled to various sections of the mercantile, only pretending to shop. Quinn led a protesting Mrs. Messinger to the shelves containing the fabric bolts and began pointing out selections. Eliza lingered.

"Th-thank you, Miss Ashworth."

"You've nothing to thank me for, Eliza." She smiled for the girl's benefit. "Hopefully the next time we meet will be under better circumstances."

Dipping her head, she rushed for the exit. Allison wished

she could follow her. How ridiculous she must look! Beneath the paint, her cheeks burned with humiliation. At least that was hidden from his view.

"I wasn't expecting you until Friday," Shane accused in a strained voice. "Where's George? Clarissa and the kids? I thought you were all set to travel together."

After all this time, Allison had expected at the very least a polite welcome. Disappointment compounded her embarrassment. "Do you mind if we discuss this after I've cleaned up?" She indicated the damp cloth. "I'd like to get this off before it dries."

Shane took hold of her arm again and, keeping a more-than-was-required amount of space between them, maneuvered her between the counters and into a darkened hallway.

Unable to deny herself the pleasure, she drank in his profile. The boyish appeal she remembered was a thing of the past. His features were lean and taut, his cheekbones more defined, his jaw a line of defiance. His piercing azure eyes emitted a subtle but very real warning—don't come too close, don't try to unearth buried secrets, don't cross the line of separation he maintained between himself and the rest of the world. Framed by a light beard, even his mouth appeared hard. Sculpted and slightly fuller than many men's, Shane's was set in a perpetual frown.

He was the type of man who expected bad things to happen. Thanks to his poor excuse for a mother, he'd long ago lost the ability to look for good in the world. The hope she'd harbored that he had overcome his unfortunate beginnings flickered out.

At the end of the hallway, one door appeared to exit the building and another led to the seamstress shop. He rapped lightly before swinging it open. The woman who greeted them was everything Allison was not—statuesque, slender and in possession of the beauty that inspired men to pen sonnets. With inky black curls, flawless skin and unusual violet eyes, Nicole Darling must've had scads of men making fools of themselves in order to win her favor. Allison had long ago accepted that she didn't have that effect. Most men liked her. The problem was they saw her as a chum, not a potential wife. The handful that had been interested in her romantically over the years hadn't been able to measure up to the one who'd deemed her irrelevant.

Nicole's sincere greeting faltered when her gaze encountered Allison. Her shock was quickly masked, but it made Allison dread peering into a mirror. Shane explained what had happened and left to fetch a wagon in which to load her trunks.

Contrary to her composed demeanor, Nicole turned out to be gracious and kind. She assisted Allison out of her ruined dress and located a cleaning solution that rid her skin of most of the paint. Washing her hair would have to wait until she reached the house Shane had arranged for her and her family to rent. Nicole riffled through the racks of clothing and found a plain black skirt and matching gray-and-black-striped blouse that a customer had decided against purchasing. The skirt was several inches too short and the blouse fit her like a circus tent. Fortunately, the cape Nicole lent her covered the ill-fitting clothes. Shane was pacing the hallway by the time she was presentable. Well, as presentable as she possibly could be.

His gaze swept her up and down, his thoughts a mystery. "The wagon's this way."

Instead of heading to the mercantile's main entrance, he led her out the rear exit and down a steep flight of stairs. The deserted lane was edged by a wide, fast-moving river over mossy rocks of varying size. The opposite bank was a steep, tree-covered hill. Most of the trees were forlorn versions of themselves, their twisted branches bare, but plenty of pines and other evergreens were sprinkled throughout.

She surveyed the team of fine-looking horses hitched to the wagon. Their giant hooves stamped the winter-hardened earth and their breaths created white clouds. At the stairs' base, she took a moment to inspect the shops' rear facades and the livery beside the mercantile.

"Is this where the deliveries are made?"

He nodded and, giving her a boost onto the high seat, circled the horses and climbed up beside her. "I thought this route would be less of a hassle."

"Meaning, you'd rather no one else see us together quite yet," she retorted, old hurts rising to the surface.

He grimaced. "You've no idea what small towns are like. Every bit of news is blown out of proportion. I can guarantee half the town will have us engaged by nightfall."

Engaged to Shane Timmons? A fluttering sensation flared in her middle, one she resolutely ignored. Once upon a time, she'd been enamored with this man and desperate for his approval—something he'd never offered.

"You wouldn't have to dodge their questions if you'd simply told them about us."

"I considered it." With reins in hand, he called a sharp command and the conveyance jerked into motion. "My friends, the O'Malleys, know our history. I told them that I lived with you and George for a time."

"Do they know why?"

His lips pursed. "Only that my mother couldn't care for me."

"You mean *wouldn't.*"

His eyes turned stormy, and she regretted her words. She allowed herself to study his uncompromising jawline and the strong cords of his neck visible above his coat collar.

He turned his head slightly. "What?"

"Nothing. I'm simply adjusting to the fact that I'm actually here with you."

A vein in his temple throbbed.

"Not here *with* you," she amended. "Here in the same state. The same town, even. I wasn't sure I'd ever see you again, to be honest. You weren't planning to return to Virginia, were you?"

"There's nothing for me there."

Allison winced. One thing about Shane, he didn't mince words to spare her feelings. "Your home is there."

"Ashworth House was not my home."

Because you wouldn't let it be, she was tempted to retort.

She could still recall the moment her father had relayed the news that a young employee of his, an orphan in desperate need of assistance, was coming to live with them. While George had been resistant to the idea, Allison had seen an opportunity to help someone less fortunate. She'd been excited about having another sibling. Older and of a serious bent, George was no longer interested in her childish pursuits. But then Shane moved in and it soon became apparent that he didn't trust either of them. What Allison had never been able to fathom was why Shane had tolerated George, who did little to encourage a relationship, and yet rebuffed her attempts at friendship.

During the five years that he lived with them, she'd tried to earn his confidence, a bit of her heart breaking with each fresh rejection. He hadn't been unkind…just resolute in his indifference. Shane had tolerated her as if she were an annoying puppy begging for scraps of affection.

Shane hadn't liked her. It appeared he still didn't.

Ignoring the pinch of sadness, she resolved to make the best of her time in Tennessee. She was here for the month of December, the most exciting weeks of the entire year. She wasn't about to let a surly lawman spoil her Christmas.

Chapter Two

He hadn't meant to hurt her feelings. Shane noticed the resignation in her eyes before she averted her face. His commitment to speak the truth, a product of having lived with a drunken mother who'd thought nothing of making promises she didn't intend to keep, sometimes made things difficult for others.

He guided the horses onto a rutted lane flanked by trees. The prickly air stole beneath his collar, making him long for his office and a mountain-sized cup of hot coffee.

"Why did you come alone?" he said.

"That wasn't my plan, trust me. A problem arose in our Riverside factory the evening before our departure, and George had to postpone his journey. He insisted I come on ahead so that you wouldn't be disappointed." She said that last bit with a touch of sarcasm. "He suggested Clarissa and the children come with me, but she preferred to wait and travel with him. She didn't want to risk spending the holidays apart."

From George's missives over the years, Shane had learned that his friend had married Clarissa Smothers. Their union was marked with respect, commitment and love. He was happy for George. If he experienced a twinge of envy whenever he read about their life together, he made sure not to dwell on it.

That George had been delayed was not welcome news. He and his brood were supposed to provide a buffer. Without them, Shane had no choice but to interact with Allison. He'd be responsible for getting her settled, seeing to her comfort, entertaining her.

"Did he say when he might arrive?"

"He promised to right matters as quickly as possible and send a telegram letting us know his arrival date."

They traveled up a shallow incline. The Wattses' farm came into view, and Allison sat up straighter, her lips parting at the sight. Satisfaction raced through him. He'd always admired this particular homestead. When he'd heard the owners would be spending their holiday in another state, he'd approached them about renting it for his visitors.

Situated in the middle of a clearing, the white clapboard farmhouse with green shutters and shingled roof stood framed by forested hills that gave way to steep mountains. A fallow vegetable garden was situated on the right, a modest-sized barn behind that. The corncrib, smokehouse and toolshed had been built alongside a snake-and-rail fence.

"Oh, Shane, this is such a charming place. How many bedrooms does it have?"

"Four. George assured me that would be plenty."

"It will do nicely. The three older children will want to be together, and George Jr. will stay with his parents. Thank you for making the arrangements."

"The Wattses decided to spend this winter with their son and his family in South Carolina. They were pleased it wouldn't be left empty."

He slowed the wagon to a halt directly in front of the house. Quickly descending, he walked to her side and helped her down, reminded again how he'd always towered over her, taller, bulkier, stronger. She'd complained about her diminutive stature and healthy figure, but compared to him, she was dainty. If he was of a mind to, he'd have no problem tossing her over his shoulder and carrying her about without working up a sweat.

From the start, Allison had evoked a powerful desire to protect and shield. A startling and unusual reaction for a boy who'd only ever looked out for himself.

As her soles reached the brown, patchy grass, her fingers tightened where they rested on his shoulders. He examined her uplifted face, taking note of her fuller lips, more pronounced cheekbones, creamy, dew-kissed skin. The years had been kind to her.

He'd recently passed his thirty-second birthday, which meant she'd soon be thirty. *Thirty.* It hardly seemed possible. In his mind, she'd remained forever seventeen—naive, optimistic, generous to a fault and completely unaware of her allure.

She took hold of his right hand and, snatching off his buckskin glove without permission, examined his palm. "I'm glad there's nothing wrong with your hand."

"Why would there be?"

"I thought you might've injured it and that was why you didn't write to me."

The arrow hit its mark. "I'm not much of a writer."

Her jutting chin challenged him. "You wrote to my brother."

"I couldn't ignore his letters."

"And yet you had no problem ignoring mine."

Her crushed velvet gloves caressed his knuckles. He frowned at the pleasurable sensation. "I didn't get any from you."

"I wrote you. Once." She released him.

"I'm sorry, Allison. I never received it."

She reached past him and retrieved her leather satchel. "It's all right. I doubt you would've answered me, anyway."

Shane stood mute as she spun, her too-large cape scraping the ground, and marched to the porch. He'd wondered if she'd changed in the intervening years since he'd seen her. Here was his answer. The old Allison wouldn't have uttered such a thing to him. She wouldn't have voiced what they both knew—he treated her differently than everyone else.

It wasn't fair. Or rational. The knowledge didn't, wouldn't, change his behavior. The reason he'd kept his distance and hadn't initiated contact with her after he left was simple—the part of him that his father's abandonment and mother's reprehensible behavior hadn't managed to blacken with disillusionment and pain, the part protected and nourished by hope, whispered lies whenever she was near.

The first lie had come the moment he met her. *Here is a girl you can trust. She wants to be your friend. Let her in.*

Thankfully, he'd recognized the untruth immediately and had taken action to thwart her efforts. More lies followed as the years passed, tempting him to relax his guard and give her a chance. He'd resisted. Better to hurt her feelings temporarily than to destroy her life with his cynicism and bitterness.

She was going to have to be more circumspect. Letting Shane know how his ongoing disregard had wounded her was not in the plan. It wouldn't be easy, but she was determined to present a friendly yet indifferent front. She could be kind without being too personal…if she really, really tried.

Allison had a good life. A loving family. Wonderful friends. Satisfying work. A supportive church. He didn't need to know that she ached for a husband and babies to love. He would never know that sometimes, when she was alone, she'd daydream about a different life, one in which he had top billing. Her favorite recurring dream featured Shane at Ashworth House, begging her forgiveness and professing his undying devotion. She especially relished the apology bit—finally hearing an explanation for his dislike would be most satisfying.

"Allison?"

She turned from the bench swing. By the look on his face, this wasn't the first time he'd called her name. "Sorry. I was woolgathering."

He waited for her to enter first. Pulling her cape panels closer together, she wandered about the room, studying photographs of the elderly couple who'd built a life here. They looked like nice, hardworking people. Their home was tidy, the furniture in good condition, handmade rugs, curtains and a quilt thrown over the sofa back providing splashes of bright color. The window views were like paintings of pastoral perfection. She could easily envision the landscape's beauty during spring, summer and autumn.

"When George told me you'd moved here, I purchased a book about Tennessee. The photographs don't do it justice."

Crouched at the fireplace, he arranged a pile of kindling. "You should see the mountains when it snows."

"Is it likely to while I'm here?"

"Hard to say." He lifted his shoulder, causing the brown duster to bunch between his shoulder blades. "The winters are unpredictable. Some years we hardly get any. Others we get snow and ice."

"I hope it does. My niece and nephews would enjoy a white Christmas."

"As would you," he observed.

"I won't deny it."

She recalled the first winter he'd spent with them. He'd been walking alone in the estate garden, as was his custom, and had come upon her making snow angels. She'd implored him to join her. He'd gone so far as to lie in the snow beside her when he'd suddenly jumped up and stormed off. It was as if he wouldn't allow himself to experience even a moment's joy.

"Promise me something. If it snows before I leave, promise you'll make snow angels with me. Just once."

He pivoted slightly in order to stare at her over his shoulder. "I'm a grown man, Allison."

"Are you immune to a little fun, Sheriff?"

He blinked at her use of his title. "Life isn't about fun. It's about duty and hard work and being a responsible citizen."

"You don't believe that." Surely he didn't.

The wood in the stacked-stone fireplace glowed orange as the flames took hold. Waving out the match, Shane discarded it. "It's not a tragedy."

"The tragedy is you don't recognize what you're missing."

With a noncommittal grunt, he removed his wheat-colored hat and balanced it atop the caramel-and-white-print sofa. He finger-combed his short locks into place. His hair changed with the seasons—sun-kissed blond in spring and summer and dark honey in the colder months. She hadn't seen him with a beard before. She wasn't sure she liked it. The stubble made him seem even more stern, more remote, than she remembered. One side of his coat gaped open, and the badge pinned to his dark vest glinted. Considering his profession, looking dangerous and formidable was no doubt a good thing.

"What about you?"

Allison had drifted to the dining room threshold. Gripping the doorjamb, she turned back to find he hadn't moved.

"What about me?"

"From what George tells me, you make little time for fun yourself."

Astonishment arrowed through her. "What did he say?"

"That you've been working for the company for nearly a decade. You're good at what you do, and the employees respect you. However, he's worried that between your work, charity organizations and the time you spend doting on his kids, you're neglecting your personal happiness."

"He's never indicated such a thing to me."

"Are his concerns well-founded?"

"Of course not."

He advanced toward her, stopping in the middle of the multicolored rug. "Why aren't you married? I thought for sure one of your many admirers would've snatched you up as soon as you were of age."

She considered how to answer. Admitting that no man could hold a candle to the enigmatic, hurting young man he'd once been was out of the question.

"I could ask the same of you. You're thirty-two and still unwed."

"I'm not the marrying kind, and we both know it. You, on the other hand, were born to be a wife and mother." As soon as he'd said the words, color etched his sharp cheekbones. "You know what? Forget I asked. It's none of my business."

"It's all right." Some part of her that yet smarted from his rejection prompted her to reveal the next part. "In truth, there is someone special. His name is Trevor Langston. As soon as I return to Virginia, I'm going to accept his offer of courtship."

She'd resisted for foolish reasons. Coming face-to-face with her past had shown her that. Shane wasn't interested in any sort of relationship. Trevor, on the other hand, had been unwavering in his desire to court her.

Shane's features remained a blank mask, but the skin around his eye twitched. What was he irritated about? He didn't care about her or her life.

"Who is he?" His voice was even. Cool. Unaffected. "Would George approve?"

"My brother is aware of his interest. Trevor works with us. He's a wonderful man. Solicitous, dedicated, too smart for words..." She trailed off, realizing she was describing his assets in terms of his value as a company employee.

"I assume he's from a respectable family?"

"His family and ours have been friends for many years. We met at church, believe it or not. His sister and I have many common interests."

"Does he treat you well?"

She cocked her head to one side. "For someone who hasn't bothered to contact me in more than a decade, you're awfully curious about my romantic prospects. Why is that?"

"No particular reason. If you don't wish to discuss him, we won't."

He started up the stairs. "Come on up and choose your room so I'll know where to put your luggage."

"Wait."

His fingers flexed on the polished banister. He sighed again, something she noticed he did a lot around her. Come to think of it, he used to do it at Ashworth House, too. What about her vexed him so?

Allison went to stand at the base of the stairs, waiting for him to turn and look at her. When he did, she said, "Who his family is doesn't matter to me as much as what kind of man he is. His character. His beliefs."

A muscle jumped in his cheek. "That's nice."

"I'm not finished." Tired of skirting around the issue, she climbed the steps until she was one below him. Standing sideways, he leaned against the wall, aiming for a casual pose that didn't fool her. "You said you're not the marrying kind. Why not?"

He rolled his eyes. "I'm not discussing this right now.

I've got to get you settled and swing by the mercantile for perishables since I didn't have time to stock the kitchen. There's nothing much to eat here, and it's nearly noon."

When he would've continued on upstairs, she put a hand on his forearm. "Allowing your mother's poor decisions and ill treatment to keep you from having a family is wrong, Shane."

His eyes turned flinty. "You've been in town an hour and you're trying to tell me how to live my life? You know nothing about me save for whatever tidbits your brother's told you. So we lived under the same roof for a few years. That doesn't make you an expert on what I need, Allison Ashworth."

Chapter Three

He'd blundered. Again. George would have his hide if he knew.

The image of David Ashworth's craggy face entered his mind, and he felt ashamed. David had extended mercy to Shane when he'd least deserved it—instead of hauling him off to jail for stealing from one of his stores, David had offered him a paying job. And months later, when the older man learned that Shane's mother had died, their home had burned and Shane was sleeping in a makeshift camp at the edge of town, he'd taken him home and made him a part of his family.

Or at least he'd tried. Shane hadn't made it easy.

He threaded his fingers through his hair. "Look, I don't like talking about my past. You know that."

"I remember."

"But that doesn't excuse my rudeness, and I'm sorry. I know how much you enjoy Christmas and all the traditions that go along with it. This is your first holiday in Tennessee, and I want you to have a pleasant visit. So let's agree to leave that particular subject buried, okay?"

She didn't look happy about his request, but she eventually nodded.

The second floor was a few degrees warmer than the first, but that wasn't saying much. He stood against the long interior wall to give her room to navigate the papered hallway and examine the rooms. The color in her cheeks was heightened, due to her vexation with him or the cold, he couldn't determine.

After peeking in all the doorways, she entered the room to the immediate right of the stairs. "I'll take this one. George, Clarissa and George Jr. can be at the opposite end of the hall and the older children next to them."

"Are you still in your old bedroom at home?"

"No. Soon after their engagement, I moved to the third floor."

Hearing the wistfulness in her voice, he said, "You liked that room. You spent hours in the window seat with your books and your diary or simply observing the world from your perch."

"I did like it." An adorable pleat formed between her golden eyebrows. "But having an entire floor to myself suits me. With four children and a passel of staff members in the house, I don't get much privacy."

Removing the borrowed cape, she draped it over the carved footboard. Peering down at her ill-fitting clothes, she shook her head in disgust. Shane watched as she walked to the mirror above the bureau and inspected her disheveled, paint-flecked hair. In the reflective glass, her gaze found his.

"I made sure my arrival didn't go unnoticed, didn't I?"

"At least the color doesn't clash with your hair."

Turning, she attempted to smooth it. "It's still straight as a stick, I'm afraid."

"Curls are overrated."

He hadn't been able to figure out why a girl like Allison would be dissatisfied with her appearance. Her self-consciousness didn't make sense. Her hair was the prettiest color he'd ever seen, her countenance sweet and agreeable.

"I'll bring your trunks up and then heat some water you can use along with the cleaning solution Nicole gave you."

She thanked him with a grateful smile, making him regret his harsh words even more. George had to get here soon. Spending time with her would be a sore test of his endurance.

Pretend she's your sister.

Not a terrible idea, but he'd already tried that. It hadn't worked all those years ago. Now that they were adults, it had even less of a chance of working.

A half hour later, he was checking the foodstuffs and making a mental list of necessary supplies when Allison entered the kitchen. Dressed in her own clothes this time—a charcoal gray skirt and flattering blouse in a bold sapphire hue—she wore her hair loose. Still damp from washing, it hung in a sleek curtain to the middle of her back.

"You don't look a day over seventeen."

Her eyebrows rose a notch, and he wished the words unsaid.

Emitting a brief, disbelieving laugh, she said wryly, "I believe your memories are clouding your judgment."

He pointed out where the supplies and cooking utensils were stored, as well as the kindling for the cast iron stove. Her slight frown surprised him.

"I know it's not as large or efficient as the kitchen at Ashworth House, but it's got everything you need."

"It's not that." She'd removed her gloves in the bedroom, and her small, pale hand skimmed the pie safe's ledge. She moved to examine the stove's cook plates and water reservoir, a dubious expression on her face. "I never learned to cook."

"You don't know how to cook?"

"I've heated water for coffee before. That's the extent of my culinary skills, I'm afraid."

He should've anticipated this. Why would Allison apply herself to such basic chores when there were paid staff members to do it for her?

"You didn't think to bring one of the estate's employees to see to the task?"

"I considered it. However, it is Christmastime and they all have families. I couldn't ask anyone to spend this most special of holidays with me instead of with their loved ones."

Of course she'd consider others' comfort above her own, even if, as in this case, it was impractical.

In the silence stretching between them, her stomach growled loud enough for them both to hear. With a grimace, she pressed her hand against her middle. "Sorry. I skipped breakfast."

Shane felt as if a noose was tightening about his neck. This wasn't how this visit was supposed to go. He'd planned on being polite, yet distant, just like the old days. He and George would catch up while the women were occupied by the children. He wasn't supposed to be responsible for her every need.

"How did you plan to eat?"

"You do have restaurants here, do you not?"

"There's the Plum Café. The quality has gone down in recent months, but the fare's passable. It's closed on Sundays."

"So I'll eat cheese and bread on those days. I'm not spoiled."

"I know that."

The Ashworths had every reason to boast—success, wealth, high standing in society. A devout Christian, David had viewed his accomplishments as blessings from God and considered it his duty to use them to help others. While they hadn't lived meagerly by any means, they hadn't hoarded their wealth. David had taught his children to love Jesus first, others second and themselves last.

"Besides, the children's nanny is coming with Clarissa, and she knows her way around a kitchen. She'll take care of the meals, as well as the holiday baking."

Shane found himself with two equally problematic choices. He could take her to the café and suffer the type of scrutiny he went out of his way to avoid. Or he could stay here in this isolated kitchen with her and fix something. Dodge questions from curious townsfolk or share a private meal with Allison?

In the end, her damp hair was the deciding factor. He couldn't risk her health simply because he was uncomfortable in this quiet house that presented zero opportunities to slink off to a secluded spot like he used to do.

Inspecting the cupboard's contents, he said, "Which one sounds more appealing? Pickled peaches or sweet butter pickles?"

Allison couldn't recall the last time she'd shared a meal with a gentleman. Mealtimes were loud, boisterous affairs in her brother and sister-in-law's home. There were stories, jokes and laughter while the children were in attendance. Once the nanny whisked them upstairs or outside to the gardens for fresh air and exercise, the conversation turned to adult topics such as their family business, society news or happenings in the city.

Not that Shane Timmons fit her view of a gentleman. He was comprised of too many rough edges and dark secrets for that. He neither looked nor acted like the men of her acquaintance. Didn't smell like them, either. The sheriff smelled like long days in the saddle, strong coffee and virile man.

Having removed his outer coat before preparing lunch,

he sat across from her in what must be typical lawman attire—trousers, vest and a long-sleeved, buttoned-up shirt, his sheriff's badge pinned over his heart. His light blue shirt was shot through with pencil-thin navy blue stripes. His vest was a coconut-shell brown that matched his trousers. Both pieces of apparel showcased his upper-body strength. Every time he lifted his coffee cup to his mouth, she watched the play of his biceps.

Before he'd left Norfolk, his physique had been whipcord lean. He'd packed on muscle in the ensuing years, and he looked solid enough to wrestle one of those black bears she'd read inhabited these East Tennessee forests. That, combined with his over six feet of height, made him a formidable adversary for the criminals who dared pass through his town.

"Are you warm enough?" He broke the silence for the first time since he'd said grace.

Heat from the kitchen stove permeated the adjoining dining room through the doorway. Lit candles positioned around the rectangular space added warmth to the ambience even if they didn't emit actual heat. Clouds had rolled in, obscuring the sun and making the candles necessary.

"Yes, thank you."

"I know this isn't what you'd call a substantial meal. As soon as we're done here, I'll leave you to unpack while I make a trip to the mercantile."

"It may not be typical, but it's filling. Besides, now I can say I've tried pickled peaches."

"I'm sure your friends will be impressed," he drawled, his eyes hooded.

Besides the preserved fruit, her plate boasted corn cakes, fried ham slices and sautéed onions. While simple, the food tasted delicious.

She dabbed the napkin to her mouth. "Since I'll be here

the duration of the holiday season, what can I expect in the way of celebrations?"

He lowered his fork. "That's not something I pay much attention to."

"Does the town host a parade?" she prompted. "Are there parties? A tree-lighting ceremony?"

"No parade that I'm aware of. I'm sure there are parties, but I have no idea who hosts them. I'll have to put you in touch with Caroline Turner. Her mother is in charge of Gatlinburg's social events. Either one of them can help you."

Frustration warred with sadness. During his years at Ashworth House, they had done everything possible to include him in their celebrations. He'd stubbornly resisted their efforts.

Folding her hands in her lap, she studied the candlelight flickering over his rugged features. "Do you actually celebrate Christmas, or do you act like it's any other day on the calendar?"

"Apart from the commemoration of Christ's birth, December 25 is like every other day of the year." He sank against the chair, his fingers rubbing circles on the worn tabletop.

Allison wanted to ask if his view of God had changed. While Shane had believed in Him as Creator, he hadn't been able to accept His unconditional love. She struggled to find the right words, and the moment was lost.

"The weeks leading up to it are not special, magical or even particularly pleasant," he said.

"The season is about family and friends, counting your blessings and loving your neighbors."

"Charity should be year-round," he countered.

"I agree. I serve on a church committee that provides for the poor throughout the year. I've witnessed how this season magnifies their lack, however. We have to be diligent to make Christmas extra special, especially for the children."

For a split second, his mouth softened and yearning surged in the azure depths. "Where were people like you when I was a boy?"

Her breath hitched at the glimpse of unexpected vulnerability. He recovered himself all too quickly, face shuttering as he tossed his napkin atop his plate.

"I'll give you a tour of the town so you'll be comfortable navigating it on your own." Pushing to his feet, he stared down at her. "I can't ignore my duties while we wait for George to arrive."

Pricked by his words, she arched a brow. "I don't require constant supervision. I am capable of entertaining myself."

"But not cooking for yourself."

She stood and spread her arms wide. "So teach me."

His head jerked back. "You're not serious."

"We don't truly know how long my brother will be delayed," she said, sweetly. "If the café's food is as mediocre as you say it is, it would be to my benefit to learn the basics."

He put a hand out as if to ward her off. "Allison—"

Pounding on the door startled her. Unruffled, Shane pivoted and strode to pull it open without bothering to inquire who was on the other side.

"Ben."

Hovering in the doorway connecting the dining room to the living room, Allison studied the visitor. A couple of inches shorter than Shane, the attractive, auburn-haired man was broader in the chest and shoulders, his legs like tree trunks. His skin was tan and freckled from the sun, his eyes green like sea glass that sometimes washed up on Norfolk's beaches.

"Sorry to interrupt," he said with a slight grimace. "I heard you had a lady friend in town." His gaze sought out the room behind Shane, flaring when it encountered her. He nodded in greeting.

Shane turned sideways. A draft of cold air traveled through the room, ruffling her skirts. "Ben MacGregor, meet Allison Ashworth."

Swiping his hat off and pressing it against his chest, he sketched a bow. "How do you do, ma'am?"

"Fine, sir. And you?"

"I'd say my day just got brighter now that you're in it." His grin was downright roguish.

She laughed at his outrageousness.

Shane's upper lip curled. "Ben's the resident flirt. He's also my one and only deputy. Did you need something in particular?"

The deputy didn't bother denying Shane's claim, she noticed. His eyes still twinkling, he addressed his boss. "Another fight's broken out over on the Oakley spread. Figured you'd want to ride along with me." He held a gun belt aloft.

"You figured right." Taking it from him, Shane fastened the tooled-leather strip around his waist. "Sorry I can't stay and help you clean up," he told her, his head bent to his task. "I'll come later to deliver the supplies."

Her attention snagged on the menacing-looking pistol on his hip. The pearl handle was worn smooth, the barrel long and skinny.

"I've never held a gun."

Both men stared at her.

"Can I go with you?"

Shane's expression was one of disbelief. "Of course you can't go with me. Why would you ask?"

"You're a lawman now. I'd like to see how you go about upholding the law."

While Ben shifted from one foot to the other, face averted to hide a smile, Shane leveled a formidable glare at her. "Until your brother gets here, you are my responsibility, understand? It's my task to make sure you have your fun." He smirked at the reference to their earlier conversation. "And that you stay safe while doing so."

"But—"

"I mean it, Allison." Putting on his Stetson, he strode for the door. "Don't step foot outside this house until I return."

Without waiting for her response, he joined his deputy on the porch and closed the door behind him, fully expecting her to follow his dictate. Annoyed at his highhandedness—he wasn't her *actual* brother, after all—Allison wondered what would happen if she didn't.

Chapter Four

The house was quiet. Too quiet.

Shane checked the first floor. No sign of Allison. Thinking she might've decided to take a nap after her long journey, he ascended the stairs and peeked into her room. The bed was made, her trunks pushed into a neat row beneath the windows on the far wall. The other bedrooms were also empty.

Determined to unload the supplies as quickly as possible and get back to the jail, impatience jabbed at him as he bypassed the unoccupied outhouse.

Where had she gotten off to?

Intent on scanning the fields to his right, he almost walked smack into the smokehouse. Scowling, he sidestepped and stopped short. A female figure was crouched half inside the smokehouse's squat entrance.

"Allison."

She lurched. Banged her head against the wood. "Ouch!" Scrambling outside, she rubbed the sore spot. "Did you have to startle me like that?"

"I've been searching everywhere for you. You weren't in the house, the barn…" He wasn't about to admit the trepidation that had roared to life inside him. "I thought I told you to stay inside."

"You did." The baleful look she shot him transformed into a grimace. "I'm not one of your locals to boss about, however."

"What were you looking for in there?" He motioned to the smokehouse.

"Nothing. I was simply curious what was inside."

Shane removed his gloves and, stuffing them in his coat pocket, moved to her side. "Let me see."

"I'm fine."

"I'll be the judge of that," he insisted, nudging her hand aside. His fingers gentle on her scalp, he examined the spot. "It didn't break the skin."

She was very close, her round shoulder butting against his chest, the fruity fragrance clinging to her person inviting him closer. She was soft and warm and feminine, traits that were nonexistent in his world of crime and punishment.

"I told you it was nothing," she whispered, her voice off-kilter.

He took a big step back, his huff creating white puffs that hovered in the air. "You've always been a troublesome female, you know that?"

Her chin whipped up. "Excuse me?"

"You kept your father and brother hopping to keep up with your antics. I was thankfully too wise to join in."

"If I was guilty of anything back then, it was trying to be your friend."

Brushing past him in a swirl of petticoats and skirts, she marched in the direction of the house. Smoke curled from both chimneys into the gray sky above. She'd restrained her mane with a single blue ribbon, and the long ponytail bounced with the force of her steps.

He watched her for a moment before going after her, wishing for the first time in a long time that he had the kind of relationship with God that David Ashworth and his friends, the O'Malleys, had. He could sure use some divine help right then. But he'd never gotten over the feeling of abandonment that had taken root in his childhood. His pleas for his pa to come and rescue him, for his ma to truly change, for someone, *anyone*, to help make things better, had gone unanswered. Ignored. So he'd stopped asking.

Catching up to her at the corner of the house, he fell into step beside her, choosing to introduce a whole new subject. The past was a prickly maze of disappointment and confusion. Best to avoid it.

"I think you're gonna like what I brought for you."

"Oh?" She got that gleam in her eye that he didn't trust. "Did you bring me a Christmas tree? A wreath? Greenery to decorate the mantel?"

His pace slowed. "Huh?"

"I think I'd like a cluster of mistletoe, as well. Maybe two."

"What do you need all that for? You're only going to be here a few weeks."

"The most important weeks of the entire year."

"Hold on." He halted beside the wagon bed. "Why would you want mistletoe?"

Her crimson lips curved into a smile that many would find winsome. To him, it meant trouble. "You never know when an eligible suitor might pay me a visit at some point during my stay. Best to be prepared."

Shane was like an unarmed man in an ambush as jealousy pummeled him. While she hadn't mentioned Ben specifically, an image of his deputy and Allison locked in each other's arms beneath the mistletoe wedged its way into his mind. Once there, he couldn't dislodge it.

"What about Trevor Langston?" he ground out.

"Trevor and I don't have an understanding," she said airily. "I haven't yet accepted his suit."

Going to the rear of the bed, she peered into the multiple crates. He followed, irritated that she was here one day and already getting under his skin. This wasn't supposed to happen.

"You're leaving within a month. That's hardly enough time to court."

She ignored him as she continued to catalog the contents.

"I hope you're not considering Ben. He's not the settling-down type," he went on. "Don't pin your hopes on the likes of him. I mean it, Allison."

"I'm not pinning my hopes on anyone." Rolling her eyes, she planted her hands on her hips. "I'm teasing, Mr. Lawman. The mistletoe is for decoration…and maybe George and Clarissa. The children descend into giggling fits whenever their parents smooch. It's quite entertaining."

Her nose wrinkled adorably, and suddenly he was thinking about someone other than Ben kissing her beneath the mistletoe. Someone like himself.

Having reached the limit of his patience, Shane stifled a groan and, loading his arms with heavy crates, made his way to the kitchen. It took several trips to unload everything. He didn't stay to help her unpack. Murmuring an excuse about work, he promised to swing by the following morning before beating a hasty retreat.

"Hurry up and get here, George," he muttered.

At the livery, Milton Warring met him at the entrance, stained fingers tugging at his scraggly beard.

"What's on your mind, Warring?"

"I've found evidence of a trespasser."

Shane climbed down and let Warring's assistant take over the rented wagon and team. When the lad was out of earshot, he said, "Show me."

The livery owner led him upstairs into the loft where mostly hay and other supplies were stored. Near the shuttered opening overlooking Main Street, he spotted an empty tin of beans and nudged it with his toe. Inside, a dirty spoon rattled. Shane bent and examined the tin and raked through the scattered straw for other clues.

"Is it possible your hired boy ate his lunch up here and forgot to clean up after himself?"

"He eats his lunch on the bench out front most days. I asked to be sure, and he denies this is his."

Shane walked the perimeter of the space, his gaze sweeping the planks. Near the ladder opening, he reached down and plucked a gold necklace from the straw. "Recognize this?"

Taking turns, they examined the locket and faded photo of a woman. "Haven't seen her before," Warring said. "You?"

"Nope." Slipping it in his pocket, Shane said, "I'll ask around. See if anyone has an idea who she might be."

He scowled. "You think he'll come back?"

"It's a lot warmer in here than it is out there. If he got away with it once, he'll try again. Unless he's moved on."

Their town saw a lot of travelers passing through on their way to or from North Carolina. Most were respectable folks. It was the disreputable few he had to worry about.

Shane put his boot on the ladder's top rung. "Ben and I'll take turns watching the place."

"Good. I want that rascal caught."

"Keep an eye out for anything else suspicious."

He left the livery and headed for his office. His deputy was warming his hands at the woodstove and looked up at his entrance.

"We have a potential problem over at Warring's." Shane related the scant details and warned him to be on alert for unfamiliar faces.

"Will do, boss." He gave a short nod. "You get Allison settled over at the Wattses' place?"

"She's Miss Ashworth to you. And I'd prefer it if you'd steer clear of her."

Folding his arms over his chest, Ben met his gaze squarely. "Because she's just here for Christmas? Or because you want her for yourself?"

When it became clear a couple of years back that he needed to hire help, he'd chosen Ben MacGregor because of his astute mind and discernment skills. They worked well together. Shane didn't approve of his deputy's flippant attitude toward women, but his personal life was none of his business.

"I don't care what you do on your own time or who you involve, as long as you uphold the reputation of this office. But I won't have you trifling with Allison's emotions."

"You didn't answer the question." From his stance and unyielding stare, it was obvious he wasn't going to drop the matter.

"There's nothing romantic between us. Never has been. She's like a sister to me." The words sounded false, even to his ears. "I don't want to see her hurt."

"I respect you, Shane. As my boss, but also as a man. I'd be an idiot to ruin our professional relationship by doing something stupid regarding your friend."

"I'm glad you understand."

"I'm not finished." He held up a hand. "Seeing as how I'm *not* an idiot, you can rest assured that any relationship I pursue with her will be respectable."

Shane curled his hands into fists, the buckskin gloves molding to his knuckles. For the first time since they started working together, he was tempted to plant his fist in the other man's face. All because of Allison.

"If you hurt her, your career in law enforcement is over."

Ben's eyes widened a fraction. "That's not going to happen."

"See that it doesn't."

Pivoting on his heel, Shane stormed out with no idea where he was headed.

The tantalizing scents of sizzling bacon and rich-bodied coffee woke her. Snuggling deeper into the cocoon of quilts, it took several moments for Allison to remember that she was not at Ashworth House. She shot up in bed.

Pushing the tangled mass out of her eyes, she blinked at the framed needlework on the opposite wall and the mountain view through the nearest window. She inhaled again, and her stomach rumbled in anticipation. Leaping out of bed and wincing at the cold shock to her stocking feet, she hurried to the wardrobe.

Shane must've paid someone to cook meals for her. He'd seemed reluctant to share a meal with her yesterday. No way would he commit to cooking for her the duration of her visit. Although a thoughtful gesture, it would've been nice if he'd alerted her to his plans.

She chose one of her favorite dresses, a soft but sturdy material of rich cream dotted with orange and green flowers and trimmed in green ribbon. The dress put her in mind of her beloved estate gardens in springtime. Once dressed, she brushed her hair until it shone and arranged it in a twist.

Descending the stairs, Allison noticed a sorrel horse hitched to the post out front. She entered the kitchen and the polite greeting died on her lips.

"What are you doing here?"

"Isn't it obvious?"

She crossed her arms, irrationally annoyed with him. "You of all people should know it's a bad idea to let yourself into someone else's house while they're sleeping."

Shane scooped a pile of fluffy eggs onto a plate, along with biscuits and a thick, white sauce. "Most intruders don't cook you breakfast." He held the plate out. "Have a seat. There's milk on the table. If you'd prefer coffee, the kettle's there."

Allison accepted the plate. The food smelled amazing, especially after the modest, cold supper of cheese and bread she'd had last evening. "What is the white stuff? Are those lumps in there?"

"You've never had sausage gravy?"

"I've had brown gravy."

"Biscuits and gravy is a common breakfast food here. Try it and see if you like it."

She carried her plate to the dining room. He joined her in a few moments with his own breakfast and, assuming the same chair he'd occupied the day before, picked up his fork and spiked a clump of eggs.

"Shouldn't we say grace?"

He looked startled. "You're right. I forgot. Would you mind?"

Allison nodded, unsure if he was too shy to pray aloud or if his reluctance stemmed from a lack of confidence in God's love. *Lord, please give me the courage to broach the subject. Give me the right words.*

Catching her off guard, Shane settled his fingers over hers atop the tablecloth. Her focus shattered. The heat from his hand seeped into hers. His skin was rougher than hers, his bones denser, his hold firm and sure. Allison curved her fingers inward, capturing his, returning the pressure. His breath hitched. Her own heart tumbled in her chest. This wasn't the first time they'd held hands.

That other time he'd been guiding her through the woods to safety and, although he'd scolded her for wandering off alone the entire trek home, he'd allowed her to cling to his hand, a lifeline in a dark and stormy night.

The rare moments of physical contact stood out in her mind because Shane either hadn't liked the connection or hadn't known how to handle it. Their chief cook, a boisterous, vivacious woman who'd been liberal with her affection, had hugged him just like she did everyone else. Instead of returning the embrace, he'd stood rock still, his arms imprisoned at his sides, looking as if he was being prodded with a hot poker. When her father had occasionally given Shane a hearty pat on the back or slung an arm about his shoulder, he'd stiffened. Allison's heart had broken each time she witnessed his reaction.

Since he refused to open up about his childhood, she was left to imagine the terrible things he must've endured.

Her prayer was brief. He tugged free of her and turned his full attention to his meal. Tension prickled between them. Allison ate without speaking, her thoughts racing. He had yet to show her where he worked and lived. Did he eat alone most of the time? The thought made her sad. And unexpectedly annoyed. If only he wasn't so stubborn, so determined to remain aloof and unaffected by the people in his life.

"How do you like the gravy?" His soft query brought her attention to his implacable blue gaze.

"It's delicious." The biscuits were large and doughy and not beneficial to her waistline. "Where did you learn to cook like this?"

"In Kansas. I didn't have a lot of extra money to spend in restaurants, and I got tired of corn mush and beans real quick. The sheriff I was working for was a widower, and he'd invite me over sometimes. I commented once how I'd wished I'd learned, and the cooking lessons commenced."

"I wish I could've seen that." She smiled at the mental image of a pair of tough lawmen puttering around a kitchen.

"I'm sure you do." One corner of his mouth tipped up. It wasn't a full-fledged smile, but it was still able to make her spirits soar.

"You could pass on a few of those lessons, you know."

"Sorry. I'm not much of a teacher."

"Like you're not much of a writer?"

Over the rim of his coffee cup, he blinked at her. When he lowered it, a wrinkle tugged his brows together and the grim set of his lips returned.

"How did you fare during the night?"

Allison allowed the change in subject. She truly didn't want to travel down this road because, first, he likely wasn't going to admit his reasons for disliking her, and second, she didn't want to be the one to put that frown on his face. She wanted to make him smile and laugh. She wanted to bring him joy.

You didn't manage that before, a voice reminded her. *Nothing has changed except for the fact he's had more practice retreating into his protective shell.*

"Not terrible. There were creaks and groans that prevented me from falling asleep right away. It will take some time to get used to being alone in a big house."

"Your brother will be here before too long."

Allison didn't tell him about the idea she'd been pondering for months. While George and Clarissa were happy with the current arrangement, she'd been thinking more and more about setting up her own household, a smaller house with fewer staff in a good section of the city. Of course, that had been before she'd decided to give Trevor a fair shot at winning her heart, a decision goaded by Shane's presence and the hurtful memories he revived.

He downed the last of his coffee and stood. "Are you interested in a trip to town?"

"Certainly. What did you have in mind?"

"I was thinking I'd introduce you to the woman I told you about... Caroline Turner. The two of you can discuss holiday stuff while I see to business."

He was pawning her off on a stranger. Allison tried not to let her disappointment show. "What kind of business?"

Striding into the kitchen, he spoke over his shoulder. "Work-related."

She swallowed the last bite and, gazing longingly at the dish of remaining biscuits, turned away and joined him by the dry sink. "Do you have to resolve another argument among neighbors?"

He took her plate and submerged it in a basin of soapy water. "No. Why?"

"My world is almost completely made up of ledgers and employee disputes and company policy. It's predictable and mundane. I'd like to see what a typical day for a sheriff is like."

"My job isn't as exciting as you might imagine. Sure, there are days when I have to break up fights or investigate crimes. But there are long stretches of inactivity that anyone would consider boring."

"At least show me the jail."

"Since the cells are unoccupied at the moment, I can do that."

"I'd like to see your home, as well."

"It's nothing special."

"Please?"

"Why is it important to you?"

"After I return to Norfolk, and George tells me what you've written in your latest letter, I'll be able to picture you in your jail or your home. Much more satisfying than a blank void."

He got a funny look on his face…like an apology. Did he regret not contacting her? Was he about to promise to change his ways after this visit? He opened his mouth, apparently searching for the right words.

"I'll take you after lunch."

Breaking eye contact, she headed for the exit. "I'll gather my things."

Maybe seeing him in his environment wasn't the best

idea. Sure, she'd be able to picture him more easily. But she'd also be able to remember being in those spaces with him. She'd wish she could return and be with him, a future that was out of the realm of possibility.

Not only would he not welcome a second visit from her, but she was determined to give a relationship with Trevor an honest try. That meant cutting all ties to her girlhood dreams.

Chapter Five

Caroline Turner was flawless.

She lived in a flawless house and wore flawless clothes that displayed her flawless figure.

Allison sat in the Turners' sumptuous parlor, sipping golden floral tea from a china cup and listening as the young woman listed Gatlinburg's holiday-themed events. She exuded quiet elegance. Her white-gold hair was scraped into a neat bun at the base of her neck. A double string of iridescent pearls complemented her off-white bodice, as did the pearl earrings at her ears. She had large, dark blue eyes, almost navy-colored, that weren't as happy as someone with a flawless life should be. Her smile wasn't happy, either. It was one a person pinned on for guests.

"We typically have a large turnout for our annual nativity unveiling." Caroline's gaze was assessing. "The sheriff doesn't attend many of our holiday functions. I wonder if that will change this year."

"He never has been one for social functions."

"While our humble festivities can't possibly measure up to what you're accustomed to, I'm certain you'd enjoy yourself."

"Norfolk has a great many events to experience, it's true.

However, I'm certain I will enjoy what Gatlinburg has to offer." Allison placed her cup and saucer on the low coffee table between them. Caroline must've seen her eyeing the tray of jumble cookies, because she picked it up and extended it her direction.

"Please, have as many as you'd like."

"I shouldn't," she said, even as the scents of juicy raisins and walnuts teased her nostrils. "I've had two already."

Caroline offered her a sincere smile then, one that lit up her entire face and made her less perfect. "I find them hard to resist myself." Taking one, she sunk her teeth into it and made a little sound of appreciation. "We only have them around the holidays."

Allison returned the smile and chose a third cookie.

"I know it's bad manners to pry, but Shane hasn't spoken of you before. Or anyone else from his past, for that matter. May I ask how you know each other?"

Having already prepared a standard answer to this exact question, she said, "Shane's a close friend of my family. He worked for my father."

"I didn't realize he'd lived in Virginia." Brushing imaginary crumbs from her pleated skirts, she remarked, "I'd heard he moved here from Kansas and assumed that was his home state."

"He's always been a private person. In fact, he'd be annoyed if he knew you and I were discussing him."

"I'm afraid he's invited more scrutiny by keeping your existence a secret."

"I told him as much myself," Allison said. "He didn't appreciate it."

A husky laugh burst out of her. "I think I'm going to like you, Allison Ashworth. I'm going to relish watching you pull the rug from beneath the staid sheriff's feet."

Unsure how to respond, she was grateful when her hostess didn't probe further. Caroline returned to the topic of

Christmas, specifically their custom of assembling gift baskets for the poor. Allison was keen to assist. Charitable endeavors took up much of her free time back home, holidays or no.

A half hour past the time of Shane's specified return, the teapot was drained dry and only crumbs remained on the plate. Besides remorse, Allison felt embarrassment for monopolizing Caroline's morning. When she caught her checking the mantel clock a second time, Allison went to retrieve her gloves from the carved hall stand.

"I appreciate your hospitality, Caroline. Shane must've gotten detained."

"I've enjoyed our chat. I hope I didn't make you feel as if you overstayed your welcome." Following her to the foyer where Allison fastened on her cloak, Caroline fiddled with her pearl necklace. "I'm waiting for my father to return from a trip. Today is my birthday, and he promised to be home no later than today."

There was a hint of vulnerability in the younger woman's expression, yet another crack in her sophisticated facade.

"Happy birthday. You're fortunate to have your father with you. Mine passed away many years ago, and I still miss him terribly."

"I'm sorry for your loss." The corners of Caroline's mouth turned down. "I'm afraid my father and I don't have the best of relationships."

Allison's hand paused on the knob. "Oh?"

Pink suffused her skin. "What could I be thinking of? My manners have deserted me today. Please forgive me, Allison. You don't want to hear about my family woes." She waved a hand in dismissal. "Don't feel as if you have to leave. You're welcome to stay for lunch."

"I appreciate the invitation, but I'd actually like to explore the town a bit. Would you mind telling Shane I've gone to do a little shopping?"

"Certainly."

"I'm looking forward to seeing you again soon."

"As am I."

The cold enveloped her as she strolled in the direction of Main Street. Fortunately, she'd been blessed with a good sense of her surroundings. On the way, the clouds parted and a shaft of sunlight warmed her.

She wished she could speak to her brother. Tell him about the rented farmhouse, the quaint mountain town, her excitement about experiencing Christmas in a new place. Like Shane, she hoped George wasn't long delayed. Spending time alone with the lawman was both heady and frustrating.

Help me guard my heart, Lord, she prayed.

Caring too much for Shane Timmons had always been a problem with no solution.

"Where's that pretty little filly of yours, Sheriff?"

Striding past the barber shop on his way to the mercantile, Shane ignored the good-natured teasing. He'd brought it upon himself. If he hadn't been so flustered by the prospect of her visit, he would've seen the wisdom in letting the news travel the grapevine before her arrival. Folks wouldn't have been as shocked.

Over the years, he'd worked hard to make the Timmons name one to be respected and revered. He'd earned his current reputation as a just, honorable, hardworking man of the law, and he wasn't about to let anything tarnish it.

He'd spent too many years carrying his sloppy drunk of a mother home through the Norfolk streets, trying to ignore the vulgar taunts and insults hurled their way. In their poverty-stricken neighborhood, he'd been known as a boy no one wanted. He'd been born to poor, unwed parents. His father hadn't cared enough to stick around and his mother detested her life to the point she had to drown her sorrows in alcohol every night. His maternal grandparents had refused to acknowledge him and moved away shortly after his birth. He'd never met his father's family. Doubted they even knew of his existence.

On the boardwalk, Shane passed a pair of young men. They waited until he was several yards away before calling after him.

"Where's the paint lady? Heard she's a real looker under all that green goo."

"Hey, Sheriff, are you two courtin'?"

Not breaking his stride, he allowed their words to bounce off him. They weren't cruel like the ones he'd endured as a youth, but they called forth excruciating memories better left in the dark shadows of his mind.

Paint lady. Allison was going to love that.

The mercantile's bell jangled as he walked in. The store was bustling with activity, as it would be until after the holiday. The scents of cinnamon, cloves and oranges permeated the air. Quinn and Nicole had complimentary cups of spiced cider available during the weeks leading up to Christmas. It helped ward off the chill, especially for those folks who traveled miles to get here.

Several people glanced his way, speculation flaring as their gazes switched from him to a point in the paper goods section. Allison's flaxen hair glistened in the natural light as she tilted her head this way and that, examining a sheaf of decorative papers. If she was aware of his scrutiny, she didn't indicate it.

His neck burning at the unwanted attention his presence was drawing, he wound his way through the crowded aisles to reach her.

"I'm sorry I ran late." He pitched his voice low. "Caroline said you might be here."

"It's all right," she said, casually holding the sheaf to her chest as she lifted her emerald gaze to his. "I figure that's standard for a sheriff."

"You're not upset?"

"No." She gave him a strange look. "I've taken advantage of the free time to do some shopping."

"What are you planning on doing with those papers?"

"You'll see." With a conspiratorial wink, she started for the counter.

He followed in her wake, aware that their every word and gesture was being monitored.

"You can assist me in my project if you'd like." Her bright smile invited him to share in her enthusiasm.

"I'm not committing to anything until I know what it is you have in mind."

They reached the long, worn-smooth counter where glass displays housed everything from razors to colored-glass bowls to jewelry. She paused before the display of cakes and pies, her eyes round. He hadn't forgotten her penchant for sweets. The Ashworth cook had catered to Allison's preferences, and he and George had both benefitted.

He pointed to an apple stack cake. "These are the finest desserts you'll ever taste."

She lifted her face to his. "Better than the Oak Street Bakery?"

"Better than that."

A breath pulsed between her shiny lips. "And who is the illustrious baker?"

"Jessica O'Malley. Well, it's Jessica Parker now. She's married to a former US Marshal. She's also Nicole Darling's sister. You'll meet all the O'Malleys eventually."

"I'd like that."

"Which one would you like to sample? My treat."

She shook her head in regret. "Oh, no. I've had my quota of sugar for the day, I'm afraid." Nodding to the window through which a vendor could be seen, she said, "But I will take some roasted chestnuts."

Shane kept his expression bland. "Whatever you'd prefer."

When she'd made her purchase, he guided her out into the now sunny day, one of those rare winter days with vivid blue skies and cheerful sun reminiscent of warmer seasons. He bought her a bag of chestnuts, but declined to get one for himself.

She sampled the first bite and hummed with delight. She offered the bag to him.

"No, thanks."

"Don't you like them?"

"I wouldn't know. Never tried one."

She stopped abruptly, forcing the man behind them to sidestep quickly in order to avoid a collision. "Then how do you know you won't like them?"

How could he explain his silly aversion to something that had taunted him during this most painful of seasons? Most days he'd had to make do with stale bread and moldy cheese or a thin broth with vegetables long past their prime. Walking past restaurants, he'd smell fresh-baked bread and grilled meat and his mouth would water. He began to dread Christmas because his lack was made even harder to bear. He'd see fathers out with their sons as they carried a fat goose home to their family. He'd see kids skipping down the street sucking on stick candy. Mothers and daughters sharing sacks of chestnuts on park benches.

He hadn't longed for the food, but for the love, acceptance and security of two devoted parents. Siblings who squabbled over toys and played kickball in the yard. A clean, warm home to live in, a soft bed to sleep in every night.

A voice inside his head tried to convince him that he

was no longer that ragged, defiant boy, but the feelings of inadequacy and bitterness drowned it out.

He pointed across the street. "There's the jail. Still want to see inside?"

Slowly her puzzled gaze left his to follow the line of his finger. "Very much."

With his hand nestled against the middle of her back, he guided her across the road and into the building where he spent a large portion of his time. To her, the space probably looked stark. To their left was a woodstove. Opposite the door was his desk, a scuffed relic handed down from the sheriff before him. A detailed topography map was nailed to the wall behind his chair, and the American flag hung on the right. One barred window overlooked Main Street.

Her gloved fingers trailed the desk's edge. "So this is where you keep the peace."

"Something like that."

She wandered to the first of three cells and, passing through the open metal door, pulled it closed behind her with a clang.

"What are you doing, Allison?"

Her grin was mischievous. "Go sit in your chair."

He dropped his hands to his sides. "Why?"

"Humor me."

The sight of Allison in one of his cells was a jarring one. Her loveliness had no place in a setting meant for thieves and carousers.

He dismissed thoughts of refusing. The quicker he obliged her, the sooner they could leave. Muttering beneath his breath, he circled the desk, slumped into his chair and crossed his arms. "Happy now?"

"Teach me how to shoot, and I will be."

He glared at her. "Not gonna happen."

"If I was one of your prisoners, I'd be intimidated by you."

Her tone was serious, but her eyes twinkled with a zest for life he'd always envied. "I'll never understand the way your mind works."

The main door swung open, and Claude bumbled inside, his jaw lolling when he caught sight of Allison behind bars. Shane shot to his feet. "Claude."

"Am I interrupting something?" The banker's incredulous, gray gaze inventoried the scene.

"Shane was indulging my sense of whimsy," Allison announced. Releasing the bars to allow the door to swing wide, she exited the cell and strode to shake Claude's hand. "I don't believe we've officially met. I'm Allison Ashworth, an old friend of Shane's."

Befuddled by her charming smile, the man stood up straighter and puffed out his chest. "Claude Jenkins. I manage the bank next door."

"A pleasure to meet you, Mr. Jenkins." His hand still in her grasp, she patted it and leaned forward. "You wouldn't mind keeping this between us, would you? I've never been in a jail before, you see, and I wanted to gain a better understanding of Shane's job."

Claude nodded with enthusiasm. "Oh, I understand, Miss Ashworth. I'm aware of how sensitive to gossip our sheriff is."

Beaming, she glanced at Shane, her expression one of satisfaction. He shook his head. The woman couldn't do anything the usual way, could she? He hoped Trevor Langston knew what he was getting himself into.

"Is there anything pressing you need help with, Claude?" he said.

"No, nothing important enough to take you away from this delightful young lady." Releasing her hand with obvious reluctance, the banker grasped the door handle. "Will I see you at the church's nativity celebration on Friday evening, Miss Ashworth?"

"That's a question better directed to Shane."

Claude pinned him with a suddenly steely gaze. "You are planning on escorting her, I hope."

Shane hid a grimace. He made a point of avoiding these types of events. Singing about Christ's miraculous birth while confronted with the nativity magnified the hollowness inside him. All those church services he'd attended with the Ashworths, the sermons about eternal destination—what would he choose, heaven or hell?—would march through his mind, making peace impossible.

"If Allison wishes to attend, I'll make sure she's there."

"That's what I wanted to hear."

When he'd left, Allison turned to him with clasped hands. "What's the next stop on the grand tour? Your house?"

Chapter Six

Allison was determined not to let Shane see her nervousness. This wasn't a romantic outing. He didn't wish for her company. He'd practically been ordered to escort her.

Descending the stairs, she gave her cranberry velvet skirts a little shake to adjust the stiff crinoline beneath. The bodice was constrictive, the long sleeves snug at the wrists, but the dress was one of her favorites. Shane turned from the mantel, his luminous gaze widening as he took in her appearance.

She ran her hand along the neat French braid trailing the middle of her back. "What? Is this not appropriate? Should I change?"

"No." Stroking his whiskered jaw, he said, "You look… Christmassy."

"Christmassy?" Like an ornament on a tree?

"Nice." He cleared his throat. "You look nice."

He turned his head away, giving her a chance to admire his dark suit. The midnight black hue made him seem more imposing than usual, but it also gave him a touch of city polish. His hair was neatly combed with a few stubborn locks falling over his forehead.

She moved closer to the fireplace, where the logs smoldered. "You don't look like a sheriff tonight."

His lips curved into a smile, an actual smile, and Allison felt as if the floor beneath her feet trembled. His austere features assumed a masculine beauty that had her inching forward and desperately wanting to trace his lips with her fingertips.

Thankfully, his deep voice shattered the strange compulsion. "You're awfully preoccupied with my profession. Norfolk has an impressive police force."

She made a dismissive gesture. "It's not the same. I know Tennessee isn't exactly the untamed West, but neither is it a sprawling metropolis. There are books written about men like you."

He snorted. "My life is not a grand adventure."

"You don't see it that way because, in your mind, you're simply doing your duty. To the people you help, you are that larger-than-life hero in the pages of a book."

"I suppose we'll have to agree to disagree." Running a finger beneath his collar, he tilted his head to the clock. "We'd better get going if you want to get there before the candle lighting begins."

As he locked the door and led her into the nippy winter evening, she soaked in the vast expanse of twinkling stars. Twin lanterns hooked to either side of the wagon emitted a soft glow. "I'm sorry you were roped into taking me tonight. I know you'd rather be doing something else."

"A few hours of Christmas carols won't kill me," he drawled, assisting her up.

He climbed up on his side and, instead of taking his seat, reached into the wagon bed and brought out a thick, multicolored quilt. Unfolding the bundle, he bent over her and tucked it about her legs and lap. His face was near enough for her to feel the brush of his cool, minty breath across her cheek.

"Thank you, Shane," she whispered, touched by his thoughtfulness.

The seat bounced a little when he lowered his large frame onto it. Seated this close beside him, she was aware of their variances in size and the fact he made her feel feminine and almost delicate.

With a nod, he issued quiet instructions to the horses. The wheels rolled over the rutted track. It was impossible not to bump into him. He shrugged off her apology. Allison glanced at his implacable profile, wishing he'd wrap his arm around her to hold her steady. Then she could snuggle into his side. But that would mean prolonged personal contact, which he didn't do. It would also indicate he felt at ease with her, that he felt affection for her, neither of which were true.

Focusing her attention on their passing surroundings—the forest on either side of the lane cloaked in mysterious shadows—she thought about her visit to his modest cabin. The one-room structure was so far removed from Ashworth House as to be laughable. Still, he took pride in his ownership. The wooden logs and chinking were in excellent condition, the puncheon floors and window glass clean of debris. What little furniture he had was of good quality. And while the single bed shoved against the wall and adorned with naught but a plain woolen blanket was a little desolate in her estimation, his home wasn't without personality.

Stacks of law journals and various periodicals had been visible on the small table beside the russet-colored cushioned chair. On a shelf near the fireplace, he'd stored a collection of games—dominoes, tabletop ninepins, chess. Years ago, during the afternoon hours after school, he and George could often be found in the estate's library playing checkers or some other board game. If the weather was nice, they'd engage in a game of kickball or football outdoors. Shane had possessed more aggression than actual skill in those physical games. Sometimes she would hide in the rose arbor and observe them, in awe of the almost frenzied energy coming off him.

"Do you still play football?"

He glanced over at her. "Mostly on holidays or special days when folks take a break from their usual chores."

"Who do you spend holidays with?"

"The O'Malleys."

Her curiosity about his relationship with them grew. "You're close to them, aren't you?"

"They're the closest thing to family I've got."

She stiffened. Her hands braced on either side of her legs, she gripped the wood to avoid bumping into him again as the conveyance traveled around a bend and left the woods behind.

He heaved a sigh. "I'm sorry. I didn't mean to imply that you and your family aren't important to me."

Allison was grateful for the darkness. "There's no reason to deny the truth." Could he detect the tiny wobble in her voice? "Your life is here. Has been for a long time."

"Your father changed the course of my life. Without him, I'd be in jail or worse."

"He loved you as if you were his own son."

The silent accusation hung between them. Her father had given Shane a job and welcomed him into their home, but she'd seen no sign that the friendless, adrift young man ever fully lowered his guard with any of them.

He kneaded his nape for long moments. "He was the best of men."

Emotion welled up inside. Some days the grief lay dormant, like a hibernating bear, and others it roared to life, reminding her of everything her father was missing. He would've liked to have seen how well his business was flourishing under George's leadership. He would've cherished being a grandfather.

"He would be proud of you, Shane."

The faint lamplight allowed her to see his initial surprise and disbelief. Sorrow, and something akin to regret, surged in his blue eyes.

"I'd give anything to be able to talk to him again." Where his hands rested atop his thighs, his gloves stretched tight across his knuckles. "I don't remember thanking him."

Stunned by the raw admission, Allison reached over and squeezed his forearm. "My father was a wise man. He saw more than you realize."

Shane's gaze returned to the lane. When he didn't acknowledge her gesture in any way, she removed her hand.

He nodded to the cluster of buildings comprising Main Street. "Almost there."

Lamps shone in several of the windows. The white clapboard church was situated at one end of town. A golden glow lit up the night around it, allowing her a glimpse of the grand steeple soaring into the sky. Shane guided their wagon to the edge of the congested churchyard.

Their arrival didn't go unnoticed. A cluster of young men strolling past called out as Shane was helping her to the ground.

"Hey, Sheriff. Evening, paint lady."

Allison stumbled. Shane's hands curved around her waist, preventing her from plowing into him. Bracing herself against his sturdy shoulders, she gaped at the retreating group.

"Did I hear that right?"

"Um, it appears you've earned yourself a nickname."

She lifted her face to gaze up at him. He bit his lip to stop a smile.

"Paint lady?"

His heat radiated outward from where he still held her.

It would be so easy to slide her hands up and around his neck...

"Could be worse."

Awareness settled across his features as his gaze roamed her face, and his fingers flexed on her waist. Yearning, intense and demanding, curled through her. *Please don't let me go,* she silently implored. *Don't pull away.*

"Here you two are. Glad to see you made it."

Claude Jenkins's intrusion brought a grimace to Shane's face. Immediately, he put her away from him and turned to acknowledge the man and his wife. Behind the couple, a handsome man with wheat-colored hair, trim mustache and goatee and a penetrating blue gaze waited to speak to them.

Claude winked at her before leading his wife away. The stranger approached and clamped a hand on Shane's shoulder in a friendly manner, all the while studying her in the most unsettling way.

"Didn't expect to see you tonight. Is your lovely guest the reason you decided to join us ordinary revelers?"

Wearing a tolerant expression, Shane inclined his head her direction. "Josh O'Malley, meet Allison Ashworth."

"One of the esteemed O'Malleys," she quipped as he enveloped her hand in a firm shake. "Shane has spoken highly of your family."

"Unfortunately, he's given us scant information about you. I'm here to rectify that." Pulling her hand through the crook of his elbow, he winked down at her. "How about I introduce you to the rest of the clan and then you can tell us about yourself?"

"Don't trust him, Allison," Shane drawled. "He's really after dirt that he can hold over me in the future."

Josh's burst of laughter drew curious looks from passersby. "He knows me too well."

She was enjoying this exchange too much to refuse. "I'd be happy to trade stories with you. As you might imagine,

Shane hasn't been forthcoming about his life here. I'm particularly interested in his professional accomplishments."

"It's a deal." Josh's eyes gleamed.

He drew her closer to the church building. Shane trailed behind them, and she sensed the weight of his attention on her. Was he worried about what she might reveal? Or did he trust her judgment?

They paused at one of several long tables to procure mugs of fragrant apple cider. Cradling the large mug, she relished the warmth seeping through her gloves. Cognizant of the curiosity she aroused in the others, Allison wondered if it was due to her being an out-of-towner or her connection to their secretive sheriff.

Josh led her to a stand of gnarled trees that resembled pitiful broomsticks. Numerous adults chatted while kids dashed after one another, shrieking and giggling. At one edge of the gathering, a beautiful brunette waved them over, a smile stretching from ear to ear.

"Allison, allow me to introduce you to the love of my life." Releasing Allison, Josh went and tugged the woman tight against his side. "My wife, Kate O'Malley."

"It's nice to meet you, Allison." Her smile was sincere. "There are quite a lot of us." She wiggled her fingers at the group of men and women, adolescents and young children. "It can be a bit overwhelming at first."

"As long as you don't expect me to remember everyone's names."

Laughing, the couple drew her deeper into the fray. Shane remained on the group's edge, engaging in conversation with a striking-looking man with raven hair and an angry scar around his eye. She learned there were three brothers—Josh, Nathan and Caleb—and their cousins, five sisters who greeted her with curiosity. The most recently married, Jessica was the only one as yet without kids.

"You're the baker, right?" Allison addressed the red-head. "Shane was bragging about your talent."

"Folks do seem to enjoy my baking."

Her husband, Grant Parker, brushed a lock of her deep-red hair behind her shoulder. "She's being modest. Jessica's desserts are highly sought after around these parts."

"My sister Jane is just as skilled." Jessica indicated her identical twin sister, who was standing a couple of yards away with a tall, distinguished fellow. "She's busy with her kids and doesn't have time to bake as much as she used to."

Allison had met only one other set of twins before, brothers in their midsixties who looked like mirror images of each other, much like Jessica and Jane. She tried to keep her fascination hidden.

"I confess to a weakness for sweets," she said. "I will no doubt prove to be a loyal customer during my stay."

The scarred man, who she'd learned was the youngest O'Malley brother, tugged a reluctant Shane to the middle of the group where she stood with Jessica and Grant.

"Interrogation time," Caleb announced with a smirk. His brown-black eyes settled on her, and she felt sure she wouldn't want him for an enemy. "Miss Ashworth, will you kindly tell us the nature of your relationship with Shane Timmons?"

Josh tapped her shoulder. "The truth, please, Miss Ashworth, not the pat answer Shane's prepped you to give."

Since Shane was standing beside her, she heard his slow exhale, sensed the flight-response of his body.

"I met Shane when I was twelve, and he was fourteen. He lived with me, my brother and father for many years."

"This was in Virginia?" Kate said.

"Yes. Norfolk. My family has lived there for generations. My father, David Ashworth, built a successful business, which he bequeathed to my brother, George."

"Allison works with George," Shane inserted. "She oversees the hiring and termination process and ensures the employees have proper working conditions. In addition to all that, she's in charge of payroll."

"I didn't realize my brother outlined my duties for you," she said.

"George likes to talk business. You're part of that world."

"What was Shane like as an adolescent?" Caleb asked, his keen gaze studying them both. She would've liked to ask what he saw that was so interesting.

She gave Shane a sideways glance. "A lot like he is today, actually. Reserved. Determined to do everything on his own. Convinced his opinion is the only right one."

"Sounds about right." Josh snorted. "You must've been terrified."

"Allison isn't terrified of anything." Shane's sardonic reply evoked laughter from the group.

Her smile felt forced. He clearly didn't know her well. He was the one who'd intimidated her from the start, the one whose good opinion she'd craved.

"My turn." Crossing her arms, she met Caleb's stare with her own. "I want to hear about Shane the lawman."

Shane hung his head and groaned. "There's really not much to tell."

"Stop being so modest." Josh socked his arm.

"If anyone has a right to boast, it's him," Jessica said with conviction.

Shane shot Allison a *help me* look. He despised being the center of attention. Not about to miss their recounting of his exploits, she shrugged. Displeasure twisted his mouth.

"Shane's the type of man who'll help anyone without thought to his own personal comfort or safety," Josh said. "He's got a will of iron and nerves of steel."

Josh listed the ways Shane had impacted their lives. He'd once hunted and captured a criminal who'd taken Nathan captive. He'd rounded up a gang of outlaws whose female leader had almost killed Caleb and his wife, Rebecca. When a series of crimes had been committed at Quinn's store and Nicole had been attacked, Shane worked with Quinn to bring the perpetrators to justice.

Grant spoke up at the end, his expression one of earnest respect. "Not so long ago, I woke up on Jessica's property with no memory of who I was. Shane could've thrown me in jail that first day. Even after I discovered evidence that pointed to a sordid past, he believed in my innocence. Things could've gone very differently if not for him."

The adults fell silent. Allison nudged Shane. "Sounds like the contents of an adventure book to me."

He kicked up a shoulder. "It's my job. I do what's required of my position, the same as any other lawman in this nation is expected to do."

"Handsome and humble…" Jessica huffed a dramatic sigh. "If only we could convince one of the single ladies around here that he's worth the effort."

Kate shot Allison a significant look. "What about you, Allison? Are you involved with anyone?"

Her cheeks blazed with heat at the implication. "Not at the moment."

Nathan elbowed Josh. Someone let loose a low whistle. "Isn't that convenient. Shane's not courting anyone."

"When has he ever?" Nathan's young brother-in-law, Will, observed with a hearty laugh.

Shane threw up his hands. "That's enough punishment for one night."

Threading his fingers through hers, he pushed past Josh, guiding her away from their group.

"You don't have to go," Caleb called after them. "We'll promise to behave."

He lifted a hand in acknowledgment. Still, he didn't slow his pace until they'd left his friends behind and were on the opposite side of the church near the cemetery. He dropped her hand the moment they stopped.

"It wasn't that bad, was it?" she said softly.

"They like to harass me sometimes. You presented a perfect opportunity."

"It's obvious how much they care about you. You're fortunate to have them."

After witnessing the evidence of their regard for him, she could only be happy to know he wasn't alone.

"I know." His attention shifted beyond her. "Evening, Ben."

"Howdy, boss." The rakish deputy took hold of her hand and, clasping it between his, pressed it to his heart. "You are as radiant as the North Star, Miss Ashworth. You put every other woman here to shame."

Allison didn't dare risk a glance at Shane. "You are quite inventive with your compliments, Mr. MacGregor."

"What can I say?" His grin widened. "You inspire me."

"You can release her hand now," Shane muttered.

Ben reluctantly did so. "Boss, I know how you feel about these types of shindigs. I don't mind keeping Miss Ashworth company if you'd like to skip out."

Dejection weighed heavily on her shoulders. Lowering her gaze to the grass beneath her feet, she waited for Shane to agree.

"That's mighty thoughtful of you, but Allie came with me, and I'll see to it that she gets home safe and sound."

She whipped her head up. In the semidarkness, his profile was impossible to read. He'd called her Allie just once, the day he left Virginia. On the verge of boarding the train, he'd taken her hand and told her to take care of herself.

Ben accepted his refusal with aplomb. "Understood." His green gaze slid to her. "I'll see you around, Miss Ashworth."

He sauntered off in the direction of the snack tables.

Shane scrubbed at the day's growth of beard shadowing his jaw. "I didn't think to ask your opinion. If you'd rather pass the time with him, I'll understand."

"I came here to visit you, Shane."

He stared at her for long moments. Holding out his bent arm, he said, "The reverend's getting in position, which means the program is about to start. Let's go and find us a spot."

About that time, the jangle of cowbells got everyone's attention. The reverend, a silver-haired man clad in a penguin's colors, went to stand near the church steps and waited until the crowd gathered around.

"Friends and neighbors, another year is drawing to a close," he said. "In this last month of 1886, let us reflect on God's blessings and His greatest gift to mankind, His Son, Jesus Christ." He gestured to the grouping of statues covered with burlap. "This year, I'm pleased to inform you that we have a new nativity. My thanks goes to Josh O'Malley, who carved each piece with his own two hands."

The people clapped as the reverend removed the burlap from each statue. Allison was amazed by the craftsmanship and detail of Mary, Joseph, baby Jesus and the animals.

"It's wonderful," she whispered. "I've never seen the like."

His face devoid of emotion, he nodded and sipped his cider. "Josh is a skilled carpenter. You'll have to visit his furniture store sometime."

"I'd like that."

Candles were handed out to the adults. When they were lit, the reverend's wife led the gathering in the singing of several carols. The flickering lights created a pretty glow in the darkness, and the sound of male and female voices blending together and singing about their Savior sent chills cascading over her skin. This was a humble church in a tiny mountain town, yet she'd never experienced the same awed emotion.

Beside her, Shane was peculiarly silent. His candle aloft, he stared into the distance, his focus far from here. Was he remembering some terrible moment from his past? Another sad, disappointing Christmas?

She touched his sleeve. "I'm ready to leave if you are."

He angled his head toward her, and it took a second for his gaze to clear. "Are you sure?"

Of course she wanted to stay, but she refused to be selfish when he was unhappy.

"I'm cold. I'd like to go back to the house and relax before a comforting fire."

Taking her candle, he extinguished them both and, discarding them in a bin, led her past awaiting horses and wagons to where his was parked. As before, he cocooned her in the quilt, his movements efficient and impersonal but wreaking the same effect as the first time. She was so busy seeing to her niece's and nephews' needs that she'd forgotten what it felt like to experience a moment of cossetting herself.

"You were uncomfortable back there," she ventured. "You don't like when I question you about your past, but you didn't say I couldn't ask about your faith. Has your viewpoint altered since you left Virginia?"

He was quiet a long time. "I want to believe that the God who created all this beauty could love someone with a soul as tarnished as mine. I want to, but..."

"It's hard for you to trust." Anxious to say the right thing, she said, "No one deserves Christ's love. Or His forgiveness. But because of His compassion and mercy, He extends it to us. It's a free gift. We can't earn it."

"I've heard these same words many times." The defeat in his voice disappointed her.

Why can't you accept them as truth? "I've never stopped praying for you, Shane."

His gaze swerved to her face, his shock evident. "I don't know what to say except thank you. That you would take the time to pray for me..." He removed his hat and thrust a hand through the blond-brown strands.

"I won't stop." Her own voice grew thick. "You can count on that."

Nodding, he didn't utter another word. At the house, he set the brake and, after helping her down, started to climb the steps.

"You're coming inside?" she blurted. "I can stoke the fireplaces without your help."

He paused with one boot braced against the bottom step. It was impossible to make out his features in the porch shadows. "I thought I'd see to the task. Unless you don't want me to."

"That depends on your reasons," she said evenly. "If you're coming in because of some perceived duty, then the answer is no. I don't need to be watched after. If you're coming in because you'd like to share a cup of coffee and my company, then the answer is yes."

His long-suffering sigh originated deep in his chest, and the tenuous bond born from her confession evaporated.

"I guess I have my answer." She ascended the steps. "Good night, Sheriff."

Chapter Seven

"Allison."

Still reeling from her revelation that he featured regularly in her prayers, Shane trailed after her. He had to tread carefully because, to him, this entire visit was a necessary but not exactly welcome intrusion into his life. He hadn't invited her here. He definitely hadn't anticipated having to keep up his guard every hour of the day.

"Wait a minute." He touched her shoulder, and she whirled on him.

"I have to be honest, Shane. I hate that you see me as a burdensome child. Every time you sigh and huff and roll your eyes, I'm tempted to throttle you."

He stared at her. "I'm sorry."

He was sorry that he wasn't a different man, one who knew how to trust and love and have normal relationships. He was sorry he hadn't done a better job of hiding his unease around her.

She began to dig in her reticule, her frustration evident. He pulled the key from his pocket and held it up.

"Looking for this?"

When she went to snatch it from him, he held it out of

reach. "For the record, I don't see you as a burdensome child."

"Oh?" Her chin jerked up, her hair gleaming in the night. "How *do* you see me, Shane?"

He strove for a rare moment of honesty between them. The fact that she couldn't see his face helped. "As an intelligent, caring, gorgeous woman who makes me wish I was a better man."

The admission hung between them. She didn't move or speak. He heard her swallow, noticed her moistening her lips with the tip of her tongue, could almost see her mind working to process the information.

Reminded of that charged moment in the churchyard and the weakening of his resolve, he sought refuge from the longing invading every part of him. One innocent touch from her was all it would take for him to succumb to the lies and haul her in his arms for a kiss that would likely tilt the world on end. His soul was like a parched desert that wouldn't be able to stop from soaking up every single drop of rain offered. If he unleashed this flood of attraction building between them, he feared he'd never surface again.

Because of his unsteady fingers, it took several attempts to unlock the door. Shoving it open, he strode to the fireplace. She entered at a more sedate pace, taking her time removing her cape and gloves. She crossed the living room and stopped behind him.

Please don't question me on this. Please.

"Would you like a cup of coffee?"

The tension between his shoulders blades eased. "Sure."

The flames were licking at the logs by the time she returned. He replaced the poker in its slot and accepted the mug she held out.

He forced himself to meet her gaze. "You aren't having any?"

"It's too late in the evening for me."

He half twisted toward the mantel, touching a finger to patterned paper pinwheel stars perched there. "This was the project you thought I could help with?"

She clasped her hands together in front of her. "It's not difficult to do. Requires more patience than skill."

There were six on the mantel, all done in shades of white, green and red. She'd hung more between the stair rail rungs.

Her features softened into a fond smile. "I placed those there so they'd be on the children's level."

"Tell me about them."

She crossed her arms. "They're a lively lot, especially the boys. Danny's seven and a miniature of his father in both looks and personality." She chuckled, no doubt picturing them in her mind's eye. "Five-year-old Peter is a firecracker but he's always eager for a hug. Lydia's four. She's the most mischievous of them all."

"Let me guess, she has George wrapped around her finger."

"Without a doubt. And then there's George Jr. He's an easygoing child. He loves to snuggle and is generous with his kisses. Since he's only just turned two, he prefers to spend most of his time with Clarissa."

Unsurprisingly, she spoke of the children with great affection. "You adore them."

"I do. I've been there for each birth and watched them grow and flourish into little people with their own unique personalities."

"You should have a brood of your own."

The words cost him. He could easily picture her with a babe in her arms and one bouncing on her knee. Her children would never question whether or not they were loved.

Her smile turned wistful. "I'd like that very much."

"Does Trevor like kids?"

"I—I haven't thought to ask." She bit her bottom lip.

Wishing the question unsaid, he set his mug on the coffee table and plucked a pinecone from a bowl full of them. "What's this?"

"My meager attempt at decoration. I gathered them from the yard. If the weather's nice enough tomorrow, I plan to search for ivy or other greenery to spruce up the space."

Shane bit back a sigh. Pacing to the far corner beside the window, he said, "This would be a good spot for a tree."

Her brow furrowed. "A tree?"

"You said the children will be disappointed without one. We'll go in the morning."

"You're serious? You're going to take me to cut down a Christmas tree?"

"Yes."

"And you're going to help me set it up? Maybe even place a few ornaments on the branches?"

He found it impossible to say no in the face of her obvious delight. "If I must."

With a little squeal, she launched herself at him, her arms going around his neck. Stunned, he registered several things at once—the fruity fragrance clinging to her hair, the curve of her cheek pressed against his neck, her breath tickling the skin above his collar. The need to return her hug, to hold her close, surged within him. She was incredibly soft and warm and sweetly alluring. It took immense effort to keep his arms at his sides.

Belatedly noticing his lack of response, Allison removed herself from his person and took great care in rearranging her skirts, her chin tipped to the floor. "What time shall I be ready?"

"Ten o'clock. Dress warmly."

His heart was out of rhythm and thumping erratically against his chest. Hopefully that was her last spontaneous show of affection. Testing the boundaries of his willpower wouldn't benefit either of them.

* * *

She shouldn't have hugged him.

Every time the memory of how he'd borne her enthusiastic thank-you came to mind, she cringed with embarrassment. Riding on horseback alongside him through the mountainous terrain, all she had to do to be reminded of her foolhardy behavior was look over at his rock-hard jaw, sculpted, stern mouth and the rigid line of his broad shoulders.

He'd been quieter than usual this morning, and it was her fault.

"I stopped by the post office on my way to your place," he said, shifting in the saddle. "Still no word from George."

"When it comes to work, he can be single-minded. I wouldn't be surprised if he forgets to contact us and simply shows up here unannounced."

Shane's lips pressed more tightly together.

"You're awfully serious today," she said. "Something particular on your mind?"

Framed by the overcast day and cream-colored Stetson, his eyes looked bluer than usual. "Seems I have something of a mystery on my hands."

"Oh?"

"I believe we may have a drifter problem. There's evidence someone has been spending nights in Mr. Warring's livery. This morning, Quinn got a delivery from a neighboring city. While he and the driver went inside to settle up, someone stole a box of oranges."

"A costly loss. Do you have any clues as to who it might've been?"

"None. When Quinn discovered it missing, he searched the riverside and discovered a pile of orange rinds. The culprit is headed for a massive stomachache if he eats them all in one sitting. Ben's doing the rounds today on the lookout for suspicious strangers."

"Were there any nonfood items taken?"

"I know what you're thinking," he said evenly. "Need doesn't make it okay to steal."

"Hunger can be a powerful motivation." Despite her thick green cloak, woolen scarf and fur-lined gloves, she was cold. The mountain air chilled her exposed skin. "What if he doesn't have a proper winter coat? No home to lodge in? If it's this cold during the day, wouldn't anyone caught out in the elements overnight be in danger of freezing to death?"

"Unfortunately, the danger is very real."

"What will you do if you catch him?"

He leveled his gaze at her. "My job."

"You'd put him in jail?"

"I don't always like what I'm required by law to do, but sometimes I don't have a choice. The best I could do is appeal to the business owners affected and ask for leniency. If they agreed, I'd be able to let him off with a warning."

Allison fell silent as she contemplated the difficulties of his position. Her horse navigated the increasingly hilly terrain. She had to concentrate on balancing atop his broad back.

Shane's mount pulled a little in front of hers. Shane twisted to look at her over his shoulder. "In these parts, it's common knowledge that the church is willing to help those who've fallen on hard times. My hunch is that this person is living on the wrong side of the law and doesn't want to draw attention to himself."

"Still, it's difficult to think of someone suffering like that. I've never had to go hungry, so I don't know what it's like."

"I do." A muscle ticked in his jaw. "When you're that hungry, your world narrows and finding food is all you can think about."

Her horror must've shown on her face, because he

turned away. Her fingers clenched on the saddle horn as a particular memory reasserted itself. The first night Shane joined them for dinner, his eyes had nearly popped out of their sockets at the sight of the luxurious seven-course meal. Even so, he'd limited himself to scant proportions. Her father had encouraged him to help himself to as much food as he'd like, but he'd declined. It had taken months for Shane to relax enough to eat a healthy amount.

"How often did you go without?"

"It was an ongoing problem. Sometimes, I'd resort to stealing, just like our drifter."

Allison knew better than to express her dismay. Thankfully, he was sitting forward in the saddle and couldn't see her reaction. "Did you ever get caught?"

"Once. When I was ten, the owner of the diner around the corner found me sneaking out the kitchen door that exited onto the back alleyway. I had a chicken leg and a roll. He marched me straight to jail." He looked back, saw her sagging jaw and smirked. "Don't feel too bad. The sheriff fed me a fine meal that evening."

"You were a child!"

"I broke the law."

"How long?"

"Was I in jail?" He shrugged. "Just the one night. The owner's wife found out what happened and insisted her husband show me mercy. Not only that, she made sure I had one hot meal a day for the remainder of the time I lived in that neighborhood."

"I don't envy you your job," she confessed, having trouble absorbing these rare revelations about his past. "Those instances when those who deserve punishment are the same ones in desperate need of help must wear on your soul."

"It doesn't happen as often as you might think. When we find our drifter, I'll check if he's wanted by local or federal authorities. If not, I'll make it my priority to get him the assistance he needs."

"I hope you find him soon." Before he dies from exposure.

"Me, too." Thumbing up his hat's brim, he tilted his head back to study the low, grayish-white clouds. "Looks like snow."

"The temperature has dropped significantly since last evening."

She'd woken to a frigid room. In this house, there weren't any maids to stoke the fires and make her morning routine comfortable. For breakfast, she'd made do with coffee and a cold slice of bread smeared with blackberry preserves, all the while picturing Clarissa and the children in the estate's elegant dining room with their porridge, eggs, ham and jelly-filled pastries. After nearly a week of separation, she missed them terribly, despite the fact that she was enjoying the peace and quiet.

"How far are we from the Wattses' land?" Her hold on the saddle horn tightened as the Wattses' horse she was borrowing navigated a steep bank. She'd likely be sore tomorrow. Her outings were confined to the estate grounds and expansive city park—easy terrain compared to this.

"A couple of miles." His gaze swept her from head to toe. "You all right?"

"I'm fine."

Pointing higher up the mountain slope to where the forest thickened, he said, "We've got about a half mile of ground to cover before we start seeing the trees you'll be interested in."

By the time they reached it, Allison was grateful for a chance to dismount and stretch her legs. She was turning a slow circle, soaking in the glorious view, when Shane appeared at her side and handed her a small, squat canteen with a hand-knitted cover.

"What's this?"

"Hot cocoa." He held out two miniature cups. "Would you mind pouring while I fetch the rest of our repast?"

"Repast. That's a big word for a lawman."

He cocked a brow. "Not for a lawman who spends his free time reading."

She grinned, unwisely thrilled at being far from civilization with him. Using a fallen log as a table, she carefully poured the rich brown liquid, her mouth watering at the aroma of sweet chocolate. Shane returned with a crushed white box and a slight frown.

Peeking beneath the lid, he said, "I brought a dessert for each of us but it appears only one survived the trip in my saddlebags."

Going to stand beside him, she inspected the hefty slice of golden cake and, beside it, what looked like a pancake. "I can't believe you brought us cake." She sniffed the contents. "What kind is it?"

"Cider cake."

"You are a very wise man, Shane Timmons," she said, grinning. "You've thought of all the essentials."

"Here." He handed it to her with a slight smile. "You eat it. The cocoa is all the *repast* I need."

Taking a fork from his hand, she scooped up a large bite and held it out. "There's no reason we can't share."

Beneath the brim of his hat, his brows tugged together. "You don't have to do that."

"I can't eat this entire thing by myself. Well, I could… but I shouldn't. Come on, you know you want to." She wiggled the fork close to his lips.

His strong fingers closed over her wrist and, his gaze melding with hers, guided her hand to her own mouth. Small clouds of white formed from his exhaled breath. "Ladies first."

The pleasant blend of flavors on her tongue—cloves, an

undertone of tart apple and juicy currants—couldn't distract her from his nearness and intense scrutiny. How did she get to this place? Alone with Shane on a frigid winter day, high in the mountains of East Tennessee, sharing a slice of cake?

A hushed expectancy shrouded the forest, the tranquility pierced occasionally by a hawk's cry or crack of a tree branch.

As she slowly chewed and swallowed, he studied her with unwavering focus. The shadow of a beard outlined his hard jaw and framed his mouth. He looked like a rugged backwoods hunter in his duster that hit him midcalf.

"Your turn."

Shane remained watchful while she fed him, his gaze burning into her. Her stomach fluttered. What did he see in her expression? She glanced into the box, wondering how she was going to keep her hand steady throughout this ordeal. Downfall by dessert.

Something cold and wet hit her cheek. Tilting her head, she gasped at the sight of white flakes drifting from the heavens and onto the leaf-strewn forest floor.

"It's snowing!"

"That it is." Shane didn't exude the same level of excitement. In fact, he looked a trifle concerned as he studied the sky. "We should finish up here and pick out a tree."

Allison followed him to the fallen log, where he swiftly downed the contents of his cup.

"You said it doesn't typically snow this early in the season. Do you think it will stick?"

Already a thin layer of white coated the ground. "Hard to say."

"What aren't you telling me?"

Deep grooves carved either side of his mouth. "The weather can be unpredictable and patchy. This elevation might see several feet of snow, while the center of town might get an inch." He held out a cup to her. "Drink. It'll help warm you."

"We don't have to get a tree today. We can head back right now."

Shane studied the horizon. "If we don't dally, we should be fine."

"Should be?"

"Let's just say this is the last place we want to be if the clouds decide to dump a significant load of snow on us."

Chapter Eight

He was questioning his decision three-quarters of an hour later. Allison had quickly made her choice, a dense Fraser fir about as tall as him, but by the time he'd gotten it cut and tied to the sled, several inches of snow coated the ground. Not a single pinch of sunlight penetrated the clouds. Fat, heavy flakes glided past them at a steady rate and gave no sign of letting up.

You were too afraid of disappointing her to heed your instincts.

Allison sat quietly on her mount, her profile solemn as she dusted the collecting snow off her sleeves.

He climbed into the saddle. "I'm going to go first so the sled will make a clear path for you. We'll take it slow and steady. You encounter any problems, speak up."

"No need to worry, Shane." Her green gaze expressed confidence. "I trust you to get us home safe."

Determined to do just that, he guided his horse between the closely spaced trees. The ground sloped downward at a gradual angle and would level out as soon as they broke free of the dense growth. Allison didn't speak, and he wondered if she was mulling over where the decorations would look best in the main floor rooms.

Minutes passed with no other sounds besides the creaking of saddles and muted slush of hooves against fresh white powder.

"There's an uneven outcrop up ahead." He pointed to where the trees thinned.

The sled bobbed and jerked as it caught on thick roots, and he worked to keep his horse calm and on task. Soon they were free of it and on flat ground. Behind him, he heard Allison cry out. He twisted around. Her horse rushed past him, its saddle empty. Seeing Allison on her back in the snow—eyes closed, body too still—sent icy fear coursing through him.

His heart threatening to burst out of his chest, Shane leaped down and scrambled to her side, dislodged snow spraying in all directions. "Allison! Can you hear me? Are you all right?"

He knelt beside her, his knees protesting the cold shock of moisture seeping through his pants. Yanking off his gloves, he gently swiped the melting flakes from her cheeks. Her skin was cool but not shockingly so. Leaning over her, he brushed a thumb lightly across her plump lower lip. "Allie, speak to me."

Her lashes fluttered open, and he was engulfed in twin pools of the deepest green.

She sucked in gulps of air. "I didn't hold on tightly enough. He shifted the opposite way of what I expected."

When she started to sit up, he put his arm around her shoulders to assist her. "Easy. Are you hurt anywhere?"

"No, merely winded from the impact." Patting the snow with her open palm, she gifted him with a weak smile. "This acted as a thin cushion. Otherwise, I'd likely be sporting some nasty bruises come tomorrow."

"You may still." Relief lessened the tightness in his chest. "Your brother would have my hide if I let anything happen to you."

He glimpsed a flash of disappointment before she dipped her head. "Right. George's good opinion is what matters." She moved to stand, and he supported her with a hand on her elbow.

"What's that supposed to mean?"

Sidestepping his hold, she straightened her bonnet and shook out her skirts, all the while avoiding his perusal. "Never mind." She finally lifted her head, her gaze going beyond his shoulder. Her lips formed an O. "Shane... where's my horse?"

Spinning, he scanned the wide open space with a sinking feeling. "I was too distracted to pay attention to him. He's got to be headed for his barn and a bucketful of oats."

"Won't he get lost?" Her worry for the welfare of the animal was obvious.

"From what I know of Martin Watts, he rides his horses out here on a regular basis. I'm confident he'll find his way home." His hands began to smart from exposure. Snagging his gloves from the ground, he plunged his fingers into the warm slots. "It does present us with a problem."

Allison looked from him to the horse and back. "We have to ride double."

Her trepidation poked his pride. "You have an issue with that?"

"I don't." She shrugged. "But I know you don't like to be touched."

He gaped at her. "And exactly how did you come by this conclusion?"

"I lived with you, remember?" Marching through the filmy curtain of snow, she laid a hand against his cheek. Despite his surprise, he couldn't help wishing her glove didn't form a barrier between his skin and hers.

What could he be thinking of? He could not *want* Allison, couldn't think of her as anything more than an old acquaintance...an adopted sister—that should smother any further thoughts of male interest in an alluring female.

Shane had trouble holding her gaze. "What are you doing?" he grated.

"Proving my point."

"I'm not going anywhere, am I? I'm not pushing your hand away."

"But it's costing you," she challenged. "When I hugged you last night, you stood there like a wooden statue."

"I'm not accustomed to spontaneous affection," he said stiffly.

Her features softened. "I'm guessing you're not accustomed to any sort, planned or spontaneous."

"It was never a part of my world."

He wasn't sure what he'd expected, but anger wasn't it. "Allison?"

Lowering her hand, she shook her head in disgust. "People like your mother shouldn't be allowed to have children if they aren't going to treasure and nurture them."

"It's in the past."

"Is it? I don't think so. Otherwise, you wouldn't insist on avoiding relationships."

"I like being alone." Now why did that statement ring false to his ears?

"I don't believe that, either." She brushed past him and went to stand beside his horse. "Do you get on first or do I?"

"Ladies first." Once she was situated, Shane hauled himself up behind her. They set out across the snowy field, and she had trouble balancing herself. He curled his left arm around her middle.

"Rest against me. You won't bob around as much."

After a short hesitation, she relaxed into his chest. A strange sense of satisfaction flooded him. It felt nice to hold her close. Better than nice. It felt wonderful. He could get used to this.

Minutes stretched into an hour. Their progress was slow, punctuated by the silence between them.

"Allison."

"Hmm?" She sounded sleepy.

He was hit with the sudden urge to nuzzle her nape, perhaps kiss her cool cheek or rest his forehead on her shoulder. His fingers automatically curved about her waist, and she turned her head so that he had a view of her profile.

"What is it?" she said, more alert this time.

"This isn't ordinary snowfall. It's heavy and piling up fast. If we continue on our current course, there's a good chance we won't make it to the Wattses'."

She considered his words. "Is it because of the tree's extra weight? Couldn't we leave the sled here and pick it up later?"

"I doubt that would make a difference. Our best option is to find shelter. There's a homestead not far from here. Fenton Blake lives there with his granddaughter, who's about eighteen years old. We could bed there for tonight and head to town in the morning."

"Will he welcome us?"

"Fenton's the sort that keeps to himself, but he won't deny hospitality to a stranger in need."

"Do what you think is best. I trust you."

Allison's confidence in him had his chest expanding with pleasure. He appreciated her calm assurance. If she'd been worried and upset about their situation, it would've made it more difficult for him to concentrate on getting them to safety.

Another hour and a half passed before he finally spotted the outline of Fenton's cabin. The peppery scent of wood smoke hung in the air, and he anticipated the heat of a roaring fire. The place where he held Allison was the only warm spot on him. The rest of him was protesting the frigid temperatures. Every few minutes, a shiver would course through her, and his arm would tighten around her, as if by holding her closer he could infuse her with some of his residual warmth.

He'd never forgive himself if she suffered because of his actions.

If not for the sting of winter air and the stiffness of her muscles, Allison would never move from this spot.

Being this close to Shane was like a dream, one she wished didn't have to end. He was solid and strong. He smelled of leather and pine and subtle spice. He held her as if he didn't mind her nearness, as if he'd do anything to keep her from falling, and it was a heady experience.

"We're here."

Her disappointment was completely unreasonable. It was imperative they take shelter from the elements. Still, she would miss this.

Shane guided the horse almost to the cabin door. She couldn't make out the structure's details through the heavy precipitation, but it struck her as small, maybe smaller than Shane's modest abode.

Dismounting, he hollered out his presence before pounding on the door. Cold rushed in where he'd been, wrapping her in its unwelcome embrace. She pressed her hands to her numb cheeks.

Shane pounded the weathered wood a second time. "Fenton Blake? You in there? It's Sheriff Timmons."

A cry filtered through the door, and Shane fell back a step. "Did you hear that?"

"Sounds like Mr. Blake has an infant in there."

He assisted her off the horse, holding her a couple of seconds longer than necessary to ensure she was steady on her feet. His hand at her elbow, he guided her through the drifts onto the small porch. The squalling sound came again, and they stared at each other.

Shane did not appear pleased. He whacked the door with the flat of his hand. "Open up, Fenton. I—"

The rest of his words were lost as they were suddenly met by a frail, elderly man who was bouncing an angry baby on his hip.

"All your racket done woke up the babies!" he accused, his steely gray gaze pinned on Shane. When he noticed Allison on the doorstep, relief gripped his features. "You're a woman. Maybe you can get 'em to stop bawling." And he promptly deposited the infant in her arms.

Allison's soft protest was swallowed up by heartwrenching sobs. Instinctively, she hugged the baby—a girl, she guessed—to her chest and kissed the halo of blond curls ringing her head.

Shane's astounded gaze swung from her face to the infant she was trying to soothe. His features puckered in disbelief. "Did you say *babies*?"

Fenton turned sideways and pointed a gnarled finger at a pair of matching cradles positioned at the foot of the single bed. From their vantage point, a pair of tiny fists punching the air were visible.

"Yep. A pair of 'em. Brother and sister."

"Fenton. What's going on here?" Shane demanded. "Where's Letty?"

The man's thin shoulders drooped and moisture filled his eyes. "She's dead, Sheriff."

Shane's features reflected shock. "Fenton, I'm sorry."

"Go see to your horse," he said gruffly. "Then we'll talk. You're lettin' all the heat escape."

After one last look at Allison and the baby, Shane left her alone with the unlikely trio. Once the door was closed, Fenton shuffled over to the ancient cookstove in the corner and set about making coffee.

Shifting the little girl to one hip, she managed to untie

her cape and hook it on a peg. Getting her bonnet off took more fancy maneuvering.

"How old are they?" She had to raise her voice to be heard. The boy in the cradle was getting angrier by the second.

"Six months."

After stomping off most of the wet clumps of snow clinging to her boots, she advanced toward the cradle and, crouching beside it, captured one fist in her hand.

"Hey there, little fella. The one in the cradle is the boy, right?"

Fenton nodded, the lamplight shining on his dull silver hair. "His name's Charlie. The girl is Izzy, short for Isabel."

Charlie's crying ceased and tear-washed blue eyes blinked up at her. His round cherub face was bright red, his straight blond hair lank where it lay across his forehead. His nightgown bore several stains.

Izzy's fussing had grown quieter, and Allison looked down into the liquid pools of chocolate brown. The combination of light hair and dark eyes was striking. They were both pretty babies. And both in desperate need of a bath and a fresh change of clothes.

Glancing about the cabin, she saw that it wasn't spotless, but nor was it filthy. Like Shane's home, there wasn't a couch, only wooden chairs pulled around a rectangular table that had seen better days. A leaning hutch pushed against the wall beside the fireplace housed lamps and assorted tools. A rifle hung above the mantel. In the kitchen area, a couple of homemade shelves attached to the wall held dishes and cups, as well as a stack of pots. A counter where a dry sink was situated held an assortment of glass baby bottles, ceramic jugs and folded towels. A stack of nappies and infant clothing occupied the bedside stand.

How long had Fenton Blake had the full care of these infants?

Shane reentered the cabin then, his expression grim. Dusting the snow from his hat onto the porch, he hung it on the empty peg beside her things and pulled the door closed behind him. When he'd removed his duster and gloves, he cupped his hands and blew on them.

"I'll have a cup of coffee ready for ya in no time."

"Appreciate it. Thanks for letting my horse share your barn space."

Charlie figured out that she wasn't picking him up and decided to squall again. Shane winced. Well, if he wanted the noise to stop, he was going to have to help out.

Allison marched over to where he stood and held out the baby girl. "Hold Izzy so I can see to her brother."

Looking like she had lost her wits, he made no move to take her. "I've never held a baby in my life."

"It doesn't require a university education, Shane."

He transferred that dubious gaze to Izzy, who was staring at him in quiet contemplation. "Uh…"

"Don't tell me you're scared of a wee human?"

"Actually, I am."

Charlie's tirade threatened to crack the windows. Fenton was either hard of hearing or had become immune, because he continued about his business at the stove.

"Do you enjoy listening to this? Because I don't. And I'm not sure I can juggle the pair of them." Without waiting for his response, she placed Izzy against his chest and physically moved his arm up to balance her there.

"Allison," he growled in protest.

Ignoring him, she hurried to the cradle, scooped up the little boy and hugged him tight. He didn't smell as most babies should, like sunny mornings, clean sheets and Ivory soap. Her nose scrunched as the odor of curdled milk rose to greet her.

"It's all right," she soothed, lightly patting his back.

Charlie cried into her shoulder, his face buried in her

dress, and Allison's heart melted. Poor darlings. What had happened to their mother and father?

She lifted her head and intercepted Shane's intent perusal, a heavy dose of caution at the back of his eyes.

Fenton turned and, taking in the scene, set three enamel cups on the table. "You look like a natural, Sheriff. Sure you ain't held a baby before?"

Shane's frown grew more pronounced as he glanced dubiously at Izzy, who he held slightly apart from him. "I think I'd remember something like that."

The elderly man came around and took her, cocking his head to the table. "Go ahead and drink your coffee while it's hot." He glanced at Allison, who'd managed to quiet Charlie. "You the sheriff's new sweetheart?"

Shane choked on his drink, coughing and sputtering and going red in the face.

Was the thought of them romantically linked that upsetting? "We're old friends."

"What're you doing in my neck of the woods?"

Since Shane was still clearing his throat, using a chair for balance, she answered for him. "We were out searching for a Christmas tree when the weather changed. We thought we could make it home, but we miscalculated." At the questioning lift of his bushy brows, she added, "I'm staying at the Wattses' place this month."

"Allison's from Virginia," Shane rasped. "She'll be returning as soon as Christmas is over."

He said it as if Christmas was something to get through, not enjoy. She'd hoped to make this one special for him, but she was beginning to think that was an impossible task.

Chapter Nine

A part of him wished he could start the day over. If he hadn't offered to cut down a tree for Allison, a tree for a house that didn't even belong to her, he wouldn't have walked into this nightmare—a blizzard, not one but *two* babies and a grieving great-grandfather. At least, he assumed they were Fenton's granddaughter Letty's offspring.

Barely able to rip his gaze from Allison with the baby boy, he took a moment to study Fenton. He appeared slighter than last he'd seen him. His eyes were bloodshot and his age-spotted hands shook slightly. Caring for infants around the clock was a demanding task that couldn't be good for the man's health, especially considering his heart condition had worsened in recent years. The last he'd heard, the medicine Doc Owens had prescribed would help preserve Fenton's quality of life as long as he got plenty of rest. When it had been just Letty and him, she'd cooked the meals and assisted with chores. Now everything fell to him, with the added burden of the twins.

As much as Shane disliked the situation he found himself in, he couldn't deny that the man was in dire need of assistance. Being in difficult spots was part of his job. Doing his duty for the residents of these mountains wasn't always pleasant, but he wasn't one to shirk his responsibilities.

"I hate to inconvenience you, Fenton, but do you mind if we bed down here for the night?" Shane said.

"You're welcome to share what I got. It ain't much, but the good Lord meets my needs."

"Izzy and Charlie. They're your kin?"

Quiet reigned while the older man struggled to contain his emotions. "I warned Letty not to get involved with the Whitaker clan, but she wouldn't listen. She fancied herself in love with their youngest boy. Convinced herself he loved her back. He filled her head with pretty lies. When she found out she was expecting, she didn't doubt he'd marry her."

"Clyde Whitaker is the babies' father?"

Righteous anger lit his gray gaze afire. His hold tightened around Izzy. "He might've sired them, but he ain't their pa."

Allison's expression revealed her opinion on the young man in question's behavior, one that matched his own.

"I know how the Whitakers operate. I'm not surprised Gentry didn't make his son do right by Letty."

"She was beside herself with grief. I went up there alone to try and reason with Gentry, but he blamed my granddaughter for leading Clyde astray." A vein throbbed in his forehead. "It's a wonder you didn't have to toss me in jail and throw away the key. Only the thought of Letty being left alone stopped me from doing something foolish."

Shane hadn't had a whole lot of dealings with Letitia Blake, but she'd impressed him as being a sweet young woman devoted to her only living relative.

"Has Clyde seen the twins?" Allison said.

Swaying from side to side, she smoothed Charlie's hair from his forehead. His blue eyes were watchful as he rested against her. Although she was a stranger, he seemed comfortable in her arms.

"Once. Letty took them up there when they were a month old. His pa said Clyde wasn't interested in seeing them. They turned her away."

Allison made a sound of distress. "She must've been crushed! What kind of unfeeling monsters are these people?"

Fenton's lined face reflected a mixture of anger and sorrow. "They're people in need of God's love and forgiveness, just like the rest of us. Only, they haven't acknowledged it yet."

His words pricked Shane's heart. He was in need of the same and more. How many times had he witnessed the power of prayer since making Gatlinburg his home? The O'Malleys were people with strong, abiding faith that didn't waver no matter what their circumstances. They weren't perfect, and neither were their lives, but they lived to serve God.

The O'Malleys aren't like you, an insidious voice inside his head reminded. *They're worthy of God's love. You aren't.*

"I'll pray for them," she said. "And you. I can't imagine how you've coped on your own."

"What happened to Letty?" Shane ventured.

"About a month ago, she got real sick. Coughing. Fever. Night sweats. The coughing settled in her chest, and she grew too weak to care for the babies." His eyes were wet. "I would've fetched the doctor from town, but she didn't want me traveling with Izzy and Charlie. And I couldn't leave them here with her alone for that long. It happened fast. One week, and she was gone."

Shane stared at the floor, sad for what the widower had endured. First the loss of his wife and adult daughter in a freak farm accident a decade earlier, leaving him with a young granddaughter to raise. And now having to bury Letty and assume the full responsibility for a pair of helpless, demanding infants.

"I thank God the babies didn't fall sick," Fenton went on, his voice uneven. "He protected them." He studied Allison and Shane. "And now He's brought the two of you here. You're an answer to prayer, that's what you are."

This entire situation had Shane rattled. Allison was convinced he'd be more comfortable staring down his gun's barrel at a ruthless outlaw than taking care of Charlie and Izzy. Fenton Blake's recent pronouncement had only made him more uptight. She was fairly sure he didn't wish to be the answer to this particular prayer.

"You sure you don't need some help?" Fenton lingered in the kitchen area, nursing what was probably lukewarm coffee.

"Go take a well-deserved rest," she insisted, noting the man's pallor. "Shane and I will be fine."

Sensing Shane's pointed stare, she smiled sweetly and waved Fenton away. He settled in the rocking chair by the fire with a battered, well-loved Bible.

"We'll be fine?" he whispered against her ear, sending what felt like a static electric charge zinging through her limbs. "Have you bathed a pair of squirming infants before?"

"As a matter of fact, I have." She angled her face toward his, which hovered inches from hers. Did he have to be so appealing? "Not a pair. I've bathed a baby before, and that's what we're going to do now. One at a time."

Between the cookstove and the fireplace, the small cabin was warm enough to bathe the babies without worrying about them catching cold. Fenton had assembled the soap, towels and clean changes of clothing for them. Shane had heated the water and poured it into a copper basin the twins' mother had used for such purposes. Since Izzy was preoccupied in her cradle with a handmade stuffed bear, Charlie was up first.

Balancing him on one hip, she tested the water temperature with her fingertip. "Feels good to me."

Laying him on his back on a towel spread out on the counter, she quickly divested him of his dirty gown and diaper. His halfhearted fussing ceased the instant she lowered him into the water. His eyes grew round with wonder.

She chuckled and gently lathered his arms and neck. "You like that, don't you?" she cooed.

Shane stood there with his arms at his sides, braced as if preparing to do major surgery. He'd removed his jacket and rolled the sleeves of his charcoal-gray-and-blue checked shirt up to his elbows, giving her a glimpse of fine dark hairs sprinkling his corded arms. His hair was ruffled from multiple finger-combings. A stubborn lock fanned across his forehead.

She resisted the impulse to smooth it into place. "I need for you to hold him steady while I wash him, all right?"

His azure gaze locked on to Charlie, he placed one hand on the baby's back and another on his shoulder. "Like this?"

"Yes, sir." She smiled. George would've gotten a kick out of this.

Charlie seemed content while she washed his skin and hair. He splashed a couple of times, raining droplets on them.

Shane didn't complain, though. He was too intent on his task to utter a word. He really was adorable, she thought. Although out of his element, he was determined to do his best.

When she lifted Charlie from the bucket and laid him on the towel, his brow puckered in dismay. She bent and rained ticklish kisses on his belly. He grinned, a single tooth flashing on his bottom gum, and grabbed a fistful of her hair.

"Shane? A little help here?"

He moved close and gently disengaged the boy's chubby fingers. "He likes when you do that."

Straightening, she smoothed her hair and laughed. "Most babies do."

Shane's slight smile held a sense of discovery. "You're a natural."

"I live with four children."

He followed her to the bed, where she laid the baby and picked up a fresh gown. "Would you like to dress him?"

He folded his arms, putting his considerable muscles on display. "I'd rather watch you do it."

Her laugh was dry, husky. "Typical answer."

In no time, she had Charlie dressed and his hair combed. She held him up. "Look at you, sweet boy! What a handsome young man you are."

"Smells better, too," Shane muttered.

"I'm glad you think so." Delivering the baby into Shane's arms, she boldly tapped his whiskered chin. "Because you're going to feed him while I give Izzy a bath."

Retrieving one of the bottles Fenton had prepared, she pushed it into his hand. "Here you are. Remember to burp him."

"But I—"

Fenton snapped his Bible closed and stood up. "You can have the rocker, Sheriff. I'm going out to the smokehouse to fetch us a slab of ham for supper."

Refusing Shane's offer to go, he donned his coat and hat and slipped outside, leaving them alone with his great-grandchildren.

Shane wanted to call him back and beg him to switch jobs. He'd be much more content in the smokehouse's cold isolation than in this stuffy, crowded cabin.

The baby in his arms reached for the bottle. Allison

wasn't paying either of them any mind. She was already undressing the tiny girl, talking in that sugary, cajoling tone all the while. Guess that was what mothers did to try and ward off crying fits. His own mother's face flashed in his mind.

Was it possible she'd been different in the beginning? Had she cooed and grinned and tickled him like Allison did with these two? Had she showered him with affection?

Since he'd never know the answer, he turned his mind to the hungry boy in his charge. He sat in the rocking chair and, tucking Charlie in the crook of his arm, lowered the bottle. Charlie latched on to it, his hands overlapping Shane's as he sucked greedily.

It had been a long time since he'd felt inadequate to a task. In those early days as a deputy, he'd had to learn his job quickly or risk getting hoodwinked or shot. He'd been in the law-keeping business so long now, there wasn't much he hadn't seen or heard. This baby opened up a whole new world. Of course, Gatlinburg had its fair share of newborns and tykes toddling about, but he didn't have any personal dealings with them. He even kept his distance from his friends' kids.

Charlie's big blue eyes, the color of a clear summer day, zeroed in on Shane's face. Shane studied him in return. His blond eyebrows were thin and sparse, his eyelashes black and as long as any girl's, his cheeks like soft pillows and his miniature fingernails in need of a trim. Now that he was clean, his hair shone and cupped his head like a soft silk cap. Allison was right. He was a good-looking boy.

A boy who'd never know his mother.

For Shane not to have known his mother would've been a good thing. For Charlie and Izzy, the opposite was true. Letty had nurtured them for five months. They appeared healthy and happy. While they didn't have much in the way of material things, she'd sewn clothes and dolls, blankets and nappies for them. Shane imagined she'd loved them so much that she'd been sure their father would love them, too.

"Don't forget to burp him halfway through," Allison reminded.

Izzy was splashing about in the basin much like her brother had done. Her chocolate-hued eyes were alight with joy. Allison dropped a kiss on the baby's forehead, and Shane's chest seized with a soul-deep yearning he recognized from his boyhood. Yearning for what he had never experienced and what so many took for granted—family, a sense of belonging to someone else, of being vital to another human being's happiness.

Because he was surrounded by families, he'd insulated his heart in a thick covering of indifference. That indifference, that conviction that he was meant to be alone, made it possible for him to survive. It didn't always stop the loneliness from creeping in, but it kept him from lamenting his lot in life. He wasn't meant to have a wife and children. He was meant to fulfill a crucial role...that of town protector and upholder of the law.

His job, along with the solid reputation he'd built, gave him plenty of satisfaction.

"Shane? Did you hear me?"

"Huh?"

"Did you burp him yet?"

He glanced at the bottle, which was more than half-gone. Hurriedly setting it on the small table beside the chair, he said, "Now what?"

"Sit him up and pat his back until he releases the air buildup."

Charlie was not pleased. His face screwed up like a prune and he waved his arms around. Shane awkwardly patted his back, amazed at the feel of his tiny rib cage and spine. Shane swiped a dribble of milk from his tiny chin.

"Do it a little harder." Allison brought a towel-wrapped Izzy over and stood observing him.

"I don't want to hurt him."

"You won't."

Once again, she regarded him with utmost confidence. She was wrong to put her confidence in him. A stolen purse or an argument between neighbors? He was equipped to handle those sorts of problems. Babies hadn't figured into his training.

The door burst open, allowing a swirl of icy wind and snow inside. Fenton shoved it closed behind him and stomped his boots on the rug. He held a large ham in his hands.

"Bad news, Sheriff. Wind's picking up, and the snow's showing no sign of stopping." His gray gaze didn't look particularly worried. In fact, Shane was pretty sure the older man was pleased with the forecast, which didn't make any sense. "Looks like you may be sticking around longer than just one night."

Chapter Ten

On a thin pallet near the banked fire, Allison huddled into the quilt, unable to get warm. Cold air clung to the floorboards. The tip of her nose was cold. And her cheeks. Her ears, too. The cabin's earlier heat had waned with the onset of evening. She could make out the jut of Shane's shoulder beneath his blanket. His pallet was situated a couple of feet from hers, close enough for her to reach if she were to stretch her arm out as far as she could.

This arrangement would've felt incredibly intimate if it hadn't been for Fenton's occasional snores and the babies' soft, steady breathing.

"Shane?" she whispered. "You asleep?"

He was lying facing away from her, his head cushioned by a small pillow. "Yep."

"You are?"

Drawing in a deep breath, he shifted onto his back and rested one arm across his forehead. "What's on your mind?"

"I'm curious what your plan is."

"Plan for what exactly?" He spoke in hushed tones.

"Helping Mr. Blake and the children. You know as well

as I do that he can't continue as he has been. He doesn't look healthy, in my opinion."

He rubbed both hands down his face and turned his head to look at her. His eyes gleamed in the near darkness. "He's not. His heart's weak. The medicine he takes helps manage the condition provided he takes good care of himself."

This was terrible news. The twins' mother was dead, and their sole caretaker was in poor health. "We have to do something."

"I'm not sure what the solution is. He's too far from town for someone to come out on a daily basis."

"Do you think he'd be willing to move closer?"

"A gentleman like him who's up in years? I seriously doubt it. The Blakes have inhabited this cove for generations."

Allison mulled over the problem. There had to be a solution that Fenton could live with. But what?

"I'll talk to him tomorrow," Shane said. "Maybe there's a distant relative who'd take the kids in."

She sat upright. "I can't see him allowing that. Charlie and Izzy are all he's got left."

He sat up, too. "We'll figure something out. You have my word."

"The people of Gatlinburg are fortunate to have you looking out for them, you know that?"

"Some might not agree with you," he drawled, "but I appreciate the sentiment."

She covered a yawn. "I wonder what George and Clarissa are doing right now."

"If they're smart? Sleeping. Like we should be." He pointed over his shoulder. "No telling if those two will snooze through the night."

"You're right." Shivering, she lay down again and tugged the frayed quilt edges to her chin. "My body's exhausted, but my mind won't settle. That ever happen to you?"

He got comfortable, this time facing her. "Sometimes. When I have a vexing puzzle to solve or an elusive criminal to capture."

Allison changed her mind...being here like this, chatting with him in the stillness of the night, felt immensely personal and private.

"What keeps you up nights?" He sounded relaxed and close to drifting off to sleep. "What worries the indomitable Allison Ashworth?"

"The things that worry me would seem silly to you."

In her early twenties, she hadn't given much thought to marriage. After her father's death, she and George had assumed the daunting responsibility of running their father's business and seeing to their employees' welfare. Her free time had been devoted to charitable work or visiting with her dearest friends. There had been several men who'd shown interest in courting her and, while she'd agreed to spend time with a few of them, she hadn't allowed anything serious to develop.

She hadn't wanted to acknowledge the truth back then, but being with Shane now made it impossible to deny. Deep in the inner recesses of her heart, she'd nursed the hope that one day Shane would return to Norfolk and finally give her a chance to love him. To heal the wounds inflicted by careless parents and life's hard knocks.

"Try me," he said.

The fact that he couldn't see her expression made it easier to confess. "My mom died when I was ten," she reminded him. "I have many wonderful memories of her. I remember her as a kind, gentle, patient woman. She had this exuberant laugh that didn't match her genteel appearance. She and my father would sit and talk for hours in his study...sharing stories, playing chess, making plans for our future." Smiling to herself, she felt for the locket she kept around her neck. A gift from her father on her thirteenth birthday, it contained miniature photographs of her parents.

"Sounds nice."

"I was blessed with parents who adored each other. They didn't exclude us, however. Mother and Father were firm in their discipline. They expected us to follow their instructions. They were also generous with their affections."

"I'm sorry you lost her, especially at so young an age."

A pang of wistfulness gripped her. "It was incredibly difficult in the first few years following her death. Her absence leached much of the happiness from our lives. Our family unit had been broken, and the loss of her nearly crippled my father emotionally. He was a changed man. His faith in God was the only thing that got him through."

"Are you worried you'll lose George like you lost your parents?"

She tucked her hand beneath the pillow. "The thought crosses my mind sometimes, but I try not to dwell on it."

"What is it, then?"

"I wonder if I'll ever experience a love like my parents shared…if I'll have a deep connection with someone." She worked to keep the emotion from her voice. "I think that's why I've focused on my profession instead of romance. I'm scared of failing. I don't want to settle for less than God's best for me."

Shane was quiet a long time. "I didn't have the opportunity to meet your mother. Is it possible you remember only the good times? That maybe your memories are better than the reality?"

"I know my parents' relationship wasn't perfect. There were times when things were strained at the supper table and afterward they'd go their separate ways. But by the next day, they were smiling at each other again."

"If anyone deserves happiness, Allie, it's you."

Her heart thrummed at the rare use of her shortened name.

"But I'd hate to see you wind up alone because you've set your expectations too high."

It was her turn to be silent. She stewed over his words. *Was wanting* him *setting her expectations too high?* she was tempted to ask.

"I don't want to be alone anymore," she whispered instead. "I want to build a life with someone. I want children. Lots of them."

"How many is a lot?" He sounded more alert than before.

"I don't have an exact number in my head." Her cheeks stung. This wasn't exactly a normal conversation to be having with a man who wasn't her intended. "All I know is that I have the means to care for a whole gaggle of children and more than enough affection to go around."

"One day you'll get the family you're longing for. They'll be mighty fortunate to have you in their lives."

Emotion clogged her throat. That was the nicest thing he had ever said to her. "Thank you, Shane."

"Good night, Allison."

Shane couldn't get their late-night conversation out of his head. He sat at the kitchen table with Fenton the following afternoon, a chessboard between them. Usually he enjoyed pitting his wits against an opponent, especially if it was someone he didn't often play with. Today was different. He couldn't focus because he kept getting distracted by Allison and the babies.

On a quilt stretched across the floorboards, she sat with her legs curled beneath her and held Izzy's stuffed bear midair. Piles of pillows supported Charlie and Izzy. They were strong enough to sit up by themselves but their balance wasn't perfect. Taking turns, Allison would lean forward and lightly tap the infants on their noses, chins or chests with the bear. The simple game thrilled them.

Shane's attention switched between their bright, round faces to Allison, who looked very happy for a woman whose Christmas holiday had gone awry. What a special woman. Instead of fretting over things she couldn't change, she made the best of whatever situation she found herself in. That was a rare quality in anyone.

The bear slipped from her fingers. As she leaned forward to retrieve it, her unbound hair spilled over her shoulders, shimmering like strands of liquid sunshine. Shane very badly wanted to test its texture. Fenton had lent her Letty's hairbrush and mirror that morning, along with a dress. The design was plain. There were no ribbons or buttons or fancy beadwork, but the fabric was a rich jewel-blue tone that made Allison's creamy complexion glow with good health. She fit in these surroundings as if born for mountain life.

"Checkmate."

Fenton's triumphant announcement brought Shane's attention to the board. Bending close, he said, "I thought you were supposed to be tough to beat. Guess you got other things on your mind." He winked so that Shane had no doubt as to his meaning.

"I guess so," he admitted sheepishly. "How about another round?"

"You in the mood to get trounced a second time?" The old man's creased face lit with humor.

He kicked up his shoulder. "What else we got to do?"

Fenton lowered his voice to a conspiratorial whisper. "You could give your sweetheart a hand."

Shane rested his hands on the table. "She's a friend."

"Shame." Turning sideways in his chair, he took in the scene before him. "The man who wins her won't live to regret it."

"How do you figure?"

"You get to be my age, you see a lot. You learn to listen to this." He tapped a bent finger to his chest, indicating his heart. "She'll be a fine mama someday."

Shane didn't disagree. Allison was a natural caretaker. Nurturing was in her blood. Look at how she'd tried to enfold him in her flock the moment he arrived at Ashworth House. Any normal person would've let her. Too bad her generosity hadn't been a match for his impenetrable defenses.

"She's worried about you, you know," Shane murmured.

Fenton's brow furrowed, and he nodded, sadness stealing over his features. "It ain't been easy. There've been moments when I thought I couldn't go on. I'm not a spring chicken anymore. Feeding and diapering twins around the clock reminded me of that fact real quick. I can't let Letty down. I'm all those babies have got, but this old ticker..." Frowning, he stared at the trio on the quilt. "I worry what might happen to them if I were to suffer an episode. No one around for miles."

"I wish I could provide someone to help out. If you lived in town—"

"Stop right there, Sheriff." He held up a hand. "I know what you're about to suggest, and I ain't leavin' my land."

"I didn't figure you would."

"I'm too old to be starting over."

"You have relatives who could come and stay? Help out for a while?"

"You mean someone who'd stick around until the twins are about five years old? Nah. I hate to admit it, but what those kids need is a young, God-fearing couple who'd raise them right."

Something in his tone put Shane on alert. The way Fenton was looking at Allison, all hopeful and expectant like she was an elusive Christmas gift he'd prayed for, filled Shane with foreboding.

Izzy and Charlie's giggles lilted through the space. Over Fenton's shoulder, Shane met Allison's gaze. She smiled, a single dimple flashing, before returning her attention to the task of playing entertainer.

Shane sank against the chair back, amazed at how much he longed to be with her on the floor, to sit close beside her and join in the game. To be a part of their group.

It was the same spot where they'd conversed the night before. He could recall the huskiness of her voice, the sweetness of her scent, the feeling that they were the only ones awake for miles. She'd opened up to him in a way no one ever had before. He'd been humbled that she'd trusted him and sorry that he'd missed out on a friendship with her.

For a moment, he'd wished her stay could be permanent. But then reason kicked in. He wasn't good enough for the likes of her, and friendship wouldn't satisfy him for long.

"What are you going to do?" Shane said at last.

The old man continued to scrutinize Allison in a way that heightened his lawman's suspicions.

"The only thing I can do. Pray and wait for the good Lord to provide an answer."

"Enjoying the peace and quiet?"

Framed by the barn stalls, Shane turned from petting one of the horses. His hat and gloves rested on a nearby hay bale. His duster was buttoned and a blue neckerchief kept his neck warm. "I needed to stretch my legs."

Allison pushed the door shut and crossed the straw-littered ground to join him. Folding her arms beneath her cape, she leaned against the stall and tilted her face up. "Admit it. The crying got to you."

"Two at once was a bit much." A slight smile graced his mouth. The growth along his jawline was heavier today.

"It wasn't long after you left that they drifted off."

After his and Fenton's second chess game, it became clear that Izzy and Charlie were ready for a nap. Allison scooped up Izzy while Fenton had taken her brother. Shane had put the board and pieces away and, mumbling an excuse about fresh air and horses, had made his escape.

"They're good babies," she said. "Especially considering they must be missing their mama."

Shane scraped a hand along his jaw. "I hadn't thought about that. They're so young…"

"Letty was their mother and primary caretaker." Pocketing her gloves, she reached out to pet the horse's face. "Did you speak to Fenton?"

"I did." Something in his tone warned her the news wasn't good.

"He won't budge from here. Can't say as I blame him. Where's he going to go? This place is all he's known. And there are no relatives in the position to give him the long-term assistance he needs."

Allison had figured as much. "What if something were to happen to him?"

Terrible ideas crowded her mind, each more dire than the next.

"Hey." He stepped closer, ducking his head to catch her gaze. "I'll figure something out. I'll send someone out here once a week to check on them. I'll even come myself if I have to."

"Once a week isn't enough." She grasped the rough edge of the stall door. "If he were to have an accident or fall ill, Izzy and Charles would starve before they were discovered."

Shane's warm hand covered hers. The gesture startled her. "Fine. I'll send someone three times a week."

She lost herself in his steady gaze. "You care what happens to them?"

"Of course, I do." He pulled away. "You think I don't want them to be safe and cared for? That's what I want for every single resident in these mountains."

"I didn't mean to offend you." Feeling bold after their late-night interaction, she captured his hand and squeezed. "I'm simply grateful that you're willing to go out of your way to help. I know taking care of infants isn't something you're familiar with."

He nodded. "You're right about that."

"Charlie didn't have any complaints about your bottle handling skills."

Instead of answering, he gave her an arch look. He slipped his hand free and pointed to her hair.

"You, ah, have something…" Shane peered closer. "Looks like dried corn mush."

She grimaced. "Charlie can't help himself. He likes to grab fistfuls of my hair."

"I noticed. Hold still while I get it out."

Allison studied his serious countenance. His fingers were gentle as he worked the bit free. Tingles radiated across her scalp when his knuckles scraped her tender nape.

"There," he breathed huskily. "I think I got it all."

Shane proceeded to smooth her heavy mane behind her shoulder, taking his time finger-combing it so that it lay against her cloak. "It's as soft as I thought it would be."

She felt unsettled. Nervous. The strong column of his throat above the neckerchief filled her vision. "It is?"

A muscle in his jaw worked as he lowered his arm to his side. "Yeah."

His searing gaze roamed her hair and face. He would deny it if asked—and she wouldn't dream of asking—but Shane Timmons was drawn to her. The evidence was reflected in his eyes, the hungry yearning he'd be horrified to know was there for her to see.

Her elation was tempered by the knowledge that he

didn't *want* to be affected by her. He wouldn't welcome these feelings, wouldn't celebrate them like she did. There was no victory in the revelation. How could there be when nothing was ever going to change between them?

Chapter Eleven

Allison's nearness, coupled with the longing in her expressive eyes, made it tough to cling to his long-held convictions. His fingers begged to sink into her silken mane a second time. Curling them into fists, he shoved them in his pockets.

His heart's pumping was fast and erratic as other thoughts bombarded him. In the deserted barn, lamps hooked on nails throughout the space gave off enough light to make it seem like evening instead of afternoon. They were alone, and she was breathtaking. Her smaller stature and form appealed to him, evoked his protective instincts and made him want to curl his arms about her waist and cradle her against his chest for hours.

He couldn't believe he'd said that out loud about her hair. The statement was of a personal nature, something he tried to avoid with her.

Allison came close and, curling her arm through his, leaned into him. With her face tilted up, he couldn't *not* look at her soft, supple lips and wonder how she'd react if he kissed her.

"Make snow angels with me."

He jerked his gaze up. "What?"

"There's no one around to see," she said diplomatically. "Besides, you owe me."

"How do you figure?"

The sparkle in her green eyes dimmed. "I haven't forgotten how you snubbed me when we were kids. A girl doesn't forget those types of things. All I wanted was your friendship."

The blood roared in his ears. He'd been so busy trying to protect himself that he hadn't cared how his behavior had impacted her.

"Allie—" His voice sounded raw.

She stopped him with a finger pressed to his lips. His throat went dry.

"I don't wish to discuss the past right now. What I want is to have a little fun, all right?"

"Fun."

"Snow angels. With you."

He didn't see the appeal of getting snow down his collar and making a fool of himself, but she was right. He did owe her.

"I let you talk me into this once before."

"You abandoned me after a minute. Stomped off muttering about little pests and foolish games."

Shane couldn't help himself. He very lightly curved his hand around her cheek, his thumb resting against the crescent below her eye. Allison held still, her lips parting.

He drew on every ounce of willpower he possessed not to kiss her.

"I was young and confused. Damaged goods. It was right that I stayed away from you."

"And now?" she whispered.

"I'm still damaged."

Her lashes drifted down. "Oh, Shane—"

"You're only here for a short while. And you're wise to

the ways of the world like you weren't back then. So let's go be silly, shall we?"

Shane turned her toward the exit before he could do something unforgiveable. He grabbed his hat and gloves and pushed the door open, squinting at the white winter wonderland that greeted them.

White powder encrusted the gigantic pines and evergreens. Those trees without leaves were also coated in snow inches thick in the crooks where the branches met the trunks. Making sure the barn door was secure, he led Allison through the knee-high drifts around the barn to where the cabin wasn't visible. There was only snow and forest and the occasional cardinal to witness their antics.

He swept his arm out like a gallant knight. "Ladies first."

She grinned, her teeth as white as the sky against her red lips. She took a handful of steps into the middle of the clearing, made a complete three-hundred-sixty turn and then, with a girlish giggle, lay flat on her back and made wide arcs with her arms and legs.

"Come on!"

Shaking his head, he laid his hat atop the snow and marched over beside her. "This stays between you and me, got it?"

He could only imagine what the good folks of Gatlinburg would say about this.

"I won't tell a soul."

With a sigh, he lay on the ground, wincing at the cold sensations greeting his body. At first he felt foolish moving about like a seal bobbing on dry land. But as Allison's laughter rose toward the heavens, he started smiling, too. The powder was soft and springy. He let some of it drift between his gloved fingers.

"This is the perfect consistency for a snowman."

Allison sat up, anticipation lighting her face and making her seem like a young girl again. "I can't remember the last time I built one. Let's do it!"

Shane could've listed several reasons why staying out here wasn't a good idea. Instead, he smothered his voice of reason and let himself take part in a custom that thousands of families performed across the country each winter season. Working together, they packed and rolled and patted snow until they'd constructed an impressive-looking figure.

"See?" She surveyed their work. "This is fun, right?"

"I suppose." He shrugged, unable to resist teasing her.

They were on their knees in front of the snowman. Her hair was disheveled, her cheeks bright pink and her eyes shone like radiant gems. "You *suppose*?"

"It beats doing paperwork."

"Is that so?"

Without warning, she barreled into him, knocking him flat on his back. Shane gasped as wet snow was smushed against his face and neck. Allison bombarded him with handfuls of the stuff, the element of surprise on her side. But she was a lightweight and no match for his strength. "You're gonna regret that, woman!"

In an instant, he had her on the ground. Crouching beside her, he retaliated, dousing her with a shower of snow. She squealed and squirmed and tried to snag his hands.

"Okay, okay, I give up!" she gasped.

Leaning over, he pinned her shoulders and bent his face close. "You sure you're done?"

All of a sudden, the lightheartedness fled, replaced with a pulsing awareness between them. Her eyes were huge in her face. She was gazing at him with longing that mirrored that which was unfurling inside him. Stunned by what he saw, he scrambled to standing.

Allison had stated that she wanted to be his friend. She hadn't indicated she was interested in anything more. It was impossible.

"Here," he said gruffly, extending his hand. "Let's get you dusted off."

Averting her face, she allowed him to help her stand. "I can do it."

While she righted her cloak and brushed the moisture from her skirts' hem, he brushed the flakes from his hair and seized his hat from where he'd left it.

Where there'd been shrieks and laughter minutes before, there was strained silence. He felt bereft, of all things. Lonelier than he could recall being, which was strange considering Allison was standing right here.

"I could go for a cup of coffee," he said. "How about you?"

She met his gaze and smiled. "I could use some warming up." Turning to look at the snowman once more, she said quietly, "I wonder who's going to build snowmen with Izzy and Charlie?"

"They're six months old."

"Soon they'll be crawling. Then walking. Talking." She fell into step beside him as he started for the cabin. "Raising children isn't solely about feeding and clothing them or teaching them their letters. It's so much more than that."

He glanced at her profile. "You're worried whether or not they'll have time for frivolous things."

They stopped at the base of the cabin steps. "Fun isn't everything," she admitted. "But it is important." Cocking her head, she considered him. "Did you have fun today, Shane?"

"I'm not going to lie."

Disappointment flitted over her face.

"Today was the most fun I can remember having. Thank you, Allie."

The disappointment transformed into joy. "That makes me happier than you can imagine."

The door opened, and Fenton stared at them in concern. "You two lookin' to catch pneumonia?" he demanded. "Come on inside and warm up before the fire. I've got soup simmering on the stove."

Shane and Allison shared a smile, and he realized something had changed between them. He wasn't sure if that was a good thing, but he liked it.

Allison tickled Izzy's soft belly and waited for the drool-filled smile. Izzy didn't disappoint. Her big doe eyes shone with contentment. Bending over the mattress again, she blew gusts of air against her middle. The baby girl cackled and, using both hands, latched on to Allison's cheeks.

"Easy, sweet girl," she said, smiling as she curled her fingers over Izzy's and moved out of reach.

"Ba-ba."

Shane's pacing ceased. Holding Charlie against his shoulder, he turned and regarded them in surprise. "That sounded like a word."

"She's trying out sounds." Allison sat her up and tugged a clean dress over Izzy's blond curls. The baby objected. Typically laid-back, Izzy didn't like having her diaper or clothing changed.

Charlie protested the lack of movement. Lightly bouncing him, Shane resumed his route from the window nearest the kitchen to the opposite wall where a wardrobe contained Fenton's clothes and personal items. Scooping Izzy into her arms, she approached the pair.

"Want to trade?"

Frowning, he shook his head. "I'm okay. I haven't worn a blister on my heel yet."

"He acts like his tummy is hurting him," she said. "Maybe he has gas."

Shane gave her a dubious look, and a bubble of laughter escaped her. Charlie decided to explore Shane's chin. His cute button nose wrinkled at the feel of his stubble.

"I think Charlie wishes you'd shave."

Ensconced in the only rocking chair, Fenton closed his Bible and observed them. "Now don't the four of you look like a picture-perfect family."

Shane appeared as startled as she felt. The observation was surprising given that his granddaughter wasn't long buried.

"The sheriff's got it in his head that he's not cut out for family life," she blurted.

Fenton raised an eyebrow. "Sometimes God has to adjust a man's thinking."

Charlie started fussing again, and Shane patted his small back. "I know how you feel, little buddy. I feel like fussing, too." He gave Allison a pointed glare.

Fenton laughed heartily. "Come sit with him. Lay him over your knees and pat his back."

Allison watched as Fenton helped Shane situate the baby. The sight was a touching one. Shane was so careful with him. His large, tanned hand looked huge as he balanced Charlie on his lap. After a few minutes, he picked him up and held him midair.

"Like the view from there?" Smiling, Shane pulled him close so that they were nose to nose and then lifted him up again.

Charlie gurgled and sucked on his fingers.

"I think he likes that," Allison said, fascinated by this first display of playfulness toward the babies.

Shane repeated the action several times before sitting Charlie in his lap. Izzy lurched toward them, and Allison lowered her beside her brother.

"There." She nodded in satisfaction. "Now this would be a perfect image for a photograph."

He smirked. "The first peep out of them and you're coming to my rescue, right?"

"Of course." Grinning, she eased onto the nearby bed. "Do you think Ben's worried about you?"

His eyes glittered. "Ben knew I was taking you out to look for a tree."

"He did?"

"Most of the time, we keep each other informed as to our whereabouts in case of emergencies."

Something about his manner implied he had made a point to tell his deputy about their plans. While he seemed to respect Ben, he didn't appear to want him associating with Allison.

"Will he organize a search party if we're gone too long?"

Using the toe of his boot, he set the rocker to moving, his arms firmly around each baby. "Depends on how bad it is in the heart of town and if he's dealing with any problems there." He rested his head against the chair slats. "Ben and I know these mountains like the backs of our hands. He no doubt assumes I've found shelter for us."

"How long would he wait?"

"Given current conditions, I'd say a week. Why?"

She glanced at Fenton, who was at the counter washing bottles. That reminded her she should probably wash the bucket of soiled nappies and clothes—not a task she was looking forward to but one she'd willingly tackle in order to give their host a break.

Leaning forward, she lowered her voice. "When were you planning on returning to town?"

He lifted his head, his gaze alert. "It hasn't snowed in a couple of hours. If it doesn't start up again between now and tomorrow morning, we should head out then."

"I've been considering asking if he'd like me to stay awhile longer."

The rocking halted. "I've got to get back—"

"Just me."

He shot a quick glance at Fenton, who was whistling

while he worked, before spearing her with a formidable stare. "Allie, I understand why you'd offer. However, this is your holiday. You're supposed to be enjoying your time away from work and responsibility. I'm sure the reason your brother sent you on ahead was because you're due a break. I admire your selflessness, but I can't let you do it."

"Let me?" Unwilling for their host to overhear, she used the rocker arm to support her weight, bringing her close to him. "I may be a guest in your town, but that doesn't mean you can dictate my actions. I've been making my own decisions for quite some time now. I can't in good conscience abandon this precious family."

Anger sparked in his eyes. "This is my responsibility, Allison, not yours. Your life is in Virginia. What are you going to do? Play house for the rest of the month? What happens after Christmas? I'll tell you. He gets used to having you around. The kids get used to having you around. And then they lose you, just like they lost Letty."

The color drained from her face. She couldn't do that to them.

"I'll tell you what else will happen," he murmured fiercely. "You'll get even more attached than you already are. Your brother won't look too kindly on me if I send you home with a broken heart."

Chapter Twelve

"The sheriff lit outta here lookin' like he sucked on a sour apple." Fenton tossed another log on the fire. Sparks danced above the flames.

Allison sat where Shane had minutes before, taking comfort from the weight of the twins on her lap. While they were relaxed and content, she was in turmoil. She'd been certain her idea was a sound one until he'd pointed out potential pitfalls. The last thing she wanted to do was cause this family more grief. And he was right. It wasn't a long-term solution.

"Shane's accustomed to bossing people about," she said, still smarting.

Fenton scratched his head. He'd taken some time to himself earlier in the day, and his silver hair shone and his cheeks were freshly shaven. His skin was deeply tanned from a lifetime of outdoor living.

"Guess it comes natural to him after all these years of being a sheriff." Drawing a chair over, he sank onto it and rubbed his hands along his thighs. His gray eyes were wise and patient. "Whatever it is you don't see eye to eye on, just remember he wants what's best for you."

She rubbed her cheek along Izzy's springy curls. "How old was Letty when her parents passed?"

"Ten."

"That's how old I was when my mother died." She knew exactly how Letty would've felt…as if her world had been taken apart and put back together wrong. And now Letty's kids wouldn't have a chance to know her. Sadness pressed in.

"What was she like?"

He blinked rapidly and sniffled.

"If you'd rather not talk about her, I understand."

"I want to. It's not easy, ya know?"

"Even though my father's been gone for more than a decade, I still get choked up sometimes when I think about all he's missed."

Fenton cleared his throat. "My Letty was a sweet girl. Quiet. What some folks would call a dreamer." His countenance bore witness to his intense sorrow. "I wanted more for her than this secluded cove. She was smart. I thought maybe the Lord would provide a way for her to have a different life. But she got mixed up with the Whitaker boy. He didn't deserve her."

"I'm so sorry, Fenton."

While he mopped his face with a handkerchief, Allison silently prayed for God to comfort this man and to provide clear answers to his dilemma.

"Shane and I are in disagreement about my wish to stay here and help you for a week or two."

When he lifted his head, his gaze was solemn. "In the short while you've been here, I've seen how you care for my great-grandchildren. Doesn't surprise me that you'd offer. And I understand why the sheriff has reservations."

Allison couldn't discern his thoughts at all. Beyond sorrowful, he looked resigned.

"So you don't want me to stay?"

"I have a different request. Don't feel bad if you'd rather not."

"What is it?"

"You're staying at the Wattses' place?"

"Yes, that's right."

"I've got to see the doctor and purchase a few things at the mercantile. Would it be a burden if Izzy and Charlie stayed with you for a day or two? The sheriff probably wouldn't mind if I bunked with him."

"No. Not at all! I'd love that."

The request wasn't what she'd expected. She'd hoped for longer time with the twins, but she'd take what she could get. In the unlikely event they returned to town and found George and Clarissa had arrived, Shane would surely know someone who'd be willing to offer temporary boarding space.

"Are you feeling all right?" She'd noticed him pausing to catch his breath at odd times throughout the day.

"Just more tired than usual." He made a dismissive motion. "I need to see him about a fresh supply of medicine."

Allison hoped it wasn't more than he was letting on. Fenton struck her as the suffer-in-silence type.

When Shane returned to the cabin a half hour later, she left the explaining to Fenton. Shane didn't comment, simply speared her with his unreadable gaze and nodded.

Their plans made, she and Fenton spent the remainder of the evening gathering the necessary supplies. Shane disappeared outside again. She assumed he was avoiding her. There was no conversation that night. He lay with his back toward her, tension radiating off his big frame.

The following morning dawned bright and clear. Once the babies were dressed and fed and the wagon loaded, Shane guided her onto the porch.

"Do you think these will work?"

A pair of wooden crates had been altered to form seats

with a slat across the top that would prevent Izzy and Charlie from toppling forward. Crouching, she patted the bunched-up blankets in the bottom.

"You made these?"

He shrugged. "Thought you might get tired holding them the entire trip."

Popping up, she hugged him, careful to keep it brief.

"You're a sweetheart for thinking of them."

Color etched his cheekbones. "It was nothing."

"Are you still angry with me?"

His eyebrows shot up. "I wasn't angry, Allie."

"You were annoyed."

"I was concerned. Still am."

Basking in his warm, blue regard, she spread her hands. "I'm not staying on here, am I?"

Presenting her with his profile, he squinted into the distance. He looked like the formidable lawman this morning in his full gear, gun belt firmly about his waist, pistols visible and badge pinned over his heart. His full beard didn't detract from his appeal one iota. "I can't put my finger on it, but something doesn't sit well about Fenton's request."

"What do you mean?"

"It's not like him, that's all. Men like him don't ask to stay in town. They go in, get what they need and get out."

"He said he had to see the doctor. I'm sure he has other business to tend to. Besides, he's got his great-grandchildren to think about now. I looked through their belongings. They don't have proper winter gear."

In the sunlight, the snow sparkled like a blanket of diamonds. "Another thing you should know—he won't look kindly upon handouts. If you're thinking of purchasing stuff for them, I suggest you broach the subject carefully."

She laid a hand on his upper arm. "Thanks for the insight. And for the seats."

He turned to her again. "You're welcome."

Allison was reminded of that charged moment between them in the snow. Being close to him was a heady experience. The feelings she'd had for him years ago couldn't hold a candle to those she was experiencing now. They weren't naive, immature kids any longer. Her reactions to him were on a whole other plane...all-consuming and difficult to fight. He was like a decadent plum pudding she shouldn't go near but couldn't stop thinking about.

Oh, if he only knew she'd compared him to a plum pudding...

He tilted his head. "You have a strange expression on your face."

"Uh, just thinking about Christmas dinner."

His brows pulled together. She was saved from further questioning by Fenton, who appeared in the doorway.

"We ready to head out?"

Shane's gaze seemed reluctant to leave her. "We are."

They reached the Wattses' property by noon. Shane's intention to make a quick escape was thwarted almost as soon as they unloaded the wagon.

Fenton pulled him aside. "I didn't expect the trip to wear me out. Allison said I could use one of the extra bedrooms. Would you mind keeping her company for a while longer? I'll be ready to head to your place once I've rested."

Shane glanced at the big white farmhouse with reluctance. He'd counted on getting Fenton settled and then going off alone to process all that had happened the last two days. He needed time and space to reclaim his former emotional distance from Allison.

He couldn't refuse the man, however. Judging by his haggard appearance, he'd benefit from a long nap. "I'll be glad to."

His gratefulness was obvious. "Sure do appreciate it, Sheriff."

Together, they crossed the yard. The Wattses' farm had received less accumulation than Blake's Cove. Still, the ground was completely covered and the buildings' roofs had about an inch of white on them. He eyed the Fraser fir propped against the porch railing.

Stifling a sigh, he grabbed the cut end and, waiting until Fenton went inside, dragged it to the living room.

"Allison?"

Passing Fenton on the stairs, she reached the bottom tread and paused.

"Are the kids asleep?" he said.

"Fenton put their cradles in my room." Dressed in the outfit she'd worn during their original outing for the tree, she'd tied her hair back with a bit of string that looked too flimsy to do the job. In spite of the past trying days, she was lovely. Maybe a little less animated than usual. "They went right to sleep."

He wasn't surprised. They'd remained awake during the trip, observing the passing scenery with interest. The seats he'd crafted had saved Allison from having to hold them. Not that she would've minded. She wouldn't think twice about sacrificing her own comfort for theirs. That was just the sort of person she was.

"Where do you want this?" he said, jabbing a finger at the tree.

Striding to the center of the room, she turned a slow circle, tapping her chin as she considered every nook and cranny. She wandered to the wall opposite the fireplace and stood in front of the window. "This is the spot you picked out the other day, isn't it? It will serve nicely."

He set it up for her. The only reason he knew what to do was because he'd helped Josh with his last year. He'd never bothered for one for himself. Seemed a waste.

When she was satisfied that it wasn't crooked, she

clasped her hands together. "It's perfect. Thank you, Shane."

Each time she thanked him with those shining eyes, he got this feeling like he was a king who'd granted her dearest wish. It was a feeling he could get used to.

That's why he asked the next question. "What are you going to decorate it with?"

"I was planning on making smaller versions of those pinwheel stars with the leftover paper." She indicated the mantel. "I can get popcorn to string later."

"Want some help?"

"You're offering to make tree ornaments with me?"

"Fenton and the kids are napping, and we've nothing else to do. Unless you'd care to challenge me in a chess game."

"That would be a short match, as you well know."

He did know. While he and George had played games, she'd been content to do needlework or simply observe their moves.

"I would enjoy having your help with the decorations, if you truly don't mind."

Cutting and pasting paper wasn't high on his list of favorite things to do. He wasn't about to tell her that, however. She'd been wonderful during their entire ordeal. This was one small way to repay her.

"Point me to the scissors," he said.

Her demeanor upbeat, she hummed a familiar Christmas tune as she brought out the supplies. They chose the dining table for their workspace.

"Let me show you how to do the first one."

Coming around to his side, Allison stood close enough that their arms brushed together, making it tough to concentrate. Crafting pinwheels wasn't what he wanted right this minute. What he wanted was to wrap his arms around her, bury his face in her hair and block out the nightmare of the past. He wanted to hold fast to her and not worry about a single thing. But the courage he employed in his job deserted him. Shane was more afraid of reaching out to Allison, of opening his heart to her, than of meting out justice to malicious criminals.

"Do you want me to make a second one?" She angled her face toward his, wholly unaware of her effect on him. Or was she? Something flickered in her eyes as they traveled his features. Was she deliberately testing his boundaries?

He dismissed the thought. Allison wasn't a calculating woman. George had indicated she had little experience with courting. The knowledge thrilled him, which was wrong for many reasons.

"Yeah. A second demonstration would be good." Subtly putting a couple of inches between them, he did his best to focus on her instructions.

She returned to the chair opposite his, and he found he could breathe easier.

"I remember the monster tree at Ashworth House," he said. "Those ornaments weren't handmade."

He recalled that first Christmas with the Ashworths and his awe at the opulence of their decorations. To him, the ornaments had appeared to have been crafted of pure gold and expensive glass. The huge red velvet ribbons adorning the stair banisters had fascinated him. Put together, there would've been enough fabric to make a hundred fancy dresses.

"True." Her expression turned fond. "However, these days we install a smaller tree in the parlor that the children and I decorate."

"I suppose they love that tradition."

"They like to be creative, and they like to feel as if they've contributed. They're also quite fond of the frosted sugar cookies and hot cocoa that's served once our work is finished."

He could picture her there in the parlor, directing her

niece and nephews in their endeavors. "Your sister-in-law hasn't made you feel unwelcome, has she?"

"Oh, no." Shaking her head vigorously, she laid her cut pieces on the tabletop in various patterns. Her hands were small and dainty and jewelry-free. "I'm fortunate in that Clarissa and I have a wonderful friendship. When she and my brother became engaged, she and I had a long talk. She told me that it wasn't her intention to move in and take over the running of things, nor did she wish for me to feel displaced or unwanted. We've worked out a system where we share the household responsibilities."

"I'm glad, Allie. Ashworth House is where you belong. I can't imagine you separate from it."

Her fingers stilled, resting flat atop her assembled pinwheel. "I won't live there forever." Her lips pressed together in dismay.

Shane realized he'd offended her. "I didn't intend to imply that you would." He gestured, the scissors still in his grip. "My memories of the estate are tied up in the past, that's all. I think of you, and all I can see is that grand house."

She slowly nodded, her gaze dropping. "While I'm content to continue on with George, I've been thinking of striking out on my own for a while."

Shane wasn't convinced she'd be happy. Imagining her all alone in an enormous house didn't make *him* happy. That wasn't her dream. "What's George's opinion?"

"I haven't told him yet." Lifting her chin, she silently dared him to keep her secret. "Besides, I don't know what the future holds. Who knows? Perhaps I will be setting up residence with Trevor in the new year."

Jealousy instantly invaded every inch of him. It was an illogical reaction. He didn't wish for her to be alone or unhappy, and yet the idea of her building a life with a stranger made him ache with regret.

"Whatever you decide," he forced himself to say, "I support you. You deserve to be happy."

Chapter Thirteen

Decorating a tree with Shane was very different from decorating one with four rambunctious children. Where the children would attack the task with haphazard gusto, he was deliberate. He studied the branches for long moments before placing each ornament.

"It doesn't have to be perfect." She softly nudged his side. "You should see our parlor tree. It may not win awards, but it's decorated with love."

The shiny ribbon dangled from his pointer finger. "I've never done this before."

Allison nodded, masking her consternation. It shouldn't come as a surprise. The estate staff had decorated the large tree in the hall, and they hadn't had a second tree then.

"Well, you're doing a fine job. I'm glad you agreed to this." She gestured toward the kitchen. "I'm only sorry I don't know how to make frosted sugar cookies."

"I don't need cookies." His steady gaze warmed her and seemingly communicated that her presence was enough to satisfy him.

Fanciful thinking, that.

He looped the pinwheel on a high branch and watched it spin and dance. They'd chosen a pretty tree, about seven feet tall with thick, full branches. Its sharp perfume competed with the smoky odor of crackling firewood.

He gestured to the coffee table. "That was my last one."

"Mine, too." Tapping her chin, she said, "It definitely needs more color. I'm thinking popcorn and cranberry strings, maybe fabric bows. And there's nothing for the top."

"Quinn stocks a small selection of Christmas merchandise. You might find a topper you like there."

She turned to him. "Will you help me finish decorating once I get more supplies?"

After a moment, he nodded in mock seriousness. "I suppose I could do that. It wasn't as tedious as I thought it would be."

"I'm relieved to hear you weren't bored," she said wryly.

"I could never be bored around you, Allie." Then, as if embarrassed at the admission, he located a broom and began sweeping up stray needles. "Did your father ever tell you how I came to work for him?"

"He didn't mention it."

Her father hadn't given them a whole lot of information about Shane's past, citing his private nature. Her father had urged them to give Shane time, probably thinking he'd share when he got ready. Only, he never did.

A sigh gusted out of him, and Allison knew it had nothing to do with her. "My mother spent most days drinking and bemoaning her lot in life. One day she got careless and, locked in the booze's haze, knocked over a lamp and started a fire. I came home to find the place burned to the ground. The police told me what happened." He stopped sweeping and rested his weight on the broom handle.

Her heart breaking for him, she forced herself to remain where she was. "I'm so sorry, Shane."

"I didn't have anywhere to go, so I spent the next couple of nights on a bench in the city park. I got tired of being hungry, so I decided to steal some items to sell on the street for profit." Memories lent him a haunted look. "I did that for a while, justifying my behavior with the thought that the folks I was stealing from had enough to spare. And then I chose one of your father's stores. The one on Federal Street." A sardonic smile twisted his mouth. "He was there for a meeting with the manager and caught me in the act."

Allison took a step closer. She could hardly believe he'd chosen to confide in her after all these years. "He must've been angry."

"He was at first. I thought he was going to march me straight to the police headquarters." He shook his head ruefully. "Instead, he took me into the store office and demanded to know why I was stealing. He chose to hear my story. And he had compassion on me."

Tears blurred her vision. "He was one of the most caring men I've ever known."

"I wish I could be like him."

The admission rocked her. Shane hadn't had the foundation she and George had enjoyed. He hadn't had anyone to love him, to instruct him in the ways of healthy relationships, to bolster his confidence. That he'd achieved as much as he had was a testament to his inner strength and determination. She liked to think her father's intervention had had a hand in that, as well.

"In many ways, you are like him," she said. "You stand for what's right. You insist on justice and fairness. You apply yourself to helping your fellow man."

He resumed his sweeping. "You're kind to say that," he said gruffly.

"It's the truth."

She wished she could make him see his own value, but she couldn't. He'd have to come to accept it for himself. She wasn't sure he ever would, and that made her sad.

Spying a stray ribbon on the floor near the coffee table,

she bent and retrieved it. When she straightened, black dots danced before her eyes. She swayed.

"Allie?" The broom handle thwacked the floor. Suddenly, he was beside her, his arm around her. "What's wrong?"

Letting him support her, she closed her eyes. "I'm a trifle light-headed. Nothing serious. I probably need to eat something."

"Sit down." He guided her to the sofa, settling her in the middle and sitting right beside her. His fingers skimmed her forehead. "Are you too hot? Do you have a headache? Are you experiencing any other symptoms?"

She opened her eyes to find him hovering close, worry churning in the stormy depths. "I'm fine, honestly." She placed a hand on his chest. "I haven't slept well the last two nights. That, combined with skipping lunch, is all that's wrong."

He glanced at the mantel clock and huffed. "One-thirty already. I should've fixed our noon meal instead of messing with the tree."

"I should've paid attention to the time."

"You sure you're okay?" Beneath her palm, the muscles of his chest contracted and released.

She was tempted to explore his strength. "I'm positive. I was simply light-headed for a moment. That happens sometimes."

His gaze zeroed in on her mouth. Yearning surged there. His hand, which had come to rest on her neck, slowly slid beneath her ponytail, his thumb stroking a mesmerizing pattern beneath her ear. She decided to throw discretion to the wind.

Her pulse racing, the tattoo of her heart loud in her ears, she reached up and framed his jaw with her hand. Surprise stirred in his gaze seconds before she pulled him down to her. His sharp inhale was cut off by her lips covering his.

Allison had no clue what she was doing, nor how to go about it. Shane didn't at first respond. He seemed frozen in shock. Then, with a rumble deep in his chest, he crushed her to him. He took charge of the kiss, and her toes curled inside her boots.

Her fingers clenched the fabric of his shirt, holding him hostage. Not that he protested. He delved into her hair, cradling her head, holding her fast. His lips were warm, firm and sweet. Being with him felt right, as if this was what was meant to happen all along, the two of them traveling on converging roads that took years to intersect.

When he gripped her shoulders to hold her apart from him, a sound of protest escaped.

"Shane?"

His eyes were on fire, his features hewn from granite. "You don't know what you've done, Allison."

Upset and confused, she blurted, "You mean what *we* did, don't you?"

"That cannot happen again."

Releasing his shirt, which was hopelessly wrinkled, she scooted to the couch's far edge. "Why not?"

"Why not?" He scraped a trembling hand through his hair. Shooting to his feet, he began to pace. "Because your life is in Virginia. Because you're going to marry Trevor Langston or some other man like him who knows how to be a husband and father. You're going to live in a house as grand as Ashworth House, and you're going to have enough kids to form a football team."

Allison gaped. Pushing to her feet, she intercepted him, blocking his path. "What if I don't want Trevor? What if that life isn't for me? What if…I want you?"

"No." He shook his head. Desperation flared. "*No.* You don't mean that."

She touched his arm, and he flinched. "I know what's in my heart."

"Stop, Allison." Backing away, he held up his hands. "I've said it before, and I'll say it again. I'm not the commitment type. I like my life the way it is. That won't change."

He was almost to the door when soft crying carried down the stairs. Hanging his head, he shot her a look full of turmoil. "I'll cook you a quick lunch while you see to them."

On the verge of tears, Allison brushed past him and practically bolted up the stairs. She'd made a grave error in judgment. She'd taken a risk and it had blown up in her face.

Shane left the house as soon as he had lunch prepared. Allison had assured him she'd be fine on her own and would tell Fenton he'd return for him later that afternoon. Craving privacy to deal with what had happened, he seized the chance of escape.

He wasn't accustomed to being with other people around the clock. Being cooped up in Fenton's cabin with four other humans had taken its toll. And now the kiss...

Just thinking about her softness, her innocence, made his middle drop to his boots. Allison had branded him with that kiss. He'd never get it out of his head. Not only was he going to have a difficult time not repeating it, he was going to have to watch her leave at the end of the month, knowing the next time he saw her she'd likely belong to another man.

None of this was supposed to have been an issue. He was supposed to have remained aloof, unaffected by her many attributes. This was bound to be the worst Christmas in the history of Christmases.

He decided against going to the jail. His mood was too foul for polite conversation. Taking the long route home, he was relieved when he didn't cross paths with anyone.

Shane took his time brushing down his horse and unpacking his saddlebags. Afterward, he took his rifle apart, cleaned each piece and reassembled it. His new copy of *American Jurist and Law* didn't appeal, so he returned outside to chop wood in hopes the physical activity would burn off his frustration.

Twenty minutes later, he was midswing when he heard a masculine greeting. He lowered the ax.

"Josh. What brings you here in the middle of the day?"

His friend strode past the outhouse and toolshed and into the wooded area behind his cabin. "I was manning the store when I heard someone say they saw you riding near town. Ben's been concerned. We all have."

"As you can see, we didn't freeze in the high elevations."

Lifting the ax above his head, he brought it down with enough force to slice through the wood like butter. The resulting thwack was satisfying. He tossed the pieces into the growing pile.

"Where'd you find shelter?"

"We passed a couple of nights on the Blake homestead."

"Fenton and Letty getting along all right?"

He wedged the blade in the wood and, resting his hands on his hips, regarded Josh.

"Some things have happened out at the Blakes'. Letty got mixed up with the youngest Whitaker boy. About six months ago, she gave birth to twins. A boy and a girl."

Josh's eyes widened. "I'm sure Fenton was fit to be tied."

"I'd say he was at first. Doesn't matter now because Letty's dead, and he's Izzy and Charlie's sole caretaker."

"I'm sorry to hear that." Somber now, he passed a gloved hand over his mouth. "He practically raised Letty. How's he gonna cope with two kids in his condition?"

"I don't know."

Allison had posed the same question. He didn't have answers then, and he didn't have any now.

The treetops rustled as a stiff breeze barreled down the mountains. Pulling his collar up, he grabbed the handle again. As Shane chopped, Josh moseyed over to the growing pile and toed it with his boot.

"You planning on hosting a bonfire for the entire town?"

"Nope."

His lower lip protruded as he nodded and inspected the stack over beside the barn. "That right there's enough to last one winter. Why the extra?"

"I need the exercise," he huffed.

"Right...because you're getting thick in the middle."

His dry tone sparked Shane's ire. "Why don't you go on back to the shop? Wouldn't want to miss any customers."

"You wanna know what I think?"

"Not particularly."

"I think you like Allison."

Shane sliced through another log, not bothering to answer.

"You like her a lot. Except you don't want to, and that's got you all worked up. Am I right?"

Josh sported an infuriating grin that Shane was tempted to wipe off his face.

"Go home to your wife and kids, O'Malley, and leave me be."

"Come on, Shane, I'm your friend. You have to talk to someone."

"No, I don't."

"So you're going to chop the entire forest down?" He held his hands out at his sides. "She's got, what? Three weeks left?"

"Twenty-four days."

"Tell me this. Does she fancy you, too?"

Laying aside the tool, he passed his coat sleeve across his forehead and paced to where he'd left a water bucket. He downed a dipper of ice-cold water. Josh was persistent. Even if Shane managed to get rid of him now, he wouldn't drop the subject.

"Why is it important that you know?" he said testily.

"Because I'm your friend, and I think you need someone special in your life. Allison's the first person I've seen you let get to you. That tells me she's different."

"She is different," he admitted. "Always has been."

"Then what's standing in your way?"

He waved for Josh to follow, and they made their way inside. Over coffee, Shane unloaded his entire life story. Josh didn't judge him. Didn't condemn his actions.

"I'm glad you finally told me. Took you long enough."

Cradling his mug in one hand, he stretched his arm along the top of the chair beside him. "I held off because it's not something to be proud of. I've worked hard to leave the boy I once was behind."

"You've achieved great things," he said, his gaze probing. "What I don't understand is what any of this has to do with you and Allison. I mean, what does the past have to do with the present?"

"Everything." He'd expected Josh, of all people, to understand. "I'm a product of my past."

"To a certain extent, yes. However, you're in control of how you live your life now." He tapped the table. "You know what *not* to do. I would argue that you'd make a more excellent husband and father than someone like me, who was fortunate enough to have good parents."

"That's absurd." While far from perfect, Josh and his brothers all had solid marriages and were doting fathers.

"Think about it, Shane. You were miserable as a kid. So miserable that you'd never put another kid through that. You witnessed what a man's carelessness and neglect can do to his wife. You wouldn't dare treat a woman you loved that way."

Pushing out of the chair, he stalked to the fireplace and propped his hand against the mantel. The orange flames licked at the fat logs just as self-doubt taunted his insides.

He'd been set on this solitary course for much of his life. Entertaining another way, one where he'd get to experience love and partnership, was peculiar and slightly frightening.

He knew how it felt to be let down again and again. To have his hopes dashed repeatedly. He couldn't do that to any woman, especially Allison. Couldn't do that to a helpless kid. The twins' faces popped into his mind, and his chest tightened.

"Have you never considered that God sent David Ashworth into your life for a reason?"

"What?" He twisted to meet his perusal. "Why would God do that? He didn't bother with me for the first thirteen years of my life."

Josh was aware of his struggles with his faith. Shane frequently sought excuses not to attend church services. Over the years, the reverend had reached out to him, as well as Josh's father, Sam O'Malley. Josh and his brothers had talked to him, urging him to take his relationship with Christ seriously. He hadn't listened.

Turning his chair around so that he could face Shane, he sat with one leg propped on the other. "The Scriptures tell us that it rains on the good and the bad. We all endure trials in this world, and many times we won't discover the reasons for those trials until we reach heaven. Other times, we can use the lessons we learn to bless others."

Bitterness rose up to choke him. "How is having an absentee father and drunk-out-of-her-mind mother supposed to enable me to help someone else?"

"I can't answer that," Josh said. "What I do know is that those experiences have shaped the man you are today, the same as living with David and his children did."

Shane fell silent. Not once had he viewed David's entrance into his life as anything other than chance. Eaten up with self-pity and rage, his soul starved for love and approval, he could've missed the greater picture.

"It's possible I was wrong."

"God loves the whole world. It'd be prideful to think you're the exception," Josh quietly pointed out.

Turning away, Shane stared at the flames. "I need to think."

His friend approached and laid a hand on his shoulder. "You should also read your Bible. Start with the book of John."

Then he let himself out, leaving Shane alone with a thousand unanswered questions.

Chapter Fourteen

Shane must've decided to avoid her for the remainder of the month. He'd left without saying goodbye yesterday, and she hadn't seen him since. Town business could be keeping him away, but Allison had her doubts. He'd been upset with her. Maybe even a little angry, which in turn made her miserable. Memories of being in his arms warred with the sting of his ultimate rejection. She'd basically offered him her heart on a platter, and he'd walked away.

Initiating that kiss had been a mistake. Revealing her feelings had been a mistake. Because even if he'd met her declaration with one of his own, they couldn't be together, not when his relationship with Christ was unresolved. Building a life with someone who didn't share her faith would bring trials and heartache. After her reckless behavior, she wasn't sure how she was supposed to act around him.

Just after feeding the babies their midday meal of warm milk and oatmeal flavored with cinnamon—thankfully she knew enough to manage the simple food—a rap sounded on the front door. Hope and dread surged.

God, please give me strength, she prayed desperately.

Her hand shook as she turned the knob and eased the

door open. Surprise followed on the heels of disappointment. Not Shane.

"Caroline? Good afternoon."

Beneath her cream hat adorned with ruby red flowers, Caroline's hair was perfectly coifed. Her cream cloak—an impractical choice given the elements but one she could obviously afford—skimmed the toes of her polished leather boots.

"I hope I'm not interrupting anything." She looked askance at the apron Allison had found in Mrs. Watts's hutch. She'd donned it to protect her dress from the twins' mess-making skills.

"Not at all." She stepped aside. "I'm afraid I haven't yet stocked the kitchen. There isn't any cocoa or tea, but I know how to fix coffee."

"No, thank you—" She stopped short on the threshold, her delicate gloved hand pressed against her chest. "What are those?"

Closing out the cold, Allison suppressed a chuckle. Caroline was staring in comical horror at Izzy and Charlie, who were confined in the crate seats Shane had crafted for them. They were close enough to the fireplace to benefit from its warmth, but out of reach of stray sparks. Izzy clutched her bear and bounced, big eyes fastened on Caroline. Charlie's own fingers were entertainment enough for him.

Smiling, she removed the apron and draped it on the chair back. "Caroline, meet Charlie and Izzy Blake, Fenton Blake's great-grandchildren."

Astounded, she couldn't seem to tear her gaze away. "Two of them? They look the same size."

"They're the same age. Twins." Feeling mischievous, she approached the babies. "Would you like to hold one?"

"No!" She snapped her jaw shut. "I mean, no, thank you." Her lips puckered. "Why do you have them?"

"Their mother passed away nearly a month ago."

"How terrible."

"Fenton had errands here in town. They're staying with me for a couple of days."

Bending to smooth Izzy's curls and wipe a stray eyelash from Charlie's cheek, Allison struggled with the thought of having to say goodbye. She'd grown used to their toothy smiles and eager morning greetings. Every time they clutched her neck and buried their faces in her hair, trusting her to meet their needs, her heart expanded with emotion. Before meeting Izzy and Charlie, she hadn't thought it possible to form an attachment so quickly. Now she knew differently. They'd take a little piece of her heart when they returned to their cove.

It was going to be impossible not to worry about them, to wonder how Fenton was faring. She hoped Shane would make good on his promise to send frequent visitors to check on the little family.

Shaking off the maudlin thoughts, she said, "Would you like to put your cloak and gloves over here?"

"I can't stay. I came to tell you that a group of us are meeting Friday afternoon to assemble the gift baskets, if you're interested."

"I'll plan to be there. Thank you for inviting me to join in."

Considering she was a short-term visitor, it really was thoughtful of Caroline to include her. She sensed there was more to Caroline Turner than the privileged, rich-girl persona she projected to the town. Too bad Allison wouldn't be sticking around to discover whether or not she was right.

"You did say that you were involved in Norfolk's charitable activities." Her navy blue gaze returned to the twins. "I thought you might be bored. I see now that's not the case."

"Still, I'd like to participate."

"I'll count on you." Inclining her head, Caroline bid her

goodbye and returned to the buggy and hired man waiting for her beneath the giant maple tree.

She watched her leave, her mind once again drifting to Shane. Would he continue to shun her? Would that be such a bad thing?

Allison touched the tip of her finger to the paper pinwheel and watched it flutter. Her tree was beautiful but incomplete. It needed more color and texture. Shane wasn't likely to fulfill his agreement to help her finish it. Not after that ill-timed kiss and his hostile reaction.

"Is this a good spot?"

Allison turned to watch Deputy Ben MacGregor balance on a chair and hold a sprig of mistletoe to the beam between the dining and living rooms. He'd dropped by in search of Shane with Fenton in tow, whom she was beginning to suspect had mischief up his sleeve. The older man had produced the mistletoe from his coat pocket and guilted the deputy into hanging it for him.

"A little to the left." Fenton stood in the dining room observing Ben.

"I wouldn't have pegged you as a romantic, Fenton," she said, coming around the sofa. The sofa where she'd kissed Sheriff Shane Timmons. Her skin flushed hot, then cold.

"I'm simply following tradition." He tried to look innocent and failed.

Allison pursed her lips. He'd made several pointed remarks about her and Shane at the cabin. If he thought he could push the two of them together, he was going to be sorely disappointed.

Footsteps on the porch alerted her to another arrival. "Busy place today."

The instant she opened the door, the breath squeezed out of her lungs. She drank in Shane's rugged features, caressing them with her gaze as her fingers itched to do.

"Allison." His azure gaze wary, he spoke into the awkward silence. "I'm looking for Ben."

Using the door for support, she stepped out of his way, giving him an unobstructed view of the room. He spotted Ben first, then the mistletoe in his hand. His expression turned icy.

"Hey, Shane." Ben greeted his boss with enthusiasm. "I need to talk to you."

Shane halted on the threshold, his hands fisted at his sides. Allison could feel waves of hostility coming off him. He obviously didn't like that Ben was here. But if he didn't want her for himself, why did he care who she spent time with?

"Best place to do that would be at the office," he snapped. "Why didn't you look for me there?"

Ben belatedly noted his ire. "Oh, I did," he said, his tone flat. "I looked in the livery, the barber shop and the mercantile. When I couldn't find you, I naturally thought you might be spending time with your visitor."

Shane's nostrils flared. The two men glared at each other until Fenton ducked past the chair supporting Ben and clapped his hands together. "What do you say, Sheriff? You wanna be the first one to try out this here mistletoe? Quinn was having a sale. I'm sure Allison wouldn't mind a peck from an old friend."

Allison heard Shane's sudden intake of air. Ben averted his face to hide a smile. Mortified, she wagged a finger at the older man. "I don't mind being caught under the mistletoe with you, Mr. Blake. These two will have to find their own volunteers."

"Aw, I'm too old for such shenanigans." He waved off her suggestion, but she could tell her words tickled him.

"Where's Izzy and Charlie?" Shane directed the question to Fenton, not sparing her a second glance.

"Upstairs asleep. Allison has them in a routine already."

"Glad to hear it."

Ben gave one tap of the hammer and stepped down off the chair. "There you go, Mr. Blake."

"Fenton, remember?"

"Yes, sir. Would you like a ride back to Shane's?"

"Nothing for me to do there. I'll go after supper."

Laying the hammer on the large table, Ben strode to fetch his hat. He held the battered Stetson against his chest and cupped Allison's upper arm. Trouble twinkled in his green eyes. "I look forward to seeing you again, Miss Allison. Next time I stop by, be prepared. It's been a long time since I've caught any lady beneath the mistletoe, let alone one as irresistible as you."

With a wink, he ambled past an annoyed-looking Shane to the porch. Fenton chuckled.

Mumbling a farewell, Shane pivoted and stalked out behind his deputy. Allison hesitated in the open doorway and overheard them talking about new evidence of their drifter. She was still there when Shane walked around his horse to climb into the saddle. He hesitated. Over the animal's broad back, he looked straight at her. Ben was talking and gesturing as he mounted up, yet Shane's gaze remained trained on her. The look was charged with emotion.

Fenton stepped up beside her, and the connection was broken. Shane bent his head so that his hat's brim blocked his face. He swung his leg up and over, fit his boots into the stirrups and nudged the animal's flank with his heel.

"Now there goes a man who could use the love of a good woman."

She didn't have to ask which man he was referring to. "He's pretty satisfied with the life he has."

"Maybe you could persuade him to see things differently."

"Me?" she squeaked, whipping her head around.

Tiny lines creased the outer corners of his eyes. "I've got eyes and ears, missy."

"You can't make someone love you, Fenton," she whispered, sorrow invading every part of her.

Sympathy mingled with understanding on his wizened face. "So it's like that, is it?"

Blinking away tears, she lowered her gaze to the rug at her feet. "I'm afraid so."

He patted her shoulder much like a caring grandfather would do. Letty was fortunate to have had him in her life. Allison wished with all her soul that her father was here to hold her. He hadn't been one to press his advice on her, but he'd willingly given it if she'd asked.

"It's plain as day he cares about you."

"He feels a responsibility for me. That's all."

He opened his mouth to respond, but no sound came out. He paled and clutched his chest.

"Fenton?" Alarmed, Allison took hold of his arm. "What's wrong?"

"Need to sit," he wheezed, fumbling for the nearest chair.

She assisted him to the sofa. "Tell me what to do. Do you need water? Medicine?"

"My satchel." Hunched forward, he pointed to the corner behind the door.

Allison brought it to him and riffled through the contents until she found a bottle. "Is this what you need?"

At his nod, she shook out a tablet and gave it to him. "I'll get water."

Unnerved, she lifted silent prayers and hurried back to his side with a cup. His color still off, Fenton sipped the liquid and, when he'd had enough, sank against the cushions and closed his eyes.

"Should I get the doctor?"

"Already seen him."

"But—"

His lids fluttered open. "No need to fret. I'll be right as rain shortly."

She felt useless, not sure what to do and wishing Shane was there. "Does this happen often?"

"Twice since Letty passed. I thank the Lord I had my medicine close at hand."

"I can't imagine how you've coped this past month."

"Prayer sustained me."

Something about his wrinkled, age-spotted hands made her want to weep. He'd endured such heartache and hardship. She hated to think of him returning to his isolated cabin.

He opened his eyes. "I've been asking God to send help. Someone who'd love my great-grandbabies as much as I do."

The hopeful glint in his eyes astonished her. "Surely you're not thinking I'm that person. Don't get me wrong, I adore Izzy and Charlie. They're precious. But I'm unwed. And my home is in Virginia."

"I didn't give God a list of attributes." His wrinkles became more pronounced with his frown. "I hate to think of them living far from me, but in my position, I can't afford to be particular. If things were different, if I was in better health, I'd never give them up. Doc told me today that I can't go on like this much longer."

Rising from the sofa, she went to the window and stared unseeing at the bleak landscape, her mind whirling with possibilities. She had resources. Position. Influence. She had the wherewithal to provide a comfortable home for them and the means to hire a nanny to assist her. She'd require a cook, of course. The twins would soon move beyond basic oatmeal. She pictured a tasteful home in her brother's neighborhood with a spacious nursery stocked with furniture and toys. A substantial garden space would do nicely, as well.

Allison's primary desire was to have a family of her own. Could this be God's way of providing one for her?

"Besides," he said in a sly tone, "I doubt you'll remain unwed for long. If Shane won't step up, there's a certain deputy who's sweet on you."

She turned around. "I can't live here, Fenton. Not with Shane nearby..."

Gatlinburg's sheriff would not be pleased in the slightest to have her underfoot. And it would be torture for her to live so close to him, to see him on a daily basis, wanting him yet knowing he was forever out of reach.

"And Ben MacGregor is a professional flirt. If I were to express an iota of serious intent, he'd run for the hills."

From upstairs, she heard the babies stirring, babbling to themselves in their sweet, singsong voices. The idea that they could be her children, that she could love and nurture them into adulthood, filled her with a rare, tentative happiness.

"Family is the most important thing to me," she said. "I've longed to be a mother since I was a young girl. My first instinct is to seize this opportunity, but I need time to think and pray. Their future is too important."

"I understand."

"Would you mind staying in town a couple of extra days?"

He sat up and nodded, his strength slowly returning. "I ain't gonna rush you on this. The idea is new to you, whereas I've been stewin' over it since the minute you and the sheriff showed up on my doorstep."

"Please don't mention this to Shane."

"And what do I tell him is the reason for us sticking around?"

"I'll explain everything to him." The decision to become

the twins' guardian was hers alone to make, but experience told her Shane would have an opinion and would feel compelled to impose it on her. "First I need to figure out how."

Chapter Fifteen

He could hear the babies bawling almost as soon as he rode up. Trying the knob and finding it locked, he pounded on the door. "Allison?"

The sound intensified. A minute later, he came face-to-face with Allison, who looked as if she'd tussled with a wild boar and lost. Dark splotches marred her cream blouse and rose-colored skirt. A hank of hair had escaped its pins and fell directly over her left eyebrow and cheek. Although her features were taut with exhaustion, he recognized her expression of determination.

"Ben's not here."

"I'm not looking for my deputy."

The red-faced baby in her arms noticed his presence and immediately lunged toward him, taking both adults by surprise. Shane caught Charlie around the ribs and, his heart lurching with something wondrous, hugged him tight. The baby's fussing ceased as he burrowed closer.

He set the small basket he'd brought inside the doorway.

"What's wrong with him?" Shane said over the crying coming from the kitchen.

Shooting him an enigmatic look, she whirled and headed

for the other room. "I haven't yet ascertained the problem. It's been a rough morning."

Shane closed the door and followed her. Maybe instead of dropping Fenton off at an old acquaintance's home for a visit, he should've brought him here. When he voiced those thoughts aloud, she dismissed them, saying he could use the break.

Making soothing noises to Izzy, who was in her make-shift high chair, Allison picked her up and swiped at the tear tracks. "Shh, my darling. It's going to be okay."

Izzy's brown eyes communicated her misery.

Charlie sniffled. Resting his cheek against Shane's chest, he began to suck his thumb. "Has he done that before?"

"Done what?" She tilted her head to try and dislodge the hair so she could see clearly. Izzy latched on to it and yanked. "Ouch."

Without thinking, Shane shifted closer and gently pried Izzy's fingers loose. "That hurts, sweetheart. Can't do that."

Suddenly he had two pairs of female eyes on him. Allison's fruity scent wound about him, erecting dangerous memories of their embrace. Memories he couldn't shake, no matter how long he avoided her.

Allison looped the stray lock behind her ear and averted her gaze.

"Has Charlie sucked his thumb before?"

She looked at the boy in surprise. "I haven't seen him do it, no. It could be a new behavior or something we missed in our brief time with them."

"What should we do?" he asked, intimidated by the massive amount of information he didn't know about infants.

"None of George's kids sucked their thumbs. The youngest has a penchant for sucking on his lower lip, and there's nothing we can do to prevent him. We should ask Fenton if this is a new behavior."

"He's left you alone with them a lot."

Her chin lifted. "It may not look like it, but I'm faring okay. They slept most of the night through." Caressing Izzy's curls, she said, "It's possible they're cutting teeth, and their gums are hurting."

"I didn't mean to imply you're not up to the challenge. You're a capable caretaker. It's just that you've had the sole responsibility since we returned to town. This is your holiday, remember?"

The kids were quiet now that they were being held. "That's right. It is my holiday, and I can spend it any way I choose." She speared him with a searching look. "Why did you come by if not to look for Ben?"

"You've had a telegram and a letter from George." *And I needed to see you.* He'd missed her in the brief time he'd stayed away...a troubling development. He wasn't supposed to get used to having her around.

He managed to get both out of his coat pocket without upsetting Charlie.

Her face lit up. "Wonderful! What does the telegram say?"

"It's addressed to you."

She shifted Izzy so she could take them. Worrying her lip as she scanned the telegram's message, her fleeting smile put him at ease. "He's set to arrive next Monday."

"Plenty of time to take part in Christmas festivities."

George's arrival would provide the remedy for Shane's current problem. Allison would be occupied by her family. Shane would no longer be obligated to keep tabs on her. The anticipated relief didn't come.

Allison's expression grew guarded, one that didn't fit the woman he knew her to be. Anxiety punched him in the gut. Whatever was on her mind was serious.

"There's something you and my brother need to know. It will be easier if I deal with you one at a time."

"Tell me."

"Fenton has asked if I would assume legal guardianship of the twins, and I'm considering it."

"What?" Shane couldn't have heard right.

Charlie shifted in his arms, and he patted his back. He had the inane thought that he shouldn't be comfortable comforting a baby, shouldn't feel as if standing in a kitchen with Allison and a set of needy infants was commonplace.

"He had an episode." Her eyes churned with disquiet. "The third one since Letty died. It scared me, Shane. The doctor warned him that his health will continue to deteriorate if he continues as he has been. He doesn't wish to give them up, but he's a practical man."

Fenton hadn't mentioned the episode or Doc Owens's diagnosis. "I understand how you feel, but you can't agree because you feel sorry for them."

"I'm not sure you do understand. You don't want a family, Shane. I do. These children need a mother, and I am willing and able to provide for them."

"You sound as if you've already made up your mind."

Lowering her gaze, she planted a kiss on Izzy's head. "I know what I want. I'm trying to be sensible, however, and consider all the ramifications. This is one of the most important decisions of my life. It will affect more than just myself." Besides the challenge in her gaze, he detected a hint of vulnerability. "I don't expect you to approve. I simply thought you should know."

Using his foot to hook the nearest chair's leg, he scooted it from beneath the table and sank into it.

"If you agree to Fenton's request, there'll be no turning back. No changing your mind."

"I know."

Charlie was starting to get antsy. Shane sat him on his knee and bounced him. The baby gnawed on his fist, trying unsuccessfully to push the whole thing inside his mouth.

"What about Trevor?"

She frowned. "What about him?"

"Could this affect your chances with him?"

"As I said before, Trevor and I don't have an understanding. I haven't yet agreed to let him come courting. Besides, if he doesn't have it in his heart to love Izzy and Charlie, then I don't want him in my life."

Shane stared out the kitchen window at the pastel blue sky. Weak sunlight did little to dispel the frigid temperatures. The thought of Allison and the twins making a home with a stranger made him ill.

"So Trevor isn't an issue. What about George? Your brother isn't going to react well. He'll throttle us both."

"It's my decision. You have nothing to do with this."

"You're wrong," he snorted. "With him in Virginia, it was my responsibility to keep you out of trouble."

The second the words left his mouth, he realized his mistake. Allison wasn't one to lose her temper often, but when she did—better duck for cover. Her entire body went rigid. Red flags appeared in her cheeks, and her eyes had a wild look about them. The only thing saving him from flying dishes was the twins' presence.

"I am an adult," she bit out. "I am perfectly capable of *staying out of trouble* with no help from you, thank you very much."

"Allie, sweetheart—" He stopped as she became more incensed.

"Sweetheart?" Advancing, she stood over him, pinning him with a fierce glare. "How dare you call me that, Shane Timmons!"

He stopped bouncing Charlie. "It was a slip—"

"You returned my kiss. You're as attracted to me as I am to you. You'd be lying if you tried to deny it. But you've decided that bachelorhood is what you want. I'm not going to try and dissuade you from that course. I *respect* your decision. As a friend, you owe me the same courtesy."

He'd never seen her so upset. He captured her wrist. "I'm sorry. I worded that wrong."

Her eyes swam with tears. "I'm not your friend, though, am I? I tried a hundred different ways to be, and you rebuffed me at every turn. Meanwhile, my brother practically ignored you, and you decided he was worthy of your time. Is it because I cared? Would you have acted differently if I'd treated your arrival in my household with disdain?"

Hurt and confusion radiated off her. His heart beat out a painful rhythm. "You know my past is complicated. I never intended to hurt you—"

Izzy whimpered. The tense atmosphere in the room likely wasn't conducive to happy babies.

Wiggling free of his hold, she edged closer to the stove. "You should go."

Anything he said right now would be wrong. "Fine." Standing, he carried the baby into the living room and situated him in one of the seats on the rug. Charlie grunted his disagreement. He waved his arms at Shane.

"Be a good boy for Allison." Patting his blond head, Shane fetched the basket he'd brought. "This is for you."

Her brows collided. "What is it?"

"Popcorn. For the tree."

"I'll repay you—"

"Consider it a late welcome-to-town gift." Striding for the door, he hesitated with his hand on the knob. He turned in time to glimpse a single tear snake down her cheek. His insides churned with guilt. "I'll go because you asked me to, but just so you know—this conversation isn't over."

"He was aimin' to poison my cattle, Sheriff!" Vernon Oakley jabbed a finger toward the man standing behind Shane. "Arrest him!"

Eddie Buchanan spat in the dirt, calmer than his neighbor and lifelong adversary. "This is the last time I'm gonna say it—I ain't done nothin' of the sort. Ought to check your facts before you go accusin' a man."

Vernon's young son—Shane guessed him to be about ten—waited inside the barn entrance, his face screwed up like a prune. The boy knew something. He just wasn't talking.

Shane's visit to Allison's place that morning seemed like a lifetime ago. Once he'd returned to town, he'd been drawn into one fiasco after another. One couple refused to pay for their meal at the Plum Café. A trio of youths who'd been playing chase on Main Street had knocked over a stand of Christmas trees for sale. The elderly widow, Mrs. Carson, who lived on the edge of town and regularly lodged complaints, insisted a mountain lion had invaded her chicken coop and what was Shane planning to do about it? The list went on. He'd eaten lunch on the go, a meager hunk of ham wedged between two slices of bread, and he hadn't gotten around to a proper supper. He was hungry and cranky and ready for this day to see its end.

Vernon's boy scuffed the ground with his boot. Dirt streaked his lean cheeks. "Pa?"

"Not now," Vernon growled, his gaze never leaving Eddie's.

Shane's thoughts turned to Allison and the twins. What would Charlie be like at this age? Would he have a kind, caring man for a father? Someone who'd teach him right from wrong, teach him to hunt and fish and what it means to be a valuable citizen of the community? Or would he have a man who ignored him...or worse?

Standing between the arguing men, Shane was too distracted to see the fist flying through the air. The blow stunned him. The force of it knocked him to the ground. He lay there a few seconds, his right eye throbbing and a headache blossoming behind his temples, pondering how he could've wound up on the Oakleys' barn floor.

Above him, the neighbors' temporary silence exploded into accusations.

"Now look what you done!"

"It wouldn't have happened if you'd left my cows alone!"

The boy crouched in front of him. "You need some help, Sheriff?"

"I can manage."

Shane levered himself up. He could feel his temper straining to be unleashed. Not once in his career had he lost focus in the middle of a volatile situation. As he dusted dirt and straw from his pant legs, the two men eyed him with a mixture of awe and trepidation.

This account was going to travel through the mountains like a hound on the hunt. For the first time, he'd allowed his personal problems to interfere with his job. He had one Allison Ashworth to thank for that. His fingers balled into fists.

"Sheriff—"

"Stop talking," he growled. "I don't want to hear another word out of either of you." To Buchanan, he said, "Get on your horse, go home and don't come back."

"Yes, sir." Hands held up in surrender, he shuffled backward until he reached the entrance. Yanking the door open, he slipped into the darkness.

"You."

Vernon retreated a step at the threat in Shane's voice. "For the sake of your family, pretend the Buchanans are on holiday until after the new year. Understand?"

His lips pressing together, he jerked a short nod.

"If you have any problems, you come to me. You do not initiate contact with your neighbor on your own."

He nodded again.

Shane switched his attention to the boy. "You got something on your mind, son?"

"FAST FIVE" READER SURVEY

Your participation entitles you to:
✳ **4 Thank-You Gifts Worth Over $20!**

Complete the survey in minutes.

Get **2 FREE** Books

Your Thank-You Gifts include **2 FREE BOOKS** and **2 MYSTERY GIFTS**. There's no obligation to purchase anything!

See inside for details.

Dear Reader,

Since you are a lover of our books, your opinions are important to us... and so is your time.

That's why we made sure your **"FAST FIVE" READER SURVEY** can be completed in just a few minutes. Your answers to the five questions will help us remain at the forefront of women's fiction.

And, as a thank-you for participating, we'd like to send you **4 FREE THANK-YOU GIFTS!**

Enjoy your gifts with our appreciation,

Pam Powers

To get your
4 FREE THANK-YOU GIFTS:

✳ Quickly complete the "Fast Five" Reader Survey and return the insert.

"FAST FIVE" READER SURVEY

1. Do you sometimes read a book a second or third time? ○ Yes ○ No

2. Do you often choose reading over other forms of entertainment such as television? ○ Yes ○ No

3. When you were a child, did someone regularly read aloud to you? ○ Yes ○ No

4. Do you sometimes take a book with you when you travel outside the home? ○ Yes ○ No

5. In addition to books, do you regularly read newspapers and magazines? ○ Yes ○ No

YES! I have completed the above Reader Survey. Please send me my 4 FREE GIFTS (gifts worth over $20 retail). I understand that I am under no obligation to buy anything, as explained on the back of this card.

102/302 IDL GLDK

FIRST NAME

LAST NAME

ADDRESS

APT.#

CITY

STATE/ PROV.

ZIP/POSTAL CODE

Accepting your 2 free Love Inspired® Historical books and 2 free gifts (gifts valued at approximately $10.00) places you under no obligation to buy anything. You may keep the books and gifts and return the shipping statement marked "cancel." If you do not cancel, about a month later we'll send you 4 additional books and bill you just $4.99 each in the U.S. or $5.49 each in Canada. That is a savings of at least 17% off the cover price. It's quite a bargain! Shipping and handling is just 50¢ per book in the U.S. and 75¢ per book in Canada.* You may cancel at any time, but if you choose to continue, every month we'll send you 4 more books, which you may either purchase at the discount price or return to us and cancel your subscription. *Terms and prices subject to change without notice. Prices do not include applicable taxes. Sales tax applicable in N.Y. Canadian residents will be charged applicable taxes. Offer not valid in Quebec. Books received may not be as shown. All orders subject to approval. Credit or debit balances in a customer's account(s) may be offset by any other outstanding balance owed by or to the customer. Please allow 4 to 6 weeks for delivery. Offer available while quantities last.

◄ If offer card is missing write to: Reader Service, P.O. Box 1867, Buffalo, NY 14240-1867 or visit www.ReaderService.com ►

BUSINESS REPLY MAIL

FIRST-CLASS MAIL   PERMIT NO. 717   BUFFALO, NY

POSTAGE WILL BE PAID BY ADDRESSEE

READER SERVICE

PO BOX 1867

BUFFALO NY 14240-9952

NO POSTAGE
NECESSARY
IF MAILED
IN THE
UNITED STATES

With a quick glance at his pa, he said, "I saw something."

"When?"

"Earlier tonight."

Sensing his unease, Shane said, "You can tell me. Your pa wants to know the truth of what happened, don't you, Vernon?"

Looking unhappy but resigned, Vernon waved for him to continue. "Tell the sheriff what you saw, Billy."

"I was in the smokehouse when I heard someone talking. It was a voice I didn't recognize, so I came out to see who was out there. I know it wasn't Mr. Buchanan."

Vernon made a noise.

"How can you be sure?" Shane said, trying not to bring his fingers up to the tender flesh surrounding his eye. It felt swollen and bruised.

"The trespasser was short. About the same size as me."

"Did you see his face?"

"No."

"Anything else you remember?"

Billy thought a minute. "Only that his voice wasn't deep and booming like Mr. Buchanan's."

Shane settled a hand on his shoulder. "You've been a big help, young man. Thank you."

A blush stole over his skin, and he ducked his head.

"Why don't you go on back to the house while I speak to your pa."

"Yes, sir."

With one last look at Vernon, Billy hustled out of the structure. Breath-stealing air crept inside at his departure, finding its way beneath Shane's collar. The tips of his ears stung. His exposed neck prickled. All he wanted at this point was a warm fire, a hot meal and solitude. A respite from thoughts of Allison would be welcome, as well.

"You swung the first punch," he told Vernon. "Assaulting a lawman is a serious offense. You're fortunate I'm not hauling you off to jail."

He visibly swallowed. "It was an accident, Sheriff. Honest."

"Next time, get the facts before tossing out accusations. Understand?"

Vernon looked as if he wanted to argue. In the end, he thought better of it. "Yeah. I understand."

"I've reason to believe we have a drifter or two in the area. Could be your trespasser was searching for a place to pass the night. Maybe helped himself to some of your food stores."

The farmer scowled. "I'll keep a lookout. Ain't no one gonna steal from Vernon Oakley and get away with it."

Shane remembered what it meant to be so hungry he could barely think straight. A man like Vernon wouldn't understand. Or maybe he simply didn't want to. Banishing the troublesome memories, he headed for the door.

"Let me know if you have any more trouble."

Outside in the tranquil night, he mounted his horse and, using the bright configuration of stars and half-moon above, searched the fields for signs of human activity. All he saw were the indistinct shapes of Vernon's cattle. Somewhere in the distant woods, a lone owl hooted.

Riding past the house, he spotted Billy on the porch, watching. Shane lifted a hand. Billy waved and slipped inside. Through the open door, he could see Billy's ma and young brothers gathering around him.

A sensation more painful than his sore eye invaded his chest. His hard-won acceptance of a solitary life was slipping away and the prospect of going home to an empty house made him want to weep.

God, are You listening? Do You care? Josh says You do. Your Scriptures say You do.

He left the homestead behind, and darkness closed in on him.

I believe in You, God, I just have a hard time accepting that You love me. *I need to believe it. I can't abide this emptiness anymore.*

The stillness of the mid-December night struck him as oppressive.

A verse he'd read recently in the book of John sprung to mind. *For God so loved the world that He gave His only begotten Son, and whosoever believeth in Him should not perish but have everlasting life.*

He pondered the verse the entire ride home. He had the cabin to himself tonight. Fenton had decided to bunk at his friend's house. Probably for the best. Shane would've been terrible company. Forgetting about his need for food, he settled at the table with his Bible—a long-ago and unused gift from David Ashworth—and opened the pages. As he read, he discovered that his friend had been right. If God loved the *whole* world, and Shane was part of it, who was he to think that he alone was beyond His reach?

Chapter Sixteen

Allison's heart was a house divided—joy and hope coex-
isting with sorrow and disappointment. On the one hand,
the prospect of becoming a mother made her giddy with
excitement. The more she considered and prayed over the
matter, the more convinced she was that God had brought
her to Gatlinburg for this very reason. However, the bright
future dangling in front of her was tempered with the
knowledge that the man she loved saw her as an inconvenience. A threat, actually, to his well-laid plans.

In the picturesque, white clapboard church, female
voices mingled with children's laughter and echoed off the
stained-glass windows. She worked at one of several makeshift tables, grateful to be in the company of other women
and to have something productive to occupy her time.

"Have you heard about Shane's mishap?"

Caroline had stationed herself across the table and was
folding knitted scarves of various colors and sizes to be
placed in the gift baskets.

Allison's hands stilled in the process of tying ribbons
around sacks of candy. She felt the color drain from her
face. "What happened?"

"He earned himself a beauty of a shiner." Leaning over,

she cupped the side of her mouth with one hand, her deep sea-colored eyes dancing with curiosity. "Shane Timmons is known for his vigilance. Something has him preoccupied."

It was plain from Caroline's manner that she thought Allison was the reason for his preoccupation. "Is he all right otherwise?"

"My guess is his pride is smarting more than anything else."

Relief unfurled in her midsection. She glanced over to the pew where the O'Malley cousins' mothers, Mary and Alice, sat entertaining Izzy and Charlie.

Her determination to maintain emotional detachment during this visit had turned into a spectacular failure. Circumstances and proximity had conspired to shatter her intentions. Allison must accept that her and Shane's paths were never going to coincide. She desired home and family. He wanted nothing to do with those things.

"Here's our chance to find out the details of what happened." Caroline's too-loud whisper interrupted her musings.

She followed the blonde's line of sight to the rear alcove. Shane had entered a step ahead of his deputy. Both men wore dusters, neckerchiefs and buckskin gloves. Deadly-looking pistols glinted at their waists. They removed their hats at the same time. While Ben smiled and chatted with young women clustered nearby, Shane fluffed his blond-brown locks, his brooding gaze scanning the crowd.

Even from this distance, his injury was visible. His entire eye socket was ringed in ugly purple. Allison longed to soothe his discomfort, but it wasn't her place.

Turning away before he spotted her, she resumed her task. Caroline commented on her reaction, of course, and Allison recalled that she was in a small town where gossip ran rampant. If she ignored him or acted out of the ordinary, the women would wonder about the cause.

Still, that didn't mean she had to rush over and greet him with a fake smile. Five minutes passed before his heavy tread resounded down the aisle in her direction. Her stomach clenched. *Pretend you're back in the Norfolk offices,* she told herself, *and you're faced with the unenviable task of firing someone.*

Schooling her features, she lifted her head and met his gaze. Unasked questions turned his eyes a murky hue. Or maybe it was the dimming of the room as, outside, clouds passed over the sun. The stained-glass pieces lost their brilliance.

"Afternoon, Caroline." He inclined his head. "Allison."

"Good afternoon, Sheriff," Caroline greeted with a catlike smile. "Are you and Ben here to take the first batch of deliveries?"

"Yes, ma'am."

He glanced at the babies. "How did the twins fare last night?"

"Fine." She forced her tone to remain light. Carefree. Let him think she was no longer affected by their heated exchange. "Thank you for asking."

His mouth turned down. Up close, his cheekbone looked red and slightly swollen. His eye was bloodshot, and the crescent of skin beneath the lower lid was yellow. It was extremely difficult not to stare, not to give in to the instinct to caress the ravaged skin.

He's not yours to nurture, she reminded herself.

His knuckles whitened about his hat's crown as the atmosphere between them grew thick.

Caroline intervened. "Would you mind taking Allison along with you? I'm sure she'd enjoy the experience."

Allison wanted to kick the conniving blonde beneath the table.

After some hesitation, he nodded. "It's not very exciting."

"I beg to differ, Sheriff. Our Virginia friend here is deeply involved in charitable work. I know she'll get a thrill seeing firsthand those families who benefit from our church members' generosity."

"Sorry." Allison shrugged. "I can't leave the twins."

"Don't worry about them." Caroline made a dismissive gesture and, coming around the table, physically manipulated Allison in Shane's direction. "They're in good hands with Mary and Alice."

Ben walked up, taking a position beside his boss. "Hello, Caroline."

"Ben."

"Allison, how are you?" He raked her with his sparkling gaze. "Might I say that outfit is most becoming on you? Before now, I never realized that the combination of blue and silver could put a man in mind of merry holidays."

The skin around Shane's eye began to twitch.

Caroline uttered a sound of disgust. "You need to lay off the honey, Deputy. There is such a thing as playing it up too sweet."

Ben lifted his hands in an innocent gesture. "I'm completely sincere."

Allison summoned a smile. "I appreciate the sentiment, Ben. Thank you."

Shane spoke up. "Caroline, will you point us to the baskets ready to be distributed?"

"Certainly."

While he and Ben loaded the baskets in the wagons outside, Allison spoke with Mary and Alice, who reassured her that they were happy to watch over Izzy and Charlie. Long before she was ready, Shane was handing her up into the wagon and settling onto the seat beside her. Since

Ben was heading in the opposite direction, he strode to the other wagon.

Shane took the reins in hand. "Warm enough?"

"Yes, thanks." Like before, he'd rustled up a quilt from the rear. This time, he left it to her to wrap it about herself. "How many homes will we be visiting?"

"Ten."

Uncomfortable silence fell between them as he guided the team along the wooded lane leading away from town. She studied his profile. "Is it as painful as it looks?"

Beneath his brim, his expression remained unchanged. "I was wondering how long it would take for you to mention it. I won't lie. It smarts."

"What happened exactly?"

"Remember the neighbors with the long-standing feud?"

"The Buchanans and the…"

"Oakleys. I was trying to sort through an argument and wound up standing in the wrong spot."

Troubled, Allison observed the passing landscape. Caroline's words had taken root, but putting voice to those questions wasn't something she was willing to do. If she was the reason he'd lost control of the situation, she didn't want to know.

Shane guided the wagon onto a narrow, overgrown path. The terrain was uneven, the mountain face jutting sharply above them. Naked trees clung to the rocky soil. A bushy-tailed squirrel darted across the path, reaching safety with seconds to spare. When they approached the dilapidated homestead, a woman peeked out a dirty window.

Allison chose to remain in the wagon. Some of the more reclusive families were wary of strangers.

After a quick exchange with the woman of the house— there was no sign of her husband—Shane returned and maneuvered the wagon around.

"Mrs. McGuire was very appreciative. I could tell she

was curious about you." Shooting her a side glance, he said wryly, "Ben was right. You look like a Montgomery Ward catalog advertisement."

She touched the matching royal blue bonnet trimmed in silver ribbon. "I wear this every year around the holidays. I'm not so vain as to insist on wearing an outfit only once. I get plenty of use out of my wardrobe."

Spreading her hands on her lap, she studied the gloves she'd ordered on a whim. Crafted of heather-gray leather, they were overlaid with intricate black lace and adorned with a single silver button at her wrists. "I suppose these are a bit impractical."

He arched a brow. "You suppose?"

Enjoying this return to lighthearted banter, she launched into accounts of her life in Norfolk. She told him about the friendships she'd forged at her church. He wasn't surprised to hear that she was part of a singing group, remarking that her singing could be heard up and down the halls of Ashworth House on a regular basis.

Shane was an attentive listener. The conversation turned to her profession, and she found herself pouring out her frustrations. He had such a calm approach that he balanced out her more passionate nature. Why couldn't he see how good they were together?

Before she could grow morose, Shane's posture changed, his fingers curling about the reins.

"What is it?"

He pointed to the house that was fourth on their list. "Fire."

It was unfortunate that Allison had to see this aspect of his job. She was a strong woman, though, and he couldn't completely shield her from the harsh realities of life.

After a quick survey of the burned-out shell of what had once been a large, dogtrot-style cabin, he returned to the wagon. Allison had gotten out and was pacing along the length of it, her polished black boots flashing with each flare of her ruffled skirts.

"We have to return to town."

She halted, her troubled gaze sliding to what was left of the structure. "Were there victims?"

"I didn't see any evidence of any." That didn't mean he wouldn't.

The tension left her. "That's a relief. But where do you think the owners could be?"

"The man who lives here, Harold Douglas, is a widower in his late fifties. It's possible he's out of town."

In the woods, birds called to one another, some singing cheery tunes that struck him as out of place on this dreary winter day.

"How long ago did this happen?" she said.

"Can't say for sure. The ashes are cold." He'd found something strange in the barn. "There aren't any animals around."

Rubbing her gloved hands together, she cupped them and blew. "Someone would've had to have released them."

Gesturing to the wagon, he took hold of her elbow and assisted her up. "Could've been a neighbor, but it's unlikely that person wouldn't have ridden to town to alert us."

He settled beside her and ordered the horses into motion.

"Wouldn't the smoke have been visible in town?"

"Depends on the wind patterns. Whether or not it happened at night. When it rains at this elevation, sometimes thick mist cloaks the peaks."

"That's why they're called Smoky Mountains."

"Another fact from your research?"

"Yes. What happens now?"

"I'll gather a group of men to help me dismantle the debris. First, I'll need to comb through it for clues."

Her exclamation startled him. "Shane! Look!" Balancing herself against his shoulder, she leaned close. "There. In the trees. I saw something."

Pulling hard on the reins, he brought the wagon to a rumbling halt. The horses bobbed their heads. "What is it?"

"I don't know. I saw movement. Someone was watching us."

"Stay here."

"Be careful."

His pistol at the ready, he entered the winter-deadened forest, dry leaves crunching beneath his boots. He could be dealing with a curious trespasser or one with more sinister motives. At this point, there was no way to know if that fire had been an accident or set deliberately. Muscles bunched with tension, he kept his finger on the trigger as he repeatedly scanned his surroundings.

Somewhere off to his left, a twig snapped. He whirled. The sound of pattering feet met his ears, and he gave chase. The runner was quick. Agile. When he topped a rise, he caught a glimpse of his prey. Brown cap. Thin. Younger than he'd expected.

"Hey!" he yelled. "I just wanna talk."

The young man didn't slow, didn't look back.

Many minutes passed before Shane admitted defeat, bracing his arm against a tree trunk and panting hard. After one last inspection of the woods, he retraced his steps, on the lookout for anything the trespasser might've dropped in his haste.

He reached the lane where Allison waited and, as always happened when he looked at her, his heart kicked against his ribs. The destruction of Harold Douglas's home wasn't his only dilemma. The widower's whereabouts and the identity of the trespasser were problems, sure, but ones he had a chance at solving. As for the feelings Allison evoked in him, he wasn't sure there was a solution.

Chapter Seventeen

"I've made my decision."

Deep in her heart, Allison had known all along what her ultimate course would be. There would be obstacles, of course, and those who'd disapprove of her choice. None of that mattered.

Standing on the threshold, Fenton's weathered features became guarded. "Well, let's hear it."

Charlie bounced in her arms and babbled at his great-grandfather.

"I was just about to put them down for a nap," she said.

"I'll give you a hand."

Removing his hat and coat, he hooked them on pegs and readjusted his suspenders. Scooping Izzy into his arms, he followed Allison upstairs and helped change the babies' diapers and dress them in sleeping gowns. When the twins had quieted in their cradles, she and Fenton went to the kitchen.

She heated the water, and Fenton pulled a golden canister from the shelf. "Would you like tea?"

"Yes, thank you."

Once the sugar and milk were on the table, they sat across from each other.

Allison set her spoon aside and smiled, aware that this moment was a huge turning point in her life. "My answer is yes. There's nothing I'd like more than to be Izzy and Charlie's mother."

His wariness melted, and his gray eyes glistened with moisture. "I hoped you'd agree. I had a feeling you would. The way you've taken to those babies…" Blinking fast, he peered down into his mug and seemed to struggle with his emotion.

Overwhelmed, Allison battled her own tears. Fenton adored his great-grandchildren. While this was a moment of celebration for her, it was one of unbearable sadness for him.

"I know Virginia sounds far away, but it's not a terrible distance." She covered his hand with hers. "I'd like for you to come and visit as often as you're able. I'd arrange for comfortable travel for you. You could even spend the winters there if you're so inclined."

He shook his head sadly. "I ain't never been out of these mountains."

"I think you'd like Norfolk. It's a beautiful place. There's the Elizabeth River or the Chesapeake Bay for fishing. Beaches to explore. Woods for hunting. Izzy and Charlie will be exposed to museums and musicals, plays and festivals. They'll have my niece and nephews for playmates."

"Sounds nice." His brows pulled together. "I'll give it some thought."

"And of course we'll visit you, too. We'll make multiple trips," she promised, wondering how she would cope with being forced to see Shane again and again.

No matter. She'd do anything to ease the pain of this separation.

"There is one thing you have to do before you leave."

A tiny arrow of unease winged through her.

"I want you to go out to the Whitakers' place and get their consent. You can take the sheriff as a witness."

"I thought they already made their stance clear. They didn't want to claim them."

"That's what they said a couple of months ago."

"Then why?" Worry eclipsed her joy. What if they refused her simply out of meanness? What little she'd heard about their family wasn't good. They could destroy her dream before she got a chance to live it.

"I'm looking out for you, missy. Save you trouble down the road," he said. "Don't you wanna leave here with a clear conscience?"

"Yes. Of course."

But she couldn't help wondering if, by doing what Fenton suggested, she'd be making a terrible mistake.

Allison was nursing a cup of coffee and wishing she knew how to prepare biscuits and gravy when someone knocked on the kitchen door. A frisson of unease skated across her skin. The sun had yet to crest the mountaintops. Who'd be paying her a visit in the dark, early-morning hours?

Approaching the door, she pressed her ear to the wood. "Who's there?"

"Allie, it's me."

Shane? Opening the door, she shivered as cold air washed over her.

"Can we talk?" he said. His features were stamped with exhaustion, and the bruises around his eye were more mottled. At least the swelling in his cheek had receded.

She quickly admitted him, grateful she'd taken the time to dress and brush her hair.

"Has something happened? Is Fenton okay?"

"He's fine. He was still asleep when I left." Standing in the middle of the kitchen, he removed his hat and finger-combed his hair. "I'm sorry for flustering you. I probably should've waited to come, but I couldn't sleep and I wanted to share some news with you."

"About the fire? Did you find Mr. Douglas?"

Moving to the stove, she readied coffee for him and held it out. His gloved fingers brushed hers as he took it with a murmured thanks.

"No. We cleaned the burn site yesterday and there was no sign of him." He took a long sip. "The neighbors didn't have any helpful information except to say Douglas had had some family visiting a while back."

"And the person we saw in the woods?"

He shook his head. "No idea who it could've been." Pulling out a chair, he said, "Do you mind if we sit?"

Allison resumed her seat and wrapped her hands around her cup. Nervousness fluttered in her middle. He looked serious. There were tired lines on his face, but his azure gaze was bright.

"Do you remember the Bible your father gave to me?"

"He gave it to you for your sixteenth birthday."

"I've been reading it."

Astonished, Allison stammered, "Y-you have?"

He'd struggled with his faith ever since she'd known him. Through the years, whenever she'd thought of him—which had been a daily event, his presence was stamped on Ashworth House—she'd talked to God about him, asking for protection first and also for his heart to be open to the truth.

"I went to Josh's last night. We prayed. Well, I prayed. He guided me." A spurt of joy transformed his austere face. "I've finally accepted that God loves me. That Jesus died for me. For the first time in my life, I know what peace feels like. Peace about where I'm headed once I leave this world, that is."

That's it. That's what was different about him. He exuded a calmness, an inner confidence that had nothing to do with his abilities and everything to do with his understanding of God's affection.

"Oh, Shane. I'm so very happy to hear that." How desperately she wished to hug him! "My father would be dancing a jig right now."

Laughter rumbled deep in his chest. "I'm not sure I can see David doing that, but I reckon he'd be as pleased as punch." Shifting in his seat, he grew serious once more. "I always thought God had abandoned me, like my pa. Now I can see how He used David to change the direction of my life. He extended not only mercy and forgiveness, but unconditional love. I just wish I hadn't been so stubborn."

Allison dared to give his hand a quick squeeze. "You were young. You'd experienced hard things."

"What's funny is I still have problems. The difference is I know I'm not alone."

She offered up a silent prayer of thanksgiving. "This is the single most important decision a person can make. You don't know how long I've prayed for this. My brother, too."

He ducked his head. "That means a lot."

Her heart was light with Shane's news. Knowing what a private man he was made the fact that he'd shared such a personal decision with her that much more special.

"I'm really, really happy you told me."

"Even if I disrupted your morning?" He smiled.

"You didn't disrupt it. You made my entire day brighter."

His gaze grew more intense, and she averted hers. The longing to hold him took root. She got up and carried her cup to the dry sink, her back to him.

"I'm eager to share my news with George."

"He'll be thrilled."

The scrape of the chair against the floor was followed by his slow tread to her side. His fingers brushed her spine, and she jumped.

"I think you have news of your own to share."

Turning, she found him watching her with expectation. "Did Fenton say something to you?"

"He didn't have to."

She squared her shoulders. "You're right. I spoke with him yesterday."

"You're going to be the twins' mother." His expression revealed nothing of his thoughts.

"Yes."

"I can't say as I'm surprised."

"You don't approve."

His forehead creased. "I didn't say that."

Chest cramping with disappointment, she made to move past him.

"Allie." Blocking her retreat, he gripped her shoulders and waited until she lifted her gaze to speak. "You're the most nurturing person I've ever known. You've got a heart made for loving. If anyone can give those children the home and security they need, it's you."

She bit down hard on her lip and commanded herself not to cry. He couldn't know how much his approval meant to her.

"You honestly think I'll make a good mother?"

His hands slid over the curve of her shoulders to her upper arms. "The best."

Between his announcement and her news, the room seemed charged with emotion. How she yearned to walk into his arms and remain there. But he didn't want that.

Stepping out of his hold, she hugged her midsection. For an instant, he looked bereft. Then he swung away, picked up his hat and went to the door.

"I'd better get to work. Thanks for the coffee."

She stayed on the opposite side of the room, wishing he could stay and hoping that didn't show on her face. "Have a good day, Shane."

* * *

Cold settled in his bones. Shane readjusted his neckerchief in an effort to cover as much exposed skin as possible. The mid-December night was lit only by a half-moon suspended in the inky sky. Every now and then, wisps of clouds passed in front of it. Positioned near the post office entrance, a dense cloak of shadows concealed him.

Come on, he silently bid the drifter. *Show yourself.*

Quinn had come to the jail that morning, having discovered more empty tins—peaches, cherries and the like—as well as a discarded container of chocolate creams in the alley between the livery and mercantile. He and the other store owners were anxious to find the perpetrator.

Determined to catch the man and put an end to the filching, Shane had decided to take the first shift of surveillance. If the drifter didn't show tonight, he and Ben would take turns keeping watch until he was apprehended.

While his body remained motionless, his muscles begging for his soft mattress, his mind refused to rest. He replayed the scene in the Wattses' kitchen, returning again to Allison's reaction to his news. He dared not examine the reason she was the first person he'd wanted to tell. Or why he'd been so impatient to see her.

Allison was going to be a mother. Fenton's subdued, contemplative mood the day before had clued him in that something had changed. Shane felt sorry for the man. He'd had to say goodbye to everyone he'd ever loved. And while he was certain Allison would do everything she could to involve Fenton in the twins' lives, the fact remained that they would soon be living hundreds of miles away. Shane had to admit he'd miss them, too.

And Allie. You'll miss her most of all.

He gritted his teeth and attempted to lock the melancholy away. Allison's dream was coming true and he was determined to be happy for her.

With effort, he turned his thoughts to the Douglas mystery. Josh and Shane had combed through the ashes looking for clues. There wasn't any evidence pointing to an act of arson. It appeared the fire started in the kitchen. In addition to the cookstove, there'd been a small stone fireplace. Sparks could've hit a rug or discarded newspaper. The presence of a trespasser bothered Shane, though. In his perusal of his favorite law journal, he'd learned that sometimes a criminal returned to the scene to see for himself the destruction he'd wrought. The idea made his gut clench with distaste. No matter how long he did this job, he'd never grow accustomed to the evil some folks visited upon others.

The wind shifted, suffusing the air where he stood with the twang of pine and holly berry garlands wrapped about the posts and windows. Movement registered in his peripheral vision. Furtive movements like that of a frightened rabbit.

Shane focused on the alley between the mercantile and livery. The slight figure that crept onto the boardwalk and peered into the store windows was too small to be a full-grown man. Not bothering to unsheath his weapon, he strode silently across the deserted street. He was mere steps away from the boardwalk when the boy's head whipped up. A squeak shredded the night. He took off toward the livery. Smothering a groan, Shane gave chase.

He pursued him around the livery's far side and down toward the river. No doubt the kid aimed to lose him in the woods. Shane had too many unhappy business owners to let that happen.

He pushed himself faster and, snaking out a hand, managed to grab hold of the boy's collar.

"Gotcha."

"Let me go!"

He tried to wriggle out of his jacket in a bid for freedom. Shane clamped down on his shoulders—wincing at the evidence of thin bones beneath—and held him in place.

"Listen to me," he barked, using his firm, don't-mess-with-the-sheriff voice. "I'm not going to hurt you, but you have to cooperate. Understand?"

"Why should I believe you?" he scoffed.

"Because I'm the sheriff. It's my job to see to it that everyone in this town obeys the law, including myself."

"You ain't takin' me to jail?"

In the absence of light, Shane couldn't decide if this was the same kid he'd chased out at the Douglas farm. Mixed in with the kid's anger over getting nabbed was a heavy dose of fear. Memories bombarded him, stirring a well of compassion. There was no telling what events had led him to stealing food and sleeping in a stable. Shane intended to find out before this night was over.

"My office is inside the jail, so in order to discuss this matter like men, we'll have to go there."

Keeping tight hold of his shoulder, Shane marched him inside the jailhouse and, closing the door, jabbed a finger at one of the chairs before his desk. "Sit."

The boy's eyes were mostly obscured by his cap. The rest of his face was coated with grime. Peeking from beneath his cap was straggly hair of an indiscriminate color. Instead of sitting down, he folded his arms over his chest and glared at the floor.

"What's your name, son?"

Shane winced again. He'd had the same exact question directed at him once upon a time. And just like this boy, he hadn't been inclined to answer.

Without really thinking about it, Shane offered up a prayer for assistance in sorting through this mystery. Despite the circumstances, he felt a glorious peace suffuse him. He wasn't working alone anymore.

Resting his weight on the desk's edge, he said, "Listen,

I know you don't trust me. My name's Shane Timmons, by the way. I've been the sheriff here for a long while."

The boy scuffed his boot along the floor.

"I'd like to call you something other than 'boy.'"

His head jerked up, caramel-hued eyes flashing. "I'm not—" He clamped his lips together and fisted his hands.

"You're not what?"

"I'm not talkin' to you."

Shane tamped down a wave of frustration. "I can't help you if you won't at least tell me why you're out on the streets at this time of night."

He tried several times to get the boy to cooperate. When a loud rumble met his questions, Shane decided they could wait.

"Come on, then." Striding to the nearest cell, he held the barred door open and fished his key ring from his belt. "This here'll be your bedroom for the night."

His eyes got huge. Fear surged. "You're lockin' me up?"

"I don't trust you to wait here while I go fetch us some grub. This way I know you'll stay put."

He looked from Shane to the cell and back.

"The quicker you do as I say, the quicker we get to eat."

Swallowing hard, he shuffled inside. Turning the cell door lock was one of the hardest things Shane had ever done. Allison would wallop him good when she got wind of this. But what other choice did he have?

"Sit tight. I'll be back as soon as I can."

Hurrying home, Shane snagged the loaf of bread he'd bought yesterday, along with three boiled eggs, a jar of pickled okra and a cheese wedge. On his way out the door, his gaze fell on the tabletop pin game. The boy could use it to entertain himself if he couldn't sleep. When he reentered the jail, his unlikely prisoner was in the same exact spot he'd left him in.

There was no denying his deep suspicion as he peered at Shane.

"It's not a hot meal, but it'll do. Help yourself to as much as you want." Shane placed the basket on the cot beside him.

"Ain't got no money."

His throat grew thick. "It's free."

Leaving the cell door open, Shane busied himself sweeping the floor that didn't need to be swept and straightening desk drawers that didn't need straightening. He'd assumed their drifter was an adult man, perhaps someone who'd fallen on hard times, someone without family to take him in. Maybe even someone trying to avoid the law. Not once had he considered they were dealing with a youth. Judging by his leanness and disheveled appearance, he'd been fending for himself for a while.

Shane snuck a peek at the cell. The kid held an egg in one hand and a hunk of bread in the other and was stuffing large bites of both into his mouth as fast as he could.

Well, he'd caught his drifter. What was he supposed to do now?

Chapter Eighteen

"**I** need your help."

Allison struggled to mask her surprise. Standing in the entryway between the kitchen and dining room, she studied the pitiful figure sitting rigidly on the couch.

"*He's* your drifter?" she whispered.

Turning to look at Shane, she found him standing far too close. The doorframe pressed into the spot between her shoulder blades, and she had nowhere to go.

"Looks that way. I haven't gotten much information out of him." His liquid blue gaze soaked her in. "I thought you'd have a better chance of success."

Seated in his high chair, Charlie whacked it and started spouting gibberish. Izzy joined in. Shane's attention slid to them, and he smiled. If he could see his reflection right now, he'd be stunned. There was no denying the unabashed affection in his expression. Whether he admitted it or not, he cared about the babies.

Her babies. That bubbly feeling of joy overtook her again.

Tilting her head in the direction of the living room, she said, "Has he had breakfast?"

He nodded. "I fetched us both plates from the café."

"You left him unattended in your home?"

"I couldn't do that."

"Then where…" She gasped, drawing the boy's attention. Leaning closer, she hissed, "Shane Timmons, please tell me you didn't lock up that poor child!"

His hands settled on her shoulders, startling her. They were warm and heavy. "I didn't have a choice."

His mouth hovered close. A day's growth of beard darkened his jaw, and she had the urge to explore the short bristles.

Focus, Allison. "What exactly do you expect me to do?"

His fingers tightened a fraction before falling away. A sigh gusted out of him. "You're good with people, kids especially. See if you can pry anything out of him. A name would be a good start."

"I'll give it my best effort."

"Thank you, Allie."

"While I'm doing that, you have to finish feeding the twins."

A furrow appeared between his brows. She studied his profile as he took in the messy kitchen scene. He was so dear, his handsome face etched upon her mind and heart. Soon George and his brood would descend upon them, and these precious moments of privacy would be nothing but a memory. The days would fly past, Christmas would come and go and it would be time to leave Gatlinburg.

While she eagerly anticipated setting up her new life with the twins, the prospect of not seeing Shane on a regular basis made her ache. She wasn't sure how she was supposed to cope with going back to hearing snippets about him from her brother.

Settling in the chair between the siblings, he picked up a bowl of oatmeal and shot her a long-suffering look. "Go on, then."

Pinning on a smile, Allison went into the living room. "Hello there. My name's Allison Ashworth."

Arms crossed tightly about his middle, the boy shrugged. "Sheriff already tol' me."

His pants were about an inch too short and nearly worn through in the knees. The thin jacket wasn't at all appropriate for winter.

Her heart squeezed painfully at the evidence of neglect and dire need. "Shane's worried about you, you know. His job is to help people. He can't do that if you refuse to talk to him."

He shrugged again.

"It would be nice to know your name."

A long pause. "If I tell ya, can I leave?" Beneath the hat, caramel-colored eyes snuck a peek at her.

"Where would you go?" she said gently. "Do you have relatives close by?"

"No family." When he finally lifted his head, he seemed fascinated with her ruby earbobs and the locket about her neck. "The name's Mattie."

Ah, progress. "Nice to meet you, Mattie."

"Are you rich?"

She couldn't help it. She laughed out loud. "That's not considered a polite question, young man."

"Why not?"

"I'll explain another time." Watching as he scratched his head, she said, "How about we chat later? You'll feel much better once you've had a bath." Smell better, too.

Popping up from the cushion, he held his hands up. "No!"

His vehemence confused her. "I promise you'll have complete privacy."

"The thing is…" His panicked gaze cast about the room for a handy escape.

"What's bothering you, Mattie?"

"M-Mattie's just a nickname. M-my full name is Matilda Rose Douglas."

Allison's jaw sagged. Beneath all that grime and the bad haircut was a girl?

"How old are you?"

"Eleven."

Tall for her age, she was extremely thin. They'd have to do something about that, Allison decided, even if she had to personally see to it.

"Well, Miss Matilda Rose, the sheriff sure is in for a surprise, is he not?"

Allison was hiding something. A smile had played about her mouth as he'd brought in pails of water to be heated on the stove and remained there until she shooed him out of the kitchen and ordered him upstairs. He could hear their muted voices but couldn't make out the words. Light streamed through her bedroom windows and shifted into patterns on the polished wood boards. It felt as if he were invading her privacy. At Ashworth House, she'd invited him to explore the dizzying array of toys and curiosities in her childhood room, but he'd resisted. He hadn't wanted to be drawn into her world.

The baby in his arms batted his shoulder. Glancing into her big brown eyes, he said, "This time I didn't have another option, did I, Izzy?"

Allison hadn't been in town two full weeks and she'd already made this house, this town, her own.

Izzy pressed her lips together and blew. She batted his shoulder again and uttered a string of unintelligible sounds. Hiking her higher, he smoothed a stray blond curl from her soft brow.

"You're a sweetheart, you know that?" he murmured.

He'd miss all of her major achievements—crawling, walking, talking. He wouldn't be the recipient of her drawings, her hugs, her kisses. He wouldn't be the one toting her about on his shoulders, swinging her in a wide circle as she laughed, buying her china dolls and miniature tea sets.

Someone else would do all that. Someone like Trevor Langston.

Sadness gripped him. Jealousy, too. He was jealous of a man he'd never met.

Forgive me, Lord.

Allison would make a wonderful mother, of that he had not a single doubt. Nurturing came natural to her. Generous with her affection, she held enough love in her heart for a hundred orphans.

What about a lonely sheriff who ached for a family to call his own but was too scared to admit it? Could she love a man like that?

Shane ceased his route about the room. Where had those thoughts come from? Love had nothing to do with their relationship. At best, what they had was a tenuous friendship. That kiss wasn't his doing, after all. *She* kissed *him.* It was only natural that he'd responded.

Light footsteps along the hall brought him out of his troubled musings. Propped into a seated position on the rug at the foot of the bed, Charlie waved his bear around.

Allison appeared in the doorway, her smile anticipatory in nature. What was so amusing?

"Sheriff Timmons, I'd like for you to meet Matilda Rose Douglas."

At Allison's urging, the child stepped into the room. It took several moments for the name to register and for him to absorb the change in appearance.

"You're wearing a dress."

From the looks of it, a brand-new dress of evergreen, paisley material with rose ribbons, the same one Allison had purchased in town last week. She'd been collecting items to take to her friends in Norfolk. This particular gift had been intended for a close friend's daughter.

Allison touched the sleeve. "Isn't it beautiful?"

Hearing the warning in her tone, he grunted in agreement.

"Your name's Matilda?"

She stood straighter, her hands clasped tightly at her waist. "No one calls me that anymore."

Now that it was washed and combed, he could see that her hair was a honey-brown hue. Cut even with her earlobes, a matching ribbon had been wound about her head and tied beneath the strands. Now that her face was squeaky clean, he could see the feminine curve of her cheek, the girlish set to her mouth.

It hit him then that he'd locked up a little girl. His hold tightened on Izzy, who protested by squirming.

"How old are you?"

"Eleven."

His head dipped. A moment later, he felt Allison's hand curving about his biceps. "Don't be so hard on yourself," she murmured. "You couldn't have known."

Transferring Izzy into Allison's arms, he scraped both hands down his face. His eyes felt gritty from lack of sleep. He'd tried to snooze in his hard desk chair last night, but the kid had tossed and turned and whimpered in the cell, making Shane wonder what nightmares were haunting him. *Her.* Matilda.

"That was you I was chasing through the woods, wasn't it? Are you kin to Harold Douglas?"

Her upper lip curled in a manner too old for her years. "I don't claim him."

He saw far too much of himself in her. "But you are related."

Her attention on the twins, she said, "He's my uncle. My

ma died when we were livin' in North Carolina. Pa said his brother would be happy for us to stay with him for a while."

Her brow knitted, and Shane heard what she didn't say. Her father must've been wrong.

Retrieving the locket he'd been keeping on his person since discovering it in the livery, he held it on his open palm. "Is this yours?"

With a soft cry, she rushed and scooped it up, prying the sides open to stare at the tiny photograph. "Momma!" Her lower lip trembled. "I thought I'd lost this forever."

"I found it at the livery."

When she didn't volunteer information, Allison spoke. "Matilda, where is your father?"

"Dead."

He sought out Allison's gaze. Sympathy radiated from her. Like she had wanted to do for him all those years ago, no doubt her first instinct was to rush in and fix things. Only, some things couldn't be rushed.

"What happened?" he said quietly.

"He and Uncle Harold were cuttin' down a tree. It fell the wrong way."

"I'm sorry, Matilda."

She appeared to be weighing his words, probably trying to decide if he was trustworthy. He had many more questions he wanted answered, but he sensed it would be better not to overwhelm her.

"Do you still have that popcorn I bought?" he asked Allison.

Her brows rose in question. "I do."

"I don't have to be at the jail until later. Why don't I pop a batch? We can string some for the tree."

Allison studied him for long moments, that familiar pleat between her brows. "Good idea. Matilda, would you mind helping me string it?"

The girl looked dumbfounded. "Me?" She tugged at the stiff collar. "I ain't never done nothin' like that."

Allison's smile was gentle. "I'll show you how."

Hope brightened her eyes. Shane waited, breath suspended. Would she seize on to it? Or, like he had done, would she crush it?

"O-okay, I guess."

"Wonderful." Allison beamed. "Shane, I'll join you after I get these two down for a nap."

"You don't need a hand?"

"No, I'll be fine." Her manner portrayed confidence.

Ushering Matilda into the hall, he closed the bedroom door. "You ever tasted fresh-popped corn?"

She shook her head, her eyes full of mystery.

Descending the stairs, he said over his shoulder, "I'll make a big batch so that we'll have plenty to sample."

When they reached the kitchen, Matilda said, "Are you and Allison hitched?"

He had a tough time not gaping at her. "No." He held up his left hand to show the bare finger. "We've known each other a long time, that's all."

Of course, it was more complicated than he'd made it sound.

She adjusted and readjusted the ribbon headband. "Oh. So she's a widow."

"No." Shane tossed wood into the stove box. He was beginning to wish he was upstairs with the twins. At least they couldn't pepper him with questions he wasn't quite sure how to answer. "Allison is Charlie and Izzy's caretaker. Their mother recently passed."

Shadows passed over her face. He gathered the supplies and explained the steps to making popcorn. Matilda didn't speak. It was possible she was entertaining the same thoughts as him. The chief one being what was he going to do about her?

Chapter Nineteen

Funny how some wishes came true, only in a skewed way—not bad, necessarily, just different than one envisioned. As a girl, Allison had daydreamed about taking part in Christmas traditions with Shane. Caroling. Decorating cookies. Wrapping presents for the charity baskets.

Not once had she imagined a scene such as this one—a comfortable living room in a rented house with Shane instructing a mystery of a girl who it seemed had no one in the world to care for her. A girl whose haunted eyes and defiant attitude reminded Allison of the young boy her father had brought to live with them so many years ago.

Seated on the sofa stringing popcorn, Allison observed the pair from beneath lowered lashes. Matilda had started out with her. An attentive student, she'd followed Allison's instructions with surprising precision. But her focus had repeatedly slipped to the sheriff, who was tying strips of red, green and gold fabric to the branch tips. Matilda appeared to be simultaneously in awe of and intrigued by him. It hadn't taken much urging to get her to join him by the tree.

Allison was touched by his incredible patience with Matilda. Watching the tough, unflappable sheriff gently guide the wisp of a girl in a timeless tradition filled her with bittersweet longing. *You have the babies*, she scolded herself. *Isn't that enough? Must you want to add these two to your brood?*

Ordering herself to be satisfied with what God had granted her, she began to hum a familiar carol.

"A shame the Wattses don't have a piano." Shane smiled over at her.

She lowered the needle. "You never enjoyed my singing."

"Wrong." Tying the fabric into a bow on one of the high branches, he glanced over his uplifted arm. "I used to sit and listen to you for hours."

Crouched on the opposite side of the tree, Matilda stopped what she was doing, her manner watchful.

"I would've remembered that."

He planted his hands on his lean hips. "You wouldn't because I didn't allow you to see me."

Shock shimmered through her. "I don't believe you."

One dark brow arched, and his expression shouted a warning. "Why would I lie, Allison?"

She thought back to those afternoons in the music room where she'd practiced for hours on end. The idea that he'd witnessed every moment without her knowing made her angry. He'd led her to think he couldn't stand to breathe the same air as she. "Why would you spy on me?"

"I wasn't spying. Exactly." Conflicted emotions passed over his face. "I—"

"Stop!" Rushing beside the coffee table, Matilda flung her arms out wide. "Don't argue!"

Shane's arms dropped to his sides, and he took a half step forward. "There's no cause to be upset, Matilda. We're not arguing." His gaze punched Allison's. "We're...discussing the past."

Setting the nearly completed string aside, Allison rose.

"There is a difference, sweetheart. Shane and I are friends, which means we sometimes have issues to work through."

Matilda shifted her weight from one foot to the other, obviously unsure if she should believe them.

"Remember I told you we've known each other a long time?" Shane said.

She nodded and slowly lowered her arms.

"We met when I was fourteen, and she was twelve."

Her eyes got round. "*I'm* almost twelve."

A lopsided smile curved his lips. "You see? Allie and I have known each other half our lives."

She grazed Matilda's sleeve with her fingers. "When you care about someone, you do everything possible to avoid hurting them."

Bowing her head, the girl fiddled with the locket around her neck. Fine strands of honey-hued hair whispered across her cheek.

Shane crouched in front of her. "How long ago did your pa die?"

"Sixty-two days. I've kept count in a ledger I found."

Allison's heart twisted with sympathy.

"And afterward, did you stay with your uncle?"

Matilda nodded.

He cleared his throat. "Did he hurt you?"

"He threatened to." Her small hands twisted in her skirt. "Mostly he yelled and threw things. He didn't ask to be saddled with his brother's kid, he said."

A vein in Shane's temple throbbed.

"I was happy when he left and didn't come back."

Shane exchanged a glance with Allison.

"When was that?" he said.

"About a month ago. He said he was ridin' over to Cades Cove to see to a business matter."

"How did the fire start, Matilda?"

"I didn't set it," she exclaimed, wrapping her thin arms about her middle. "Honest!"

"I wasn't implying you did. I'd just like to know what happened."

Allison listened as she haltingly recounted the events. It had been early, shortly after dawn, and she'd been in the barn milking cows, trying to carry on as if her uncle had never left. If he returned and found that she'd shirked her duties, he'd yell again and possibly make good his threats to punish her. When a stray dog happened by, she'd followed him into the fields and spent a good while making friends with him. By the time she returned, the cabin had been engulfed in flames. Frightened, she'd bolted into the woods.

Remembered terror turned her eyes dark. "I didn't know what to do."

Shane looked grim. "There was nothing you could do."

Allison could well imagine the girl's distress. After losing her father, her one trusted caregiver, she'd been in an unfamiliar town with a man who hadn't made her feel safe. Then to be left alone and homeless in the world…no wonder she hadn't approached any of the locals for help. She couldn't have known if she'd wind up in a worse situation than before.

"You like animals, huh?" Shane said, stroking the bristles along his jaw in a contemplative gesture.

Matilda didn't blink at the change in subject. "Cats are my favorite. I like dogs, too. And foxes."

"Do you like cows?"

She shrugged. "I like 'em more than chickens."

Hiding a smile, Allison wondered at the reason for his questions.

"They're much better than chickens," he agreed. "Did you make friends with any of the cows on the farms close to town?"

Understanding lit in her gaze. "You wanna know if it was me that boy saw that night, don't ya?"

"His name is Billy Oakley, and I think his pa, Vernon, would rest easier if he knew who'd been on his property."

She stared at the floor. "Will I get in trouble?"

"No, Matilda." His gaze locked with Allison's. "Allie and I want to help you."

"I was just passin' through. I didn't see any harm in pettin' them." Her features were strained. "Are you takin' me back to jail?"

"No. You're not going there again." He awkwardly patted her hand. "Unless it's to visit me, of course."

"Where will I go?" Her voice quivered.

Shane's gaze centered on Allison again and, at his unspoken question, she nodded.

"For tonight, you'll stay here with Miss Allison. We've got time to figure out what happens after that."

"Uncle Harold will thrash me if he comes back and sees his cabin's gone."

"Try not to worry, sweetheart," Allison said. "Shane and I will make sure you're safe. For now, we have a tree to finish decorating. The twins won't sleep for much longer. What do you say?"

The girl looked at both adults. "Okay."

They resumed their task. Allison attempted to lighten the mood by regaling Matilda with tales of her childhood escapades. Shane remained quiet. When they were satisfied every visible branch was properly adorned, he instructed the girl to remain in the living room and led Allison into the kitchen.

"What's on your mind, Sheriff?"

"Thanks for letting her stay."

He stood so close. Did he realize he was breaching her space?

"Of course. She's a sweet girl. I hate that she's had to endure such trials."

"I'm going to send out a search party. We need to locate Harold as quickly as possible."

"You're not going to make her go back to that monster, are you?"

"He's her guardian, Allie."

"A rotten one. It's your job to protect the innocent, remember?" Glaring, she tapped his badge.

His fingers closed over hers, warm and work-roughened, and despite her anger, she reacted to his touch as usual.

"I don't want her with him any more than you do."

"Then why would you let him have her?"

"I didn't say I was." His thumb grazed her knuckles. "Let's focus on locating him first. Then I'll work on finding Matilda a more suitable living situation."

Allison tugged on her hand. Shane let go and sunk his hands in his pockets.

"A word of advice. Don't go entertaining wild ideas."

She bristled. "What are you talking about?"

"I know how you think. I'd guess you're already furnishing a bedroom for her in your future home."

He was wrong. "*If* that were true, why would you care?"

"Taking on six-month-old twins by yourself is one thing. Add a confused, hurting girl like Matilda, and you'd be in over your head."

"Your confidence is reassuring," she sniped, stung by his utter lack of faith in her decision-making skills and potential as a mother. She wasn't rash. She'd just met the girl.

"Sometimes, Allie, I want to…" Huffing out his exasperation, he thrust his fingers in his hair.

Jamming her fists into her hips, she jerked up her chin. "Spit it out, Sheriff. You want to what?"

Shane erased the distance between them. Her heart stuttered. One of his hands found a home in the curve of her neck, fingers splayed wide, thumb pressing her jaw upward. The other settled heavily on her shoulder. His heat registered through her blouse.

His dear face was inches from hers, his eyes a blazing inferno, his uneven breathing loud in the room.

"You should think about what you're doing, Shane Timmons."

Allison wanted his kiss with a physical ache, but she'd tasted its destruction once already and wasn't prepared to do so again.

He didn't respond. Didn't move. He appeared locked in an internal war.

She reached up and covered his hand with her own. Her lids slid shut. Drawing on the pain of past rejection, she curled her fingers beneath his and tugged them down.

"*This* isn't what you truly want." The words scraped at her throat like razor blades.

Allison opened her eyes in time to see him bow his head in defeat. Moving away before her willpower crumbled and she threw herself into his arms, she was at the dining room entrance when his gruff voice stopped her.

"I'm staying here tonight."

She whirled. It hurt to look at him. "What? No."

His jaw worked. "Fenton can sleep in one of the spare rooms upstairs. I'll sleep on the couch."

"No."

"Yes."

"Why?"

"Because I remember what it feels like to be alone, scared and at the mercy of others. I don't trust her not to run."

Sleep refused to come. His body begged for rest, but his mind wouldn't succumb. The fact that his legs were about six inches too long for the sofa didn't help matters. Instead of lying on his back as he was accustomed, he had to lie on his side, his legs curled into the cushions. Add to that the knowledge that Allison was at the top of the stairs, and he didn't stand a chance.

What had he been thinking? He couldn't explain what had overcome him, couldn't fathom what it was that always flared between them like a lit match to a pile of hay. One minute he'd been worried for her, concerned her big, malleable heart was leading her into trouble, and the next his mind had been empty save for the need to hold her.

He couldn't wait for George to arrive. George would bring with him distraction and a hefty dose of common sense. No way would Shane be tempted to act like a sixteen-year-old boy with Allison's older brother around. Of course, his presence meant the end of their relative privacy. Her company was going to be in high demand, what with her sister-in-law and niece and nephews added to an already full house.

Above him, a floorboard creaked. Faint whimpering followed. Shane pushed the quilt aside and sat up. He couldn't distinguish which room the sound was coming from. A doorknob clicked. The mournful sobs grew more distinct. *Charlie.* He'd gotten fussy after supper. Allison's soft shushing and murmurs reached him as she padded up and down the long upstairs hallway.

Without giving his decision too much thought, he snapped his suspenders into place and climbed the stairs. The treads beneath his stocking feet were cold. He gripped the smooth banister near the top and stepped into the darkness.

"Allie?"

Her stride faltered. "I thought you'd be snoring by now," she whispered.

"Unfortunately, no. What's the matter?"

"He feels warm to the touch. I think he's cutting a tooth."

The prospect of a fever sent rivulets of apprehension through him. "I'll fetch a lamp."

He went to the kitchen and lit one. By the time he returned, she'd resumed her circuitous trek, the baby snuggled to her chest. Her hair formed a straight curtain of pale gold down to the middle of her back. She'd donned a Christmas-red housecoat, complete with white ruffles at the collar, wrists and hem. She looked like a Christmas package.

His attention transferred to the baby. Until this moment, he hadn't taken note of how the twins' hair color matched hers. No one would think to question their parentage. They'd assume they were her natural children.

"Fevers are dangerous," he said, setting the lamp beside the wall. "Should I fetch the doc?"

The flickering light reflected in her large green eyes. "George's kids developed slight fevers when they were teething. It's nothing to be too concerned over."

The need to hold the boy overtook him. He held out his arms. "Let me."

The baby came to him without complaint, his pudgy fingers fisting in Shane's collar. Charlie's fine hair tickled his cheek. Shane began to walk along the hall, passing Fenton's closed door first and then Matilda's. Was she comfortable in the warm bed? Or was she wide awake, alert to her unfamiliar surroundings?

Allison leaned against the railing, crossed her arms and silently watched his progression.

After a couple of turns, he worked up the nerve to speak what was on his mind. "I apologize for earlier. I jumped to conclusions. Despite evidence to the contrary, I do trust your judgment."

Her expression was unreadable. "Apology accepted."

He continued walking, and Charlie drooled on his shirt. When he came near again, she murmured, "What are her options? If Harold consents to give her up, I mean."

Moving beside her, he spoke in hushed tones so as not to be overheard if the little girl was awake in her room. "Possibly find a local family to take her in."

The corners of her mouth turned down. "But not as a means to get free labor, right? You'd find a family who wants her to be an important part of their lives? Maybe a couple who hasn't been able to have children on their own."

"I'll do my best."

Allison angled toward him. "I don't like the sound of that. I want you to promise me, Shane."

"I can't do that. Trust me, I will do everything in my power to find her a good home."

"Why don't you take her in?"

His chin met his chest. "*Me?* What do I know about adolescent girls?"

Preposterous. How could she suggest it?

"You can relate to her in a way few others can. You understand how she feels and what she requires to feel safe." Her gaze implored him to see things her way. "You can give her security, guidance and love—the kind of childhood you never had."

He shook his head, actively rejecting her reasoning. Failure loomed like a crouching mountain lion ready to pounce and devour him. He knew how to be a lawman: how to manage disputes, investigate arson and murders, track outlaws and effect daring rescues. Home life, family relationships, *love*…those weren't part of his language. Never had been.

Despair invaded him. "I'm not like you, Allison. I don't have what it takes to be a family man."

She opened her mouth to argue, so he handed a sleepy Charlie to her.

"There's no use trying to change me, Allie. You'll have to accept that some things are simply not meant to be."

Chapter Twenty

"George!" Allison squealed and threw her arms about his neck. His familiar shaving soap suffused her senses. She didn't care that Main Street was bustling with shoppers and holiday deliveries and that Shane was looking on, awaiting his turn to greet her brother. "I'm so happy you're here at last," she breathed into his itchy plaid scarf.

Laughing his hearty laugh, George pulled back, his expression slightly quizzical. "You act as if it's been a year since you've seen me."

"Believe me, it feels like an entire year has passed since I arrived."

He gave her an odd look.

Dressed in a bulky wool coat and smart gray bowler hat, he looked the same as always—his round, boyish face with lively bluish-gray eyes like their father's and thinning brown hair. Perhaps her great relief at seeing him had to do with the emotional ups and downs of the past weeks. He represented home and normalcy.

Shane chose that moment to step forward, gloved hand outstretched and a welcoming smile on his face. "George Ashworth. It's been too long."

Allison edged out of their way. George gripped Shane's

hand, pumped it several times and pulled him in for a brief hug. Around them, people stared and whispered on their walk along the boardwalk.

"I can't express how wonderful it is to see you, old friend." Glancing about at the festooned storefronts and the majestic mountain peaks towering over the town, he said, "You've chosen a right beautiful place to settle, I see."

"It is at that."

"What happened to your eye?"

"Got in the middle of an altercation between neighbors." He shrugged.

George gestured to Allison. "She give you any trouble?"

Shane's smile slipped. Not looking at her, he quipped, "No more than I expected."

George's thick brows crinkled. "What have you been up to, sister?"

Suddenly, explaining the huge life change she was about to undertake struck her as a daunting task. In her mind's playing out of events, George's reaction to her news had gone smoothly. Leaving the twins at home with Fenton had been a wise choice. It would give her time to sort through her speech and gather the courage to deliver it.

Instead of answering him, Allison peered around him at the stagecoach. "George, where's Clarissa and the children?"

He smoothed his mustache. "I'm afraid they aren't coming. George Jr. came down with a cough and fever earlier in the week. She didn't want to risk traveling with him."

Allison masked her disappointment. "Of course. I would've made the same decision."

He patted her arm. "I'm sorry, but I can't stay for Christmas. I'll be here through the week, and then I'll have to return home."

"Not staying for Christmas?"

"The kids would be devastated if I wasn't there to see them open their presents," he said.

She shifted her gaze to the narrow alleyway beside the post office, where a pair of young lads were petting a calico cat. "Yes, I know."

"Will you be returning with me?"

She sensed the immediate shift in Shane's posture, the intensity of his full focus on her. What did he want her answer to be? Was he ready to bid her goodbye? Or was there a small part of him that wished she'd stay?

"I'll have to give the matter some thought," she demurred.

One week. She wasn't prepared to leave that soon. She'd counted on attending the Christmas Eve pageant. And now with Matilda in their lives—the search party hadn't yet located Harold Douglas—she'd started planning a lavish Christmas morning breakfast complete with gifts for the orphaned girl. And what about Fenton? She'd developed a deep well of affection for the older man. Taking the twins away sooner than planned wouldn't be fair.

Then there was the one piece of unfinished business to tend to—paying the Whitakers a visit. She'd wrestled with Fenton's request, unsure if she should fulfill it. They'd already decided to cut Izzy and Charlie from their lives. What good would it do for her to revisit the issue?

Pushing the troubling thoughts from her mind, she linked arms with George as they followed Shane to the wagon. "I know what we'll do. We'll host a party. You'll have the opportunity to meet Shane's friends and a few of the acquaintances I've made."

George considered the idea. "What do you say, Shane?"

Stowing her brother's single trunk in the wagon bed, Shane turned, his breath creating a fog in the crisp air. "I say let Allison have her party. She usually gets whatever she sets her mind to, anyway."

Her brother looked at them both as if working out a puzzle. Uh-oh. While he didn't usually intrude into her personal affairs, she wasn't sure how he'd react if he knew what had transpired between her and Shane.

"Oh, don't mind him," she said airily. "He's playing the part of the grumpy lawman today."

Shane stalked past them both and climbed into the wagon, leaving George to assist her. Unfortunately, she wound up sandwiched between the two and, because of their size, there wasn't an inch of free space on the narrow seat.

Hands folded tightly in her lap, she remained silent as they caught up, talking over her as if she was invisible. Not that she truly minded. Her mind was a whirlwind of unrest. Between the torturous closeness of Shane—she registered his every movement, smushed as she was against his shoulder, thigh and knee—the worry over the Whitakers and imparting her news to George, she was anxious to the point of being nauseated.

George appreciated the beauty of the Wattses' homestead as much as she did. Seeing the farmhouse and surrounding fields and mountains through his eyes, Allison acknowledged how much she'd miss this place. She would've taken great pleasure in seeing spring transform the land. And later, summer yielding its bounty. Perhaps when she brought the twins to see Fenton, she could pay the Wattses a visit.

Guiding the team to a halt alongside the porch, Shane set the brake and quickly disembarked. He strode to the rear and, untethering his horse, secured the animal to the hitching post.

He'd been distant the past few days. When he wasn't out doing his job, he divided his time between Fenton and the children. A couple of times she'd caught him staring, but she hadn't been able to decipher his thoughts. And she wasn't inclined to ask. Not after his stinging rebuke.

Before ascending the steps, Allison informed George that there were some people inside she'd like him to meet. At his unspoken question, she said, "I'll explain everything later."

After introductions, Fenton greeted George with a toothy smile. "So you're Allison's brother. She's had nothing but high praise for you."

George shook his hand. "That's a relief." He chuckled. "Between living with me and working in the same building, she's bound to get tired of me."

Shane strode past them, George's trunk wedged on his shoulder as he carried it upstairs.

George spotted Matilda, who was seated on the rug between the twins. The girl had formed a quick bond with the twins and took great pride in helping Allison and Fenton with them.

"And who might this beautiful young lady be?" Walking over, he bent to her level.

Her honey-brown eyes were huge. Watchful. "I'm Matilda Rose Douglas."

"A pretty name to match its owner." He nodded sagely. "I have a little girl at home, but she's a lot younger than you." He switched his attention to the infants. "And who are these fine-looking babies? Your brother and sister?"

"No," she said solemnly. After giving their names, she said, "Miss Allison is their guardian."

George was silent a beat. Then, twisting slightly, he looked at her with a world of inquiry in his eyes. Allison twisted her fingers into knots. She felt like such a coward all of a sudden.

Fenton stepped forward. "Izzy and Charlie are my great-grandchildren. Their ma recently passed, and your sister has been helping me care for them."

"I see." His gaze promised this wasn't the end of the conversation.

Shane returned to the living room. Fenton pointed to the mistletoe not far from where he stood. "Still got all its berries, Sheriff. Something's wrong if you need an old man to remind you to take advantage of the moment."

Color climbed up his neck. "I don't need any reminders, thank you," he gritted.

George went over and clapped him on the back. "That's one thing I failed to ask you about. Are there any romantic prospects on the horizon? Perhaps some pretty mountain filly who's caught your eye?"

Allison's midsection tightened further. She backed toward the door. "I—I believe I forgot something in the wagon. I'll return in a moment."

Sagging against the closed door, she relished the bracing air washing over her. The distant chatter of birds greeted her, as did the lowing of cattle. In Norfolk, she'd be greeted with the blowing of ships' horns, seagulls' crying and horses' hooves clattering against the cobblestones.

She descended the steps and wandered away from the house with no particular direction in mind. A quarter of an hour later, George found her in the barn.

"Allison? What are you doing out here?"

Stroking the horse's strong neck one last time, she faced him, silently offering up a request for divine strength. His stocky frame outlined by the entrance, he gave the small structure's interior a cursory inspection before returning his gaze to her.

"What are you hiding from, my dear?" he said.

"You."

"Excuse me?" He tugged on his earlobe. "I'm quite certain I must have clogged ears."

She took a deep breath. "A lot has happened since I

arrived. Amazing, wondrous things. I couldn't have predicted any of it."

Serious now, he came closer. "You've piqued my curiosity. What sort of things?"

"I need for you to listen with an open mind."

"Go on."

"I always thought I'd get married young. I thought…" She pressed a hand to her throat as her voice grew scratchy. "I assumed by the time I reached thirty that I'd have four or five children and more on the way. As it turns out, I was wrong."

He tilted his head to the side as their father had done, which made her even more emotional. "There's time enough for children, Allison. You just have to give some poor fellow a chance at winning you."

"I don't need a husband in order to have children."

He let that sink in. "What Matilda said was true, then? About the twins?"

"It's not official, of course. I have to visit a lawyer when I return to Norfolk. However, Fenton has asked me to adopt them, and I agreed."

Allison held her breath as he paced the straw-covered ground. At one point, he removed his hat and smoothed his hand over his balding head.

"Aren't you going to say something?" she demanded.

Halting, he said, "I'm trying to figure out what Father's response would've been."

"Father took in Shane, didn't he? He taught us to act out the Bible's teachings. He said that authentic love was more than mere words, remember?"

"He was a widower when he took Shane in."

"Why is that important?"

"He'd experienced marriage and had decided he didn't wish to remarry. What if, by taking them in, your prospects become limited?"

"You sound like Shane. I didn't mention it, but I've been considering setting up my own residence for quite some time. Long before I came here."

"You're not happy at the estate? Have we done something?"

"No!" Going to him, she clutched his arms. "George, I've adored sharing a home with you and your family. Can't you understand how important it is to me to have one of my own?"

His eyes searched hers. "You'll be a fine mother to those kids." His voice was noticeably gruff.

With an exclamation of relief, she threw her arms around his neck and kissed his smooth cheek. "Thank you."

"For what?"

She released him. "For believing in me."

A throat cleared behind them, and Shane entered. "Sorry for interrupting. Fenton sent me to tell you he has potato soup and cornbread ready if either of you are hungry."

George patted his stomach. "I could eat. What about you, sis?"

"Not just yet." Her emotions were still running high.

When George started for the door, she hung back, intending to remain in the barn alone. She was surprised to hear Shane say he'd be along later. He'd been avoiding her for days. What could he possibly want?

Shane waited until he was sure George was gone. "You told him of your intentions?"

"I did."

Allison's wary expression reminded him of how folks who were distrustful of the law regarded him. He missed her shining eyes. Her bright smile. This was proof he hadn't a clue what he was doing when it came to relationships. He'd pushed her away again, like he had countless times in their youth, and it felt both familiar and wrong.

Having the siblings here together had unleashed memories of the past, memories he'd fought to keep contained, not only because they reminded him of the desperate-to-protect-himself boy he'd once been but because of all those times he'd hurt Allison. She'd been such a sweet, pure-hearted girl. Her only crime had been attempting to be his friend.

The expression she was wearing now took him back to those days, and he was amazed that David hadn't banished him for his bad behavior. The mere idea of anyone making Matilda sad, or Izzy or Charlie, made his blood boil.

He advanced and, instead of taking her hand like he was tempted to, turned to pet the horse. "He's not angry?"

"Not at all. He didn't say as much, but I know he has reservations."

"George loves you and wants nothing but good for you."

Shane paused in stroking the soft mane. *He* wanted Allison to be happy. In the deepest parts of him, he acknowledged that he'd do anything, sacrifice anything, to ensure her safety and well-being. That didn't mean he loved her, though. Did it?

He had no experience with love, so he questioned his ability to recognize it.

Behind him, her measured footsteps carried her toward the entrance. She was leaving already?

He quickly turned, relieved to see her resting her arms on the milk cow's stall. Presented with her profile, he soaked it in, gaze lingering on her pert nose and soft crimson lips. The Christmas-red, fur-lined half-cape matched the red-and-white ribbon choker about her neck. The creamy softness of her skin was imprinted on his memory.

"I'm blessed to have a brother like George. He's given me opportunities not available to many women. When I expressed interest in working for the company, he could've laughed it off as a ridiculous notion. Instead, he taught me the various aspects of the business and suggested positions he thought might be a good fit." She angled her face in his direction. "He respects my judgment in our professional environment. I shouldn't be surprised then that he does so regarding my personal life."

"I'm happy for you, Allie."

Not crossing to her and taking her in his arms cost him. "Are you truly?"

He straightened but kept a tight grip on the stall slats. That she'd question him on this cut deep. "I've given you the impression I don't care about you." He sucked in a ragged breath, his hold on the slats weakening along with his willpower. Words weren't his strong suit. "I'm sorry about that." He let go. Took three steps her direction. Never in his existence had he felt this intense pull to another person, this craving for connection. He'd gone his whole life without affection. Now he couldn't seem to get enough. "Despite what you might think, I want your dreams to become reality."

"Thank you for saying that."

"I mean every word."

She lifted her chin. "I haven't told George what happened between us, nor do I plan to."

"Are you hinting I should do the same?"

A dry laugh escaped her. "I'm confident you won't breathe a word to him. I'm telling you so you won't worry that I'm spilling secrets."

"I agree he doesn't need to know."

"Especially considering nothing will come of it."

Shane schooled his features. What if he wanted something to come of it?

Closing his eyes, he pinched the bridge of his nose. *No. You can't think like that.*

Think about what's best for Allison...and that's not you.

"I'm going inside," she said quietly.

"Good idea." Opening his eyes, he followed her through the double-wide door.

The sight of his deputy galloping along the lane put him on alert.

"Are you expecting Ben?" Allison shot him a sideways glance.

"No." He strode to intercept him. "What's happened?" he called.

"Tommy Marsh and his buddies were messing around and accidentally set the Christmas tree alight." Ben's jaw was set in hard lines as he reined in his horse. "Whole thing went up in flames. The churchyard's full of squalling kids and mamas bent on retribution."

Beside him, Allison gasped. "How horrible! And so close to Christmas."

Scowling, Ben shoved tangled auburn strands out of his eyes. "The townsfolk worked hard on the decorations. Wasn't an easy tree to set up, much less arrange all those ribbons and hand-painted ornaments on it."

Shane turned to Allison. "I've got to sort this out. Tell George I'll see him later?"

"Of course."

After instructing Ben to wait for him, Shane took her elbow and guided her toward the house. "Now that George is here, there's no need for me to occupy your sofa any longer."

While he'd missed his soft bed, he found it comforting to be near Allison and the kids. He could protect them. Not that they needed protecting. It just felt good to be close in case they did need him.

Her eyes churning with anxiety, she said, "I think the chances of Matilda running away have lessened, don't you? She's relaxed around the both of us. She treats Fenton like a stand-in grandfather, and she adores Izzy and Charlie."

Instead of reassuring him, her words caused uneasi-

ness to settle between his ribs. A bond was quickly forming between Allison and Matilda. They were both bound
to be hurt.

He wished the search party would send word of their
findings.

"I agree. I think she feels safe here." On impulse, he
pulled her close for a hug. As the scent of her wrapped
around him, he reminded himself to keep it brief. And
friend-like.

"What was that for?" she said, astounded.

"A thank-you for allowing her to stay longer and for
making her feel welcome."

Not giving her a chance to respond, he hauled himself
into the saddle and urged his horse into motion. When he
reached Ben, the younger man was staring at him with
open curiosity. Shane had forgotten all about the deputy's
presence. That's how muddled Allison had him.

"Not a word, MacGregor," he warned. "Not one word."

Chapter Twenty-One

There were days when he gained great satisfaction from his job. This wasn't one of them.

The Christmas tree mishap had dampened the town's holiday spirit. When he'd reached the church, the crowd had immediately surrounded him five and six people deep on all sides. He hadn't even had room to dismount. They wanted Tommy and his friends to suffer for their carelessness.

The men were fit to be tied. He couldn't blame them. Chopping down a tree that large, dragging it here and then erecting it had amounted to several days' work. The women were outraged, not so much for themselves, but for the children. Their tearstained faces still remained in his mind.

Christmas was eleven days away.

Thankfully, Reverend Munroe and his wife had assumed the job of consoling the crowd. Jessica Parker, having heard the news, passed out free cookies to every single child there. Quinn and Nicole brought complimentary cups of apple cider. By the time it had been decided to put up a new tree, with Tommy and his friends charged with helping to make a new batch of decorations, the high emotions had waned and hope restored.

Shane tossed his pencil on his desk and rubbed his pounding forehead. He eyed the dark sky through the window and prayed for no more complaints that night.

A figure passed by.

"Keep walking," he muttered.

The knob twisted. He prayed for forbearance. *Please God, I'm not sure I can maintain a civil attitude. I'm exhausted from too many sleepless nights, and I haven't eaten since breakfast.*

When the door scraped open and Fenton walked in, Shane nudged his chair and stood up. "Fenton." Rounding the desk, he searched for signs of physical distress. "Is everything all right?"

His color looked good, and he didn't seem as exhausted as he had at the cabin. "Fine and dandy." He lifted a basket. "Allison was worried you hadn't had a chance to eat. She asked George to deliver this, but I volunteered to do it since I'm bunking with you once again."

Pleasure at her thoughtfulness filled him. Taking his burden, Shane placed it on the desk and began to unpack the contents. "I sure do appreciate you bringing it by," he said. "I was beginning to get as churlish as a bear coming out of hibernation."

Fenton chose a chair to ease his frame into. "Nice, ain't it? Having a beautiful woman worry over ya?"

Snagging a slice of cornbread, he bit off a hefty portion and chewed. "You can stop the matchmaking, old man."

His teeth flashed white against his sun-branded skin. "You don't have to be alone the whole of your life, ya know. You got a ready-made family ripe for the pickin'. Allison cares about you. She deserves a man who'll take good care of her."

Shane finished off the slice and folded his arms. "I'm not the right man for the job."

The truth hurt. Mere weeks ago, he'd been content with

his lot. Now he yearned for a petite, blond-haired spitfire to be part of his life. Allison had unleashed hopes he had no means of fulfilling.

Fenton studied him with his perceptive gaze. "You'd keep her from making fool decisions, I know that."

Shane replaced the plate he had started to lift out. "What fool decisions?"

"She's intending on leaving Gatlinburg without squaring things with the Whitakers. I'd hate to see her heart broken if they found out afterward and decided to act out of spite."

His appetite vanished. Fenton had a point. The Whitakers might not claim the twins, but there was a chance they'd cry foul if they got wind someone else wanted them.

"I'll talk to her."

Fenton slapped his knee. "If she'll listen to anybody, it's you."

Long after the old man had gone, his parting words lingered. Why would Allison listen to him? Was his opinion that important to her?

Lost in thought on his way home, he didn't hear anyone approaching until the last moment. A big hand came down on his shoulder. Shane whirled and reached for his pistol.

"Hold on," the shadowed figure exclaimed. "It's me. Ben."

The tension left his body. "What were you thinking?" he demanded, annoyed with himself for having lost awareness of his surroundings. As a lawman, he was considered a target by some. He'd learned early to always be on guard.

"I called your name several times," Ben said with a hint of exasperation.

He eyed his deputy's scruffy appearance and dirt-streaked boots. "Did you just get back? Where are the others? More importantly, where's Douglas?"

"About twenty minutes ago. As for the rest of the search party, they're at the reverend's arranging for a coffin."

"Harold Douglas is dead?" While he'd briefly considered the possibility, he'd expected to find Douglas holed up with a friend, delaying his return to Gatlinburg and the responsibility of his niece's care.

"We found him about a mile outside of Cades Cove." Ben's breath formed white puffs in the frigid air. "Couldn't find any signs that he hadn't died of natural causes. Snow's on the ground. Could've been exposure. Or maybe his heart gave out."

"Thanks for taking charge of this."

His deputy's expression reflected surprise. "It's my job to help you. What will happen to the girl?"

"That's a very good question." One he didn't have the answer to.

Shane rode out to the Wattses' farm the following morning. Understandably, the news of her uncle's death didn't sadden Matilda. She was worried, however, that she was going to be shipped off to a foundling home. He'd assured both her and Allison that no arrangements would be made without her knowledge. Before he left, Allison reminded him of his promise to find the best home possible.

With her words ringing in his ears, he'd gone to the reverend for recommendations and then spent the day visiting those folks with potential. He'd dismissed a few outright. The ones he saw promise in went on his list of candidates. The weight of his decision rode heavy on his mind. Matilda's future depended on him, and he refused to rush the process. She deserved to be in a place she felt safe and cherished.

That evening, he was locking up the jail when Josh hailed him. "You busy?"

"Nope. Heading home. What's on your mind?"

"I heard about Harold Douglas."

"News like that doesn't take long to spread." He gestured to the lane. "Walk with me?"

"What will you do about his property?"

"Try to sell it. Any money we get will be kept in trust for Matilda."

"Maybe one of the neighbors will be interested."

"Maybe."

Josh's lantern light bounced along the uneven track. Around them, the forest gave the impression of being asleep. Stars winked above them. It was going to be a frigid night, likely below freezing. He hoped the Wattses' upstairs would remain warm enough. Infants were susceptible to illness. And Matilda was skin and bones. At the cabin, Shane tended the fire while Josh drifted around the room. "I thought Fenton was staying with you."

"He's been a bit of a nomad. Since George arrived, he's been staying in one of the guest bedrooms. It's a sight more comfortable than this place."

"He's probably happy to spend time with the twins, considering."

Josh's initial surprise at Allison's decision had turned into support. More times than Shane could count, his friend had expressed his admiration for her, along with not-so-subtle hints.

"A shame she can't find a local man to settle down with," Josh said now. "Fenton wouldn't have to be separated from his great-grandchildren. If only I had another brother. Or a friend who isn't yet wed…"

A spark shot out and landed on Shane's wrist. Jerking, he rubbed at the sore spot. "Give it up, O'Malley," he growled.

Huffing an exaggerated sigh, he moved to stand beside the mantel. "You need some holiday cheer in here."

He turned to regard him, brows raised. "Have you ever known me to care about sentimental stuff?"

His blue gaze was searching. "I thought maybe this year would be different."

"It's been a long day. State your business so I can get to sleep."

No doubt sensing his impatience, Josh got serious. "I came to see if you've found a home for Matilda yet."

Shane removed his gloves and hat. "I've a few people in mind. Why?"

"Have you considered Megan and Lucian? They've got the space and the desire for lots of kids."

Crossing the room, he shucked his duster and hooked it on a peg. Josh's cousin Megan hadn't been able to have kids the natural way. She and her husband had adopted a little girl from New Orleans. They'd also taken in older siblings who'd needed a home. The couple treated those kids as if they were their own flesh and blood. Matilda would be loved.

For some unknown reason, he held back. "I'll think about it."

Josh observed him for several beats. He opened his mouth, then closed it again. He went to the door. "Sleep on it."

"Josh?"

"Yeah?"

"Thanks for thinking of her. It's just—" He kneaded the tight muscles along the ridge of his shoulder, his tired mind scrambling for the right words.

"You don't have to say anything." Josh smiled. "Get some rest, friend."

He exhaled. "Tell Kate and the kids hello for me."

"Done."

Josh slipped into the night. Shane watched his bobbing light until it was no longer visible. Allison's suggestion that he take in Matilda refused to leave him in peace. The idea was ludicrous. He was a bachelor with zero experience with kids. If that wasn't enough reason, his profession as town sheriff sealed it. He worked odd hours and dealt with sticky situations. There was no guarantee he'd make it home each night. He couldn't do that to a kid.

Seeking His heavenly Father's wisdom, he uttered a prayer for direction.

Matilda needs a home, Lord. I want her to have a good one. Please help me make the right decision.

"You're coming with me."

A disbelieving laugh burst out of Allison at Shane's proclamation seconds after she opened her door. "Let's try this again, shall we? You knock. I greet you. You address me as you would a law abiding citizen."

In the face of her lightheartedness, Shane found himself grinning at her. "I suppose I could do that." He dipped his head and glanced at her through his eyelashes. "Miss Allison Ashworth, I'd like for you to come riding with me."

"Riding? In this cold?" She peered past him to the gray sky. "Are you aiming to get us stranded a second time?"

"It's not gonna snow."

Her green eyes twinkled with merriment. "Ah, so you fancy yourself a weather predictor now?"

"I'll saddle your horse for you."

Tugging her lower lip between her teeth, she pondered his request. They hadn't exactly been on the best of terms recently. No doubt she was suspicious of his motives.

She had a right to be.

Chatter punctuated with an occasional infant's shriek filtered out onto the porch. The living room was empty. Everyone was probably congregated in the kitchen. He would've liked to see the kids, but this errand was too important to delay.

"What? You don't trust George and Fenton to keep a

proper eye on them?" Shifting his weight, he said, "Or are you not inclined to ride alongside a lawman?"

She waved a hand to indicate her skirt and blouse. "I'll go change into something warmer while you ready my horse."

Pivoting, he spoke over his shoulder. "Ten minutes, Allie."

Her annoyed huff was followed by the snap of the door in its frame. Before the day was out, he was going to be on the receiving end of far more than that. A pity he hadn't thought to bring a piece of cake along to sweeten her mood once it soured.

This is for her own good, he reminded himself.

They set out at a leisurely pace. She asked if he'd resolved the tree situation, and he asked after George and her day. If not for the hard knot of anxiety in the pit of his stomach, he might've enjoyed himself. Allison was good company. Intelligent, witty, observant. As they traversed the hilly terrain, he related the details of a particularly intriguing criminal case he'd read about. Listening attentively, she provided insights that hadn't occurred to him. He could discuss almost anything with her, which put her in elite company. There were less than a handful of people on this earth he could say that about.

Allison shifted in the saddle to inspect their surroundings. "This looks familiar. Where are we headed exactly?"

Shane met her gaze head-on. "The Whitakers' homestead."

He braced himself as first confusion crossed her face, then understanding and finally full-blown anger. Yanking on the reins, she urged her horse to a stop. Shane followed suit.

"I thought you wanted to spend time with me." Her forehead creased and mouth pulled into a frown. The real hurt he witnessed had him sliding to the ground.

He rested a hand on the saddle cantle. The other he curved around her wrist. "I did, Allie. I do."

"No, you wanted to trick me into doing something I'm not prepared to do." She tried to wiggle free, but he held on.

"I'm sorry I hurt you. Please, hear me out."

Ceasing her struggling, she stared straight ahead, her lips a tight line and bright flags of color high in her cheeks.

He disliked upsetting her. He much preferred making her smile. "It'd be easier if we could talk face-to-face. If I release you, will you give me a chance to explain?" Instead of galloping off into parts unknown, he added silently.

"You can talk," she said stiffly. "Then I'm returning to the house. Where you go doesn't really matter."

He released her and stepped back, half expecting her to dig her heels into the horse's flank. Still not looking at him, she gracefully dismounted. She stood sideways to the way he was standing, her arms huddled about her midsection.

Clenching his fists, he battled the urge to wrap her in his arms. No question how that would go. He liked his nose the way it was currently situated on his face.

"I didn't tell you earlier because I knew you wouldn't budge from the house," he said quietly. "I thought…if I got you out here, you'd be more willing to listen."

"You manipulated me."

"You have a right to be angry. But I know how people like Gentry Whitaker and his clan operate. They're petty and closed-minded. They're miserable and want everyone around them to be, too."

"Then why risk it?" she demanded, glaring at him. "Why should I allow them to decide Izzy and Charlie's future? Fenton is their blood relative, too. He's been with them since their birth. The Whitakers have seen them once!"

"They'll find out. Sooner or later, one of them will come to town, and someone will take great pleasure in informing them that a well-to-do lady from Virginia has taken custody of their kin. Even though they've had nothing to do with the twins, they'll view it as an outsider getting one over on them," he said. "Besides, Fenton wants you to do this."

Allison buried her face in her hands. "What if they forbid me to take them? What then?" Her words were mumbled, but her desperation came through loud and clear.

Taking hold of her upper arms, he gently urged her toward him. "I'll hire a lawyer. We'll fight this together."

She lifted her head. Her misery struck him like a physical blow. After praying the whole night through for a positive outcome, Shane was pretty sure God was tired of hearing about this. He prayed again, anyway. *Please let the Whitakers do what's right by those babies.*

"I'm not family. They are."

"Think about it, sweetheart." He rubbed his hands lightly up and down the length of her arms. "As things stand now, a judge would look favorably on you. The Whitakers have proved their apathy. If you flee the state, then Clyde Whitaker will be portrayed as a wronged father desperate to have his children returned."

She took a shuddering breath and moved away, forcing him to drop his arms.

"The choice is yours," he said, wishing she'd let him comfort her. "We can ride back the way we came. Or we can continue on."

Shane was right.

Allison knew it deep down in her soul, where hurt and anger couldn't drown out sound reasoning. Trepidation wrapped its tentacles around her, suffocating the bright hope inside. *You have to fight it,* she silently scolded herself. *God put you in Izzy and Charlie's lives for a reason. He has a plan. It may not turn out to be the plan you want, but He knows what's best.*

Resuming her place on the horse's broad back, she urged

him onward. Knowing Shane would follow, she didn't bother looking back.

Even though his intentions were good, she couldn't help but feel wounded by the fact he'd misled her. He hadn't wanted to simply *be* with her. Not like she yearned to be with him…every minute of every day.

Wake up, Allison. He's never going to want that.

She should be grateful he was willing to help her in this, especially since he hadn't initially approved of her plan. After half an hour of letting her take the lead, Shane edged his horse alongside hers. He pointed out a wisp of smoke curling through the crooked treetops.

"We're almost there."

Allison's tummy flipped on itself. Unable to speak, she nodded.

As they drew closer, she began to notice the discarded tools half-buried in dirt and leaves and rusted farm equipment that looked as if it hadn't been used in decades. The chicken coop was a mess of twisted wire. One good, stiff wind could topple the open stable. Was this family too destitute to do repairs? Or did they simply not take pride in their ownership?

They came around to the ramshackle cabin's front side. Allison heard the click of a rifle. Beside her, Shane stiffened as a grizzly bear of a man loped off the porch, his gun leveled at them.

"What brings you all the way out here, Sheriff?" His upper lip curled in contempt.

"Afternoon, Gentry." Shane positioned his horse slightly in front of hers. "The lady and I have business to discuss with you and your son."

He flicked a careless glance her way. The flatness of his eyes sent cold dread through her.

"She ain't expectin', is she?"

His crude manner sparked her temper. How dare he insinuate such a thing!

Splayed against his thigh, Shane's fingers curled into a tight fist. Before she knew what was happening, he had his weapon drawn.

"Watch your mouth, Whitaker." His voice dripped with venom.

Allison shivered at this rare glimpse of Shane's ruthless side.

Inch by inch, Gentry lowered his rifle. "Last time a female came 'round here lookin' for Clyde, she claimed he'd ruined her."

"You're talking about Letitia Blake, I presume." Shane kept his pistol trained on the man. "She's the reason we're here."

Snorting, he scratched his nose. "She send you? I done told her and her grandpa that we don't want anything to do with those brats."

Allison found herself hoping Shane's finger would slip on the trigger. Hateful, hateful man.

"Letitia Blake is dead."

The news didn't evoke sorrow or regret. Gentry's mouth twisted, but he remained silent. Did he possess a heart?

Taking his time holstering his pistol, Shane drawled, "Since the twins are without a mother, you don't mind if Miss Ashworth here takes them in permanently?"

Surprise registered on his face. His eyes narrowed as he took renewed interest in her. Allison returned his gaze and tried not to let her distaste show.

Spitting a stream of tobacco juice on the ground, he said, "Don't matter to me."

She blinked. It was that easy? He was willing to hand over his grandchildren to a total stranger?

Shane pulled a piece of paper from his duster pocket. "Mind putting that in writing?"

"Can't do that."

The tension radiating from Shane had his horse prancing to the side. Soothing the animal with a soft command, Shane leveled an impatient stare at Gentry. "Why not?"

"Clyde's the one who has the final say."

"And where is Clyde?"

"No idea." His crooked-tooth grin bore the stamp of meanness. "He took off over a week ago. But I'll be sure to tell him you stopped by when I see him."

Chapter Twenty-Two

"Telling you not to worry won't help, will it?"

Allison followed Shane out of the barn, her mood as bleak as the winter day. Somewhere along the way, she'd lost her holiday spirit. She'd let her problems eclipse the wonder of Christ's birth and the celebration of family and friends.

"You're worried, too," she responded, looking over at him. "I can see it."

His brows lifted. "A sheriff doesn't worry."

"Underneath that badge, Shane Timmons, you're human like the rest of us."

"Thought I was doing a good job of hiding it," he muttered, tugging his Stetson lower. "I haven't had much interaction with Clyde," he said. "Not knowing what to expect from him bothers me."

"Not knowing when he'll return bothers me."

They reached the back stoop and the door leading to the kitchen. Shane reached for the knob but didn't turn it. His deep blue gaze roamed her features. "Guess this means you aren't leaving with George."

"I have no choice but to stay, do I?"

His nearness made her head swim. She didn't have

to touch him to know how the light scruff along his jaw would feel beneath her fingertips. They itched to explore the hard planes of his face and smooth texture of his beautiful mouth.

He visibly swallowed. Releasing the knob, he edged closer. "You still angry with me, Allie?"

"No."

"Not even a little?"

"Maybe a little," she conceded. "But I understand your reasons."

During the quiet trek home, her thoughts had turned to Shane's position in the community and the demands placed upon him. He regularly dealt with unsavory characters and challenging situations. When he wasn't risking his life to protect others, he was seeking to solve mysteries or having to restore peace after instances such as a torched Christmas tree.

Placing her hand on his chest, she said softly, "You spend so much of your time fixing other people's problems. Who do you turn to for help? Who listens when you need to talk?"

A furrow appeared between his brows. Undefinable emotion surged in his eyes. "You're the first person to ask me that."

"It upsets me to think of you shouldering your burdens alone."

He'd been alone for most of his life. He deserved companionship. More than that, he deserved to experience the give and take of a loving relationship. Allison would give anything to fulfill that role.

Having stuffed his gloves in his pocket while in the barn, he now lifted a bare hand to her cheek. The sensation of his warm, work-roughened hand gingerly scraping across her skin as he curved a stray tendril behind her ear sent a shiver of longing through her. If he tried to kiss her, she wouldn't have the strength to heed common sense.

"I have Josh and his brothers," he murmured.

"But they have wives and children. Haven't you ever wondered what it would be like to have that for yourself?"

His gaze lifted from her mouth to delve into hers. "Allie, I—"

The door swung open, startling them both. George stood there, his expression turning speculative as he took in Shane's proximity to her. "I thought I heard voices out here."

Pretending nothing was amiss, Allison walked past him into the house. "How is everything?"

George scooted closer to the stove to give Shane room to enter. "Izzy and Charlie are napping. Matilda and Fenton are in the living room playing their third round of checkers."

Untying her bonnet ribbons, she removed it and set it on a chair. "Did they eat their mashed potatoes?"

He nodded. "And guzzled their milk." To Shane, he said, "Did you enjoy your ride?"

Shane's hat landed on the tabletop. His blond-streaked hair bore the indentation of the hat. He ran his fingers through it. "It wasn't exactly a pleasure outing." He addressed Allison. "Do you want to explain or shall I?"

"Go ahead."

She listened as he relayed the events to George. When he had finished, George folded his arms over his chest and stroked his mustache in a contemplative gesture. "Sounds like a tricky business." He turned to her. "I'm assuming you're going to stay until it's resolved."

"You understand, don't you?"

"Of course. Stay as long as you have to. I'll situate things at the office."

Relief rushed through her. "Thank you, George."

Matilda entered the dining room and paused on the kitchen's threshold, her big brown eyes fastened on Shane.

He gifted her with a smile. "Hello, Matilda. Who won the game?"

She twisted her fingers together. "Me."

"Good job."

"I think Mr. Blake let me win," she said solemnly.

George made an excuse to slip away, leaving the three of them alone.

Shane pulled out a chair first for Allison, then for the girl. He waved her over. "You sure about that? He hasn't been inclined to let me win."

When they were all seated, Matilda traced invisible shapes on the polished wood. "You're an adult," she mumbled. "I'm just a kid."

"Did you enjoy playing with him?" Allison asked.

"Sure."

"Then that's all that matters." She smiled.

Shane nodded his agreement. "I have a little more time before I need to get back to the office. How about you and I play a game?"

"You don't really want to," she blurted, unhappiness etched onto her features. "You're just putting up with me because there's no one else to do it!"

Scraping her chair back, she raced for the door.

"Matilda!" Allison exclaimed, stunned at her outburst and uncertain how to make things better. She started to rise.

Shane stopped her with a hand on her shoulder. "It's okay. I'll talk to her."

"I'll accompany you if you want."

His chin was set at a determined angle. "Josh said something not long ago that's beginning to make sense. He said that God might've allowed me to go through what I did so that I could help someone else."

The similarities between his childhood and hers were clear. "Matilda," she said.

"Yep." He strode for the door. "Pray for me?"

"You have my prayers, Shane. Always."

He found her out at the fence line using a young dogwood tree as her refuge. "Awful cold to be out here without a coat."

She didn't acknowledge his presence. Her chin dipped low, her short hair fanned over her nose and cheeks. He hoped she wasn't crying. Slipping off his duster, he draped it around her shoulders. The hem dragged the ground.

"There. That should keep you warm. Just don't try and walk in it."

Slowly, she lifted her head. In place of tears, he saw apprehension and a hint of suspicion. The man who'd had charge of her had placed that mistrust there.

"You haven't found anyone willing to take me in yet, have you?"

"I'll be honest with you, Matilda. I've spoken to several couples, and two of them are excited to meet you."

Her jaw went slack.

"The Murrays are in their midfifties. Their kids have all married and moved out of the house, and they're open to the possibility of raising another." Stepping over to the snake-and-rail fence, he rested his hand on the highest post and gazed out at the green fields with brown patches where the grass had withered. "The Johnsons are in their early forties. They've always wanted children but haven't been blessed with any. I believe you'd be well-treated in either home."

Matilda didn't speak, probably trying to accept what she'd been so sure couldn't possibly be true.

"There's a third family, friends of mine actually, who have several adopted children. I haven't yet talked to them, but I'm planning on it. The thing is, this isn't a decision that should be rushed. I want the very best for you."

Holding the sides of his duster together, she shuffled closer. "Can I tell you a secret?"

"Shoot."

"I like living with Miss Allison and the babies. I always thought I'd like a younger brother or sister. With them, I could have both."

Shane closed his eyes for a brief moment. He'd expected this might happen. "Allison doesn't live here. Her home is in Virginia. When she leaves, she'll take Izzy and Charlie with her."

Her pointed chin jutted. "I don't mind. I'm sure I'd like it there." A hint of desperation stole into her eyes. "I can help Miss Allison. I'd do anything she asked."

"Matilda, it's not as easy or straightforward as you think. I—"

"She'd stay if you married her." She seized his hand, stunning him into silence. "Then I could live with you, too."

His heart cracked down the middle. She couldn't know that the idea had crossed his mind. More than once. Risking his happiness, he could do...but theirs? Four people he cared deeply about? It wouldn't be right.

Shane searched his brain for an appropriate response and came up short. What could he say that wouldn't devastate her?

"Allison's life is in Virginia. Mine's here. I'm sorry, Matilda."

Blinking rapidly, she released his hand and, shrugging out of his duster, thrust it at him.

She pivoted and started marching across the yard.

"We'll figure this out," he called after her. But by then, she was running for the house, and he wasn't sure if she'd heard him.

* * *

"Are you enjoying the party?" Allison sidled up to George, who'd slipped away from a group of men near the bonfire and was heading for the house.

He smiled down at her, his mustache curving above his mouth. "It's a nice party. Thank you, sis."

They meandered to the corner closest to the kitchen stoop. Since the house wasn't spacious enough to hold everyone, guests drifted between the inside, close to the food and drink, and the rear yard, where a huge bonfire chased away the night's chill. On the other side of the fire, a group of fiddle and guitar players performed a lilting Christmas melody. Every once in a while, one of them would bring out a harmonica.

Closer to the barn, youngsters jumped rope and engaged in games of hide-and-seek. Most of the adults gathered in clusters to converse, mugs of apple cider or coffee aiding the fire in warming them.

"Gatlinburg has a strong sense of community, doesn't it?" he said. "And the townsfolk admire Shane. He's come so far since those early days. Father would be amazed at what he's accomplished."

"More importantly, he'd rejoice that Shane has finally accepted that God loves him."

Allison was thrilled to see the change in his way of thinking, to hear him speak of spiritual matters and pray with confidence.

Searching the crowd for what seemed the hundredth time, she said, "He's still not here."

"You know he's not all that interested in parties."

"He promised he'd come." The night was nearly half-over. She plucked at the wrists of her cranberry-colored dress.

"Maybe he got held up. His job keeps him busy, I'm sure."

"I hope he hasn't stumbled into trouble. You should hear some of the tales the O'Malleys related to me. He faces danger so often that I worry it's become commonplace. He can't ever truly let his guard down."

George turned to face her. The dancing flames cast flickering shadows over his round face. "You're still in love with him, aren't you?"

Allison gasped. "Why would you say such a thing?"

"You've been smitten since the moment you laid eyes on him. I suspected he was the reason you dodged interested suitors, but I wasn't entirely sure. That's why I insisted on you coming ahead without me. I thought spending time with him would cure you of your infatuation. I had hoped you'd return to Norfolk having put Shane Timmons out of your head." He blew out a long breath. "I see now that I was wrong."

Her mouth worked but no sound came out. There was no use denying it.

"How does he feel about you?" George asked gently.

Chafing her arms, she shook her head and gazed at her boots. "I'm not sure. Whatever he feels isn't strong enough for him to take a chance on us." Despair invaded her. "Shane has no plans to marry."

George enveloped her in a hug. "I'm sorry, Allie," he murmured against her hair. "I truly am."

"It's not your fault." Willing away the tears, she wiggled free. She didn't want to arouse the others' curiosity. "I'll have to deal with my dashed hopes later. Right now, I have a party to host."

"Let's go inside and check on the children, shall we?"

"Last time I saw them, they were being entertained by Caleb's young sister-in-law, Amy, and Megan's daughter, Lillian."

The warmth inside welcomed them as laughter and a jumble of conversations carried through the house. Allison smiled at the people circled around the dining table. They had a lot to choose from among platters of meats, assorted vegetables, homemade breads and a variety of pies, cookies and cakes.

When she reached the doorway, Caroline noticed and waved from a spot near the fireplace. Sophisticated in a dress of midnight blue overlaid with silver netting, the blonde was in deep conversation with twin sisters Jessica Parker and Jane Leighton. Allison started to join them but was waylaid by a tap on her shoulder.

Turning around, she was surprised to see the handsome deputy. "Ben, I had no idea you'd arrived."

Did that mean Shane was here, too? Cutting off the questions before they could form on her lips, she pasted on what she hoped was a serene smile. "I'm glad you could make it. Have you eaten yet?"

"Not yet." Green eyes dancing, his wavy auburn locks tamed into submission, he grinned. "I apologize for arriving late. I have a demanding boss."

Behind her, the main door scraped open. Her skin prickled, and she knew without looking who had entered. Her pulse sped up. Would he come and speak to her right away? Would he avoid her? They hadn't been alone since that charged moment on the stoop. She'd replayed the moment in her mind many times, trying to guess what he'd been about to say.

Ben bent closer, mischief stamping his features. "Did you happen to notice where we're standing, Miss Allison?"

Her heart skipped a beat. The mistletoe. It had been up there for so long she'd forgotten about it. "Uh, I don't believe anyone expects us to observe tradition."

"What's the fun in that?" he exclaimed softly. "Besides, I can't ignore the chance to make the good sheriff squirm."

"Look!" a youthful voice rang out. "They're underneath the mistletoe."

"Don't just stand there, MacGregor. Kiss the woman!"

Male laughter assaulted her ears. Hot color flooded her cheeks. Ben kissing her in front of Shane was the worst of nightmares come true.

Well and truly caught, Allison froze as Ben lowered his head.

Chapter Twenty-Three

White-hot jealousy seared him. His vision clouded as his deputy took hold of Allison's hand and bent to kiss her.

I can't watch this.

Not caring who saw him leave or what significance they attached to it, he spun and pushed outside. Descending the steps, he strode for his horse waiting with others beneath a copse of trees farther down the lane.

"Shane."

"I've decided not to stay, George," he tossed over his shoulder, not slowing his pace.

The hasty footsteps behind him didn't falter. When he reached his mount, he pivoted. Dark shadows obscured his friend's features.

"That must've been the shortest attendance on record. Didn't take you long to decide you weren't having fun."

"Figured out I wasn't in the mood to socialize."

All he could picture was Ben's satisfied grin seconds before he swooped toward Allison. His gut churned with the need to march back inside and rip them apart.

George stroked the horse between its ears. "He didn't kiss her. Not a real kiss, anyway. It was more like a brotherly peck on the cheek."

Brotherly? Not likely.

Shane wished he could make out the other man's expression. It didn't signify, he supposed. George wasn't stupid. Even if he hadn't discovered them on the stoop, he knew his sister better than anyone.

"Allison's free to do as she pleases." Just not in front of him. It hurt too much.

"She's in love with you, you know."

Shane's heart squeezed into a painful mass. Scraping a weary hand over his jaw, he shook his head. "You're wrong."

"Then tell me why she lost her joy once you left town. Tell me why she's turned down suitor after suitor—good men who would've treasured her. Tell me why she was crushed each time I got a letter from you, and you didn't have a word to spare for her. Did you know that sometimes I find her revisiting your favorite spots in the house? The look on her face…" He trailed off.

"No. It can't be true." Shane took a few halting paces away. He could hardly breathe for all the waves of emotion pummeling him.

"Why not?" he said patiently. "You were able to accept that God, who knows you better than you know yourself, loves you. Why is it so impossible to believe my sister would?"

Whirling back, he sliced the air with his hand. "I don't deserve her! I wouldn't know the first thing about making her happy. I'd wind up disappointing her, and that would destroy the both of us." He slapped his fist into his opposite palm. "You should've warned her. Should've insisted she accept another man's suit years ago."

"You think I could simply *command* her to stop caring about you?" he said, incredulous. "Love isn't something you control."

Oh, he didn't have to be told that. His love for Allison

was so much a part of him there'd be no rooting it out. He wasn't sure where he ended and it began. Perhaps that's why it had taken him so long to recognize his feelings for what they were.

"I've been married a long while," he continued. "It's not about making the other person happy. It's about putting their needs above your own. It's a partnership. I love my wife in a romantic sense, but she's also my best friend. There's no one else I'd rather have at my side through good times and in bad."

What his friend described sounded perfect and exactly what he wished he could have with Allie.

Shane thrust his foot in the stirrup and, grabbing hold of the saddle horn, hauled himself up. "I need time."

George moved out of the way. "Think about what I said."

With a wave, he left the yard and entered the deserted lane. His thoughts a chaotic mess, he took his time getting home. The quiet cabin that had been his refuge until she arrived now struck him as forlorn. Desolate. Pitiful.

He could easily picture Allie in the cushioned chair, the babies in her lap. And Matilda sitting on the rug at her feet, playing with a doll.

Calling himself a fool for allowing such thoughts to taunt him, he removed his duster, suit coat and vest and went to the kitchen to fix himself coffee. He preferred peace and quiet, he reminded himself. He had enough trouble at work. What did he want with soiled nappies and milk bottles and drooling, teething babies, not to mention an eleven-year-old girl who'd soon be interested in boys?

Settling into the chair, he chose the periodical on top of the stack and tried to lose himself in his reading. An hour passed and he hadn't progressed beyond the first article. He was riffling listlessly through the pages when a rap on the door startled him. Fishing out his pocket watch, he frowned at the clock face. Visitors at this time of night meant there was trouble somewhere.

Please let it be anyone except Ben. Shane was pretty sure he wouldn't manage to be civil.

Tugging the door open as he was snapping his suspenders in place, he couldn't mask his surprise. "Allie. What are you doing here?"

"I came to see if you were all right."

Resplendent in a white-trimmed cranberry cloak that swirled around her fitted dress of the same hue, she was too beautiful for words. Her deep green eyes and ruby-red lips complemented her milky skin. Her blond hair was parted along one side and pulled into a thick, shining twist. George's words pounded inside his head. *She loves you.*

Shane searched her countenance, peered into her eyes for proof. How was he supposed to believe she loved him if she didn't tell him herself?

What good would come of it, anyway?

She took in his informal attire and stocking feet. "I know it's late. I would've come earlier but I had to wait until the guests left and Izzy and Charlie were asleep." A tentative smile graced her mouth. "They won't allow anyone else besides me to put them in bed now."

He glanced past her to the lone horse. "You shouldn't be out alone at night."

"George accompanied me as far as Main Street. He's waiting for me at the jail."

"With Ben?"

Her features tensed. "Are you going to invite me in, Shane?"

Gesturing for her to enter, he leaned against the closed door as she stopped in the middle of the room and completed a slow circle. This wasn't the first time she'd been here, but a lot had happened since that initial visit. The late-ness of the hour created a sense of seclusion, as if the entire town slumbered and only he and Allison were awake.

"Why did you really come, Allie? Your brother could've told you I simply decided not to stick around."

Lowering her hood, she tugged off her gloves and stuffed them into her cloak pocket. "I know the reason you didn't stay. I wanted to be certain you weren't planning to punish Ben in some awful way."

The sight of them together flashed in his mind, and the ire he hadn't managed to fully quell built to a new high. Deliberately shoving his hands deep in his pockets, he prowled to where she was standing. She lifted her chin, fully meeting his gaze.

"You're worried about my deputy, are you?" His voice was deceptively soft.

"We *were* standing beneath the mistletoe," she pointed out. Her nonchalant manner grated.

"He didn't have to enjoy himself quite so much," he gritted, aware such sentiment was more suited to an adolescent than a full-grown man.

She lifted a single eyebrow. "He was trying to get a rise out of you. Looks like he succeeded."

"Like I told your brother, you're free to kiss anyone you please."

"You don't mean that."

Shane's pulse skittered, sped up. "In fact, I do."

"Be honest, Shane. You left because you wanted to be the one beneath that mistletoe with me."

She was right and wrong. He did want to be there with her...just not with an audience. The fact that they were completely alone right now, with no chance of interruption by Fenton or an inquisitive young girl, tested Shane's determination to avoid hurting her further. All he had to do was lower his head a couple of inches...

The blood rushed in his ears. Surely she could hear his

heart whacking against his chest cavity. He slipped his hands free of his pockets. So close.

She licked her lips, lending them a high shine. He swallowed a groan.

Remember what's best for her, Timmons. Can you afford to throw common sense out the window?

Shane gathered the willpower slipping away and, turning his back to her, stalked to the door.

"Go home, Allie." He jerked the door open and, not looking at her, sucked in the biting air. "George has two days left. Go Christmas shopping. Wrap presents and drink hot cocoa. Forget about the upheaval of the past few weeks, if only for a little while."

She didn't move at first. Just when his self-control was starting to splinter into tiny pieces, she barreled past him into the moonlit night. Once in the saddle, her face hidden by the cloak's hood, she said, "You're welcome to see George off on Monday, but I'd appreciate it if you'd keep your visits to the Wattses' at a minimum. Official business only."

Shane stepped off the stoop. "Allie—"

Her horse leaped into motion, leaving him alone with a heap of regrets and low-burning resentment for the parents who'd bequeathed him this legacy.

"Have a safe trip." Allison hugged him even more tightly than she had one week ago.

"Keep us informed of your plans," George said against the scarf wound about her neck. "Clarissa and I will be praying morning, noon and night."

Releasing him, she smiled at the phrase her father had often said.

His brows pulled together. "Have you found alternate lodging in case your stay extends past the new year?"

She prayed that wouldn't happen. "One option is to

stay with Megan and Lucian Beaumont. Or rent a place in town."

Out of the corner of her eye, she noted the tall, commanding figure striding their way. Clutching her brother's arm, she pecked his cheek and lifted her skirts. "I'll see you soon. Give Clarissa and the kids a kiss for me!"

Acknowledging his slightly baffled farewell with an uplifted hand, she made her way to the crowded boardwalk and hurried in the opposite direction. She hadn't seen Shane in two days and wasn't prepared to see him now. Allison had come to the painful conclusion that there was no use spending time together because, sooner or later, their brief moments of harmony always ended. Being at odds with him made her miserable. More miserable than being near him, wanting him and knowing he would never be hers.

Nearing the post office, she noticed an unfamiliar man staring at her with peculiar intensity. She glanced away. When she looked that way again, he was gone.

Continuing on to the Wattses' homestead, the exercise helping to dispel her edginess, she let her mind drift to Norfolk and potential neighborhoods she should consider. Shane would not be pleased to know she was imagining a bedroom for Matilda done up in the little girl's favorite colors—yellow and white. With occasional rocks crunching beneath her boot soles, she jerked her chin up even though he wasn't around to see.

"It's my life," she announced to the vacant lane. Throwing out her arms, she startled a pair of pretty deep-blue and brown birds. "He has no say in what I do."

The instant the words left her mouth, she experienced misgivings. In the twins' case, that was so, she supposed. But Shane was in charge of finding Matilda a permanent home. She had huge doubts he'd agree to let her take Matilda in. He'd assume she couldn't provide enough love and attention for a third child. Well, he was wrong. Just like he was wrong about his potential as a spouse and father.

Allison didn't hear the stranger's approach. One minute she was walking along, lost in thought, and the next he loomed large in her path.

She stopped short, a cry slipping through her parted lips. "Who are you?"

It was the middle of the day. Surely he didn't have evil intentions...but they were alone here, nothing but trees and wildlife around for miles.

Beneath his battered hat, his hazel eyes burned with anger and some other emotion she couldn't pinpoint. "The father of the babies you stole."

Her stomach dropped to her toes. "Clyde Whitaker?"

He was young. She should've expected it, knowing Letty's age, but he was fresh-faced, clean-shaven and handsome in a mountain-man sort of way. Far different from his unkempt father.

"I've been watching you. Waiting for a chance to get you alone."

Unease lodged in her chest. "That was you at the post office."

"I wanna see my kids," he scraped out. Feet planted wide, he towered over her.

Nodding, she managed, "Of course. Come to the house anytime." Scooting to the right, she made to walk past him. "They're likely napping, but you could wait with Fenton—"

He seized her arm. "I want to see them without any nosy onlookers, understand?"

Annoyance sparked inside. "That may be difficult, considering Fenton is their great-grandfather and he's practically raised them."

Clyde scowled and lifted his fingers from her flesh. "Meet me at the old Lowell gristmill tomorrow afternoon.

It's not far from the Wattses' place. A mile at most." He gave her the directions. "Three o'clock."

"Why would I do that?"

Anguish surged in his gaze. For a moment, his hard attitude slipped, and she glimpsed a vulnerable young man wrestling with grief. Then he clenched his fists. "Because, Miss Ashworth, in the eyes of the law, those are my kids. Not yours."

She stiffened. His implication was clear. "Can you give them the life they deserve? One that Letty would approve of?"

His mouth tightened. "If you don't let me see them—alone—you won't be leaving Tennessee with them. Not without a fight. Is that what you want for them?"

"No," she whispered.

"Lowell's gristmill," he repeated. "And make sure your good friend the sheriff stays home, you hear?"

Pivoting, he loped toward the woods.

Allison didn't linger to watch him disappear. Upset, she hurried home, needing to see the twins and reassure herself they were okay. Fenton and Matilda looked up in surprise when she burst through the door.

He lumbered up from the sofa. "Everything all right?"

"Yes." Affecting nonchalance, she deliberately smoothed the folds of her dress. "Everything is peachy. I, uh, was in need of a bit of exercise." Pointing to the stairs, she said, "The twins asleep?"

Matilda nodded, her gaze bouncing from Allison to Fenton. "I looked in on them five minutes ago."

Allison rubbed her hands together. "Thank you, Matilda. You're a devoted helper."

Avoiding Fenton's narrowed gaze, she drifted to the stairs. "Well, I think I'll go and rest a bit, as well."

She tiptoed into the bedroom she shared with the twins and spent several minutes soaking in their sweet, innocent faces relaxed in sleep. Clyde's threat still rang in her ears. If she didn't do as he wished, he was going to take them away. It was a risk she wasn't willing to take.

Chapter Twenty-Four

Three days until Christmas. In a normal year, Allison would be shopping for last-minute gifts and preparing for her trio's annual church performance of assorted carols. The level of excitement in the house would be palpable. The children weren't the only ones impatient for December 25 to arrive. The estate staff looked forward to the presents she and Clarissa chose for them—unique and specific to each person—and spending Christmas Day with their families.

A pang of homesickness hit her. Dismissing it, she finished bundling Izzy and Charlie into their gear and carried them to the living room below.

Fenton reentered the house, his hat low over his eyes and coat collar pulled up to shield his neck. *He could use a new scarf,* she thought inanely. *A useful Christmas gift.*

"Sure you don't want me to keep 'em here?"

"They've been cooped up too long." She fastened her green cloak's buttons with shaky fingers. Perspiration dampened her nape. "The sun's shining, and it's warmer today than it has been. A change of scenery will do them good."

"I don't mind manning the wagon for ya."

"I've driven plenty of buggies around Norfolk's busy streets. I can handle these mountain lanes."

Matilda descended the stairs. In spite of Allison's anxiety, she registered the girl's healthy color and the slight difference in the fullness of her cheeks. Regular meals were doing wonders for her. While her physical condition was improving, the uncertainty of her future meant her emotional state remained fragile. As soon as Allison had handled Clyde—*if* she managed that—she would speak to Shane. Enough delaying. Matilda needed a solution.

"Can I go with you?" She slid the locket between her two fingers back and forth on its chain.

Aware of the mantel clock's ticking, Allison went to her and squeezed her shoulder. "Not this time, sweetie." Seeing the crestfallen look Matilda tried to hide, she said, "I have an idea. Why don't you and I go to town one afternoon before Christmas?" Bending at the waist, she whispered, "We'll pick out something special for Fenton."

Interest leaped to life. "And for the sheriff?"

Straightening, she nodded. "Sure."

She tied her bonnet's strings into a neat bow and scooped Charlie into her arms.

Countless times in the hours since their isolated encounter, she'd considered seeking out Shane. But Clyde had insisted she come alone. No telling how he'd react if she flouted his wishes.

"Would you mind bringing Izzy outside?"

Fenton complied, following her into the yard and placing Izzy in one of the makeshift cradles, long boxes made comfy with a nest of blankets. Allison situated Charlie, leaning down to give him a quick kiss on his velvet-soft cheek. Her throat was so thick she could hardly breathe. What if Clyde decided he wanted them for himself?

In those brief moments in his presence, she'd sensed there was goodness in him not present in his father. Working on a daily basis with people from all sorts of backgrounds had helped her develop discernment. She had to trust he simply wished to see that his children were all right.

Besides, there had to be something redeemable in him if Letty had loved him. She'd sought him out before and after the twins' birth. No way would the young mother have done that if she'd feared for her or her children's safety.

Pulse racing, she rounded the bed and, lodging her boot atop the wheel, climbed onto the seat and gathered the reins.

Fenton bid her goodbye. Matilda emerged from the house and latched on to a porch post. Allison waved and managed a tight smile.

The babies were quiet as the wagon rolled along the lane. Their stomachs full of warm milk and grits, they would likely drift to sleep before she reached the appointed meeting spot.

It wasn't long before the abandoned, overgrown gristmill came into view. At the sight of the lone figure pacing a line into the grass, she started to whip the horses around and flee. Instead, she eased them to a stop and waited.

Muscle jumping in his jaw, Clyde strode forward, hazel gaze wary. "You alone?"

She jerked a nod.

He craned his neck toward the bed. "Are they with you?"

"Yes."

When he started that way, she scrambled down and blocked his path.

Shame dawned in his green-brown gaze. "You don't trust me. I understand. But I promise I'm not a threat to you or my children. They're my flesh and blood. I'd never hurt them. I simply need to see them. Just once."

Convinced his earnestness was sincere, Allison stepped aside.

He walked to the rear of the bed. She followed on his heels and was afforded an unobstructed view of the raw emotion passing over Clyde's attractive features. His throat convulsed. Gingerly lifting a still-awake Charlie from his makeshift crib, he tucked him against his chest and peered intently into his face.

"Hey, little man. You look like your momma, you know that?" His voice cracked and, burying his face in Charlie's wispy hair, he exhaled a shuddery breath.

Allison's anxiety diminished. In fact, she felt as if she were intruding on a personal moment between father and son.

"He's a good baby," she said unnecessarily. "They both are."

Clyde's eyes were wet when he lifted his head. Reaching out, he fingered one of Izzy's curls. She blinked up at him.

His large, tanned hand anchored Charlie against his chest. Continuing to caress Izzy's hair, he scraped out, "I should've been there for her. For them."

Allison was quiet. A hawk soared in a circular pattern overhead, its cry shrill. "Why weren't you?"

His features hardened. He started to put Charlie back in his bed. When the baby fussed, Clyde shot her an uneasy glance. "I wanna hold my daughter."

"Give Charlie to me." He passed his son awkwardly to her and picked up Izzy. Still too young to be wary of strangers, the infant swatted his cheek with her chubby hand and let loose a stream of gibberish. A rumble of laughter shook his chest. "You take after your momma, don't ya, little one?"

Allison's heart was torn. Anyone could see the man had regrets, and his fascination with his offspring was undeniable. But what did that mean for her and the twins' future? No matter what Shane said, if Clyde truly wanted to raise his children, no judge would deny him that.

"They look healthy," he said, looking to her for confirmation.

Shifting Charlie onto her other shoulder, she nodded. "They are."

"You probably won't believe me, but I loved Letty. I wanted to marry her."

"Based on your behavior, it is difficult to believe."

His expression could only be described as tormented. "We had no place to go. Her grandpa despised me. And my parents...they never approved of her. They insisted she was trying to trap me. I should've stood up to my pa. If I had a chance to do it over again, I would," he said fiercely.

Allison reminded herself of his youth. He and Letty had been engaged in a forbidden relationship. Without family support and the means to sustain themselves in the face of an unplanned pregnancy, their options must've seemed nonexistent.

He hugged his daughter closer. "I should've tried harder to convince her to run off with me."

"You were willing to leave your home?" Shock punched through her. She'd assumed he shared his father's views.

"Wasn't sure how I'd earn enough to support a family, but I knew I wanted to be with her. But she wouldn't leave her grandpa." Unhappiness tugged at his mouth. "I got angry. I accused her of not loving me enough. We argued, and I told her to leave me alone."

Hurting for a girl she'd never met, Allison said, "What about when she came to see you after the birth? You refused to even meet the twins."

"What?" Astonishment mingled with denial. "No. She didn't do that."

"Fenton told me. He has no reason to lie," she said gently.

Shaking his head, he put Izzy in her bed and stalked into the field. Ripping off his hat, he put it over his face and suddenly his shoulders were quaking. Tears welled in

Allison's eyes. She faced the other direction to give him privacy. Gentry was behind this. He had to be.

Charlie plucked at the cluster of blossoms on her bonnet. Dislodging his fingers, she put his hand to her lips and kissed his fingers. He smiled and babbled. Her heart fissured. There was so much more to this story than she'd imagined. The players were flawed, three-dimensional humans with real feelings. Both Clyde and Letty had made mistakes. Neither were blameless.

Clyde wasn't the evil blackguard she'd made him out to be.

Many minutes passed before his muted sobs ceased. When he returned to the wagon, he refused to meet her gaze. His skin was mottled.

"I've got matters to tend to at home." His hands balled into fists. "Once that's settled, I'll come to the Wattses'. You and I have decisions to make."

Momentous, painful decisions. Allison desperately wanted to ask him exactly what he intended to do. She refrained. This wasn't the time.

She prayed he'd visit her soon, because she wasn't sure how long she could wait and wonder and imagine the worst without losing her mind.

"You're gonna wear a hole in the floor." Pausing in his Bible reading, one finger marking his spot on the page, Fenton shot Shane a resigned glance.

Matilda sat cross-legged at the foot of the tree, playing with a set of paper cutout dolls she'd crafted from Allison's decorative paper scraps. He'd known something was amiss the moment she entered his office. Matilda didn't like the jail and wouldn't have come unless something big was troubling her. If she hadn't gone outside and seen the wagon turn in the opposite direction of town, he wouldn't have known to be concerned.

He crossed to the window for probably the fiftieth time. "If she's not home in ten minutes, I'm going to ride through these mountains and knock on every single door until I find her."

Starting with the Whitakers. His well-honed instincts told him Gentry or Clyde had something to do with her prolonged absence. What other reason would she have had to mislead Fenton and Matilda?

Staring out at the desolate landscape, he worked to contain the fear eroding his composure. Panic was there beneath the fear, waiting for him to weaken. He'd dealt with thieves, kidnappers and murderers. He'd even come close to meeting his Maker a time or two. None of that compared to what he was experiencing now. This past hour had been the longest of his life. If anything happened to her—

He bowed his head, his fingers digging into the windowsill. *I love her, God. So much that it hurts to look at her sometimes. I beg You to preserve her life. Keep her safe. Keep the twins from harm.*

Pivoting, he strode for his duster and Stetson. "I can't wait around any longer."

"How do you know where to start?"

"Gentry's will be my first stop." Anything was better than staying here and allowing his mind to catalog every single scenario.

"Maybe you should take your deputy with you."

"No time."

Temperatures in the high forties swirled around him as he pulled open the door. A blue jay fluttered into flight, taking refuge in the maple's high branches. The indistinct jingle of harnesses stopped him in his tracks. Squinting down the lane, he waited, heart hammering out an impatient rhythm. *Please be her. Please—*

At long last, the team and wagon came into view. Calling the news to Fenton, he bounded into the yard, his gaze pinned to the woman whose well-being meant more to him than his own life.

Beneath her bonnet's brim, Allison's features were drawn and pale. The evidence of her tears tightened his gut. She looked extremely fragile, an unusual sight that filled him with foreboding. As soon as she guided the team to a stop, he inspected the wagon's rear space, his shoulders loosening at the sight of the sleeping infants.

Helping her down, he asked Fenton and Matilda to carry the children inside. "Allison and I are going for a short stroll," he murmured to the older man. "We'll be inside in a few minutes."

"Take all the time you need." Fenton's concerned gray gaze tracked Allison, who hadn't uttered a single word.

Wrapping his arm protectively around her waist, he guided her to the side of the house.

"I know you're angry with me." She turned toward him, eyes shimmering with emotion. "I can't bear it right this minute, Shane—"

"Shh." Urging her against him, he traced her quivering lips with his finger. "Sweetheart, angry is the last thing I'm feeling."

He brushed her inviting mouth with his and exhaled soul-deep relief. Allie was safe and sound in his arms. *Safe.* That's all he could focus on for several long moments. Then he registered her arms snaking around his neck, her fingers knocking his hat to the ground and whispering through his hair, the extraordinary sweetness of her kiss as she wriggled closer.

Joy exploded in his chest. What he felt for her was unlike anything he'd ever known…innocent and hopeful and noble. This love made him forget, if only for a little while, the nightmares dominating his past.

He skimmed her spine in search of the stray tendrils along her nape. If he had his way, he'd untie the ribbons beneath her chin and expose her flaxen hair to his exploration. But it was cold. And he needed to find out what had transpired to upset her so.

Trailing his fingers beneath her ears, over the ribbons and along her cheekbones, he registered her shiver as he eased the kiss to lingering, featherlight sweeps against her lips.

She murmured his name before lifting her head. Her happy gaze was tempered with a hint of perplexity. Wasn't hard to guess that she was searching for an indication from him that this embrace was significant, that it meant he had forever on his mind.

The joy he'd experienced minutes before fizzled out like firecrackers' ashes flickering to the earth.

That he loved her didn't matter. Didn't cancel out his lacking formative years. What mattered was that he *would* fail her. He had no doubt of that.

Sliding his hands along her sleeves, he gently disengaged her arms and, bringing her hands to his mouth, kissed each one in turn.

"Tell me what happened, Allison," he urged. "Where did you go? Why didn't you come to me for help?"

Chapter Twenty-Five

The resignation in Shane's hooded eyes was unexpected. After the tender kiss they'd shared, it was the last thing she wished to see. Disappointment spiraled through her. Nothing had changed.

"What happened?" she repeated dully, the brief spurt of happiness fading. She curled her arms about her middle. "Clyde Whitaker happened."

His gaze sharpened. "He approached you?"

"Yesterday. On my way home from seeing George off."

Biting out an exclamation, he edged closer. "He didn't harm you, did he?" His worried gaze swept the length of her.

"He's not like his father. We were mistaken, Shane. Fenton was wrong about him." Turning toward the mountains, she relived Clyde's emotional outburst. She told him everything that had transpired at the abandoned gristmill. "He loved Letty and planned to marry her. They argued, and Gentry used that to drive them apart."

She found it difficult to fathom how any father could willingly hurt his child.

"Does he…" He remained behind her. "Does he intend to raise them?"

"I don't know." Her voice sounded small and vulnerable, bruised like her heart.

He urged her around to face him. The evidence of his turmoil deepened her worry. "I'll help in any way I can, Allie."

A fresh onslaught of tears clogged her throat. The situation was impossible. *Nothing is impossible with God, remember?*

I trust You, Father, but I see my dreams slipping away. Izzy and Charlie. Shane. Will I be returning to Virginia the same as I left? Alone?

"What are you thinking?" he said.

"Why did you kiss me?" she blurted.

His lids flared before a shutter descended, closing her out. Shaking his head, he bent to retrieve his hat.

"I know you, Shane Timmons." She refused to let him retreat. Getting into his space, she declared, "You wouldn't have crossed that line if you didn't care about me."

"Our relationship is the last thing you should be worrying about."

"You admit we have one?"

"We're friends." Flicking a stray blade of grass from the crown, he put his hat on and speared her with an enigmatic gaze. "You're right. I do care. Very much."

Hope sprung to life. She reached out to him. "Shane."

"It's not enough." He flinched away, and she caught a glimpse of his misery. "No matter what happens with the twins, you're going home to Norfolk," he bit out.

"I could stay here." Desperation forced the words from her lips.

Visibly agitated, he flung his arms wide. "I can't be the man you want me to be, Allison. Why can't you get that into your head?"

She wrapped her arms around his strong body. "You already are," she exclaimed against his chest. "You simply can't see it. Your view of yourself is warped. Please let go of the past."

Beneath her cheek, his heart raced. His muscles twitched. When his arms came around her, she thought he was relenting. But he set her apart from him.

"I'm never going to marry you." His chest heaved. "Do you hear me?"

Aching clear down to her soul, she bit down hard on her lip to keep from crying. She nodded.

"I want to hear you say the words." His fingers tightened on her shoulders. "Say it, Allie."

Her vision blurred. Why was he bent on torturing them both? "Y-you won't m-marry me."

Shane's features twisted. He bowed his head in defeat. Releasing her, he turned and left without another word, and her heart broke for the second time that day.

On Christmas Eve, Allison woke before dawn with a vague headache that had persisted for days. She'd lain in her bed the night before, staring at the rafters and yearning for a few hours of blissful, mind-numbing sleep. What she hadn't counted on was reality invading her dreams. While Shane had dominated them, Clyde had made an appearance, too. Both men had been upset with her, and she'd woken with a heavy spirit.

Pulling on her housecoat, she padded over to the cradles and, crouching down, listened for the reassuring sounds of their breathing. It was too dark to make out their faces, and she didn't want to light a lamp and risk disturbing them. Uncertainty her constant companion, she pressed her face into her hands and prayed yet again for answers. Clyde hadn't come that first day. Or the next. Yesterday she'd been convinced he'd appear.

Matilda and the children had picked up on her distress, despite her efforts to maintain a calm front. Matilda had retreated into subdued silence, and Izzy and Charlie had been fussy and refused to take their afternoon nap.

Drifting to the window, she pulled the curtain aside and soaked in the star-studded expanse. Was Shane warm in his bed, oblivious to the world around him? Was he, like her, having trouble sleeping? Or was he out there in the night somewhere, doing what lawmen do?

He'd left almost immediately after their excruciating exchange, stopping only to instruct Fenton to fetch him if Clyde showed up. What he was supposed to do if Clyde demanded she return his children, she didn't know.

The predawn hours were marked with tranquility. So when her peripheral vision registered movement, she clapped her hand over her mouth. Beneath the lone maple near the porch, a figure separated from the shadows. A single flame flared, and she recognized Clyde's youthful features.

Struggling into the first outfit her fingers encountered in the wardrobe, she tiptoed down the stairs and tugged her boots on, not bothering to lace them. Slipping outside, she winced as cold enveloped her. Allison marched across the yard.

"What do you think you're doing?" she whisper-shouted.

The flame had gone out, but she saw his body stiffen. "I, uh…"

"This is hardly appropriate." Folding her arms across her chest, she glared at him even though he wouldn't see the proof of her ire. She didn't have a younger sibling, but in that moment, she understood what it might be like to be a big sister. "Lurking around someone else's residence in the wee morning hours could get you shot!"

"No one was supposed to see me."

"Well, I did. You're fortunate I didn't scream the house down." Belatedly noticing the bundle at the tree's base, she softened her tone. "What's going on, Clyde?"

"I wanted to be near them," he admitted.

"You've been spying on me?"

He bristled. "They are *my* children."

Without her cloak, Allison was already chilled. The tips of her ears stung. "Let's go inside. I'll fix coffee."

After a long beat of silence, he nodded and gathered his belongings. Trying to be as quiet as possible, she led him through to the kitchen and lit several lamps before turning her attention to the stove. He paced behind her.

The kettle warming and cups set out, she said, "Why don't you have a seat?"

Another hesitation, and he sank into one of the chairs. Placing his hat on the one beside him, he smoothed his wavy, sandy blond hair. His eyes were the exact hue as Charlie's. Had he noticed how much his son favored him?

Joining him, she folded her hands in her lap. "I've been wondering what's been keeping you. Did you sort things with your father?"

Sliding his hands along his thighs, his upper lip curled. "There ain't no sorting things with him."

"I'm sorry to hear that." She noticed his ears and nose were bright pink, as were his cheeks. "Did you spend the night out there?"

"Not the whole night."

She raised an eyebrow.

He shrugged. "I've been here the past three evenings. Got here shortly after sunset and left after the last light went out in the house."

"What was different about tonight?"

"I don't know." Lashes sweeping down, he studied a spot on the floor. Odd how she couldn't find any of her initial dislike. Shane would probably think her naive, but she couldn't help it. She was sorry he'd endured heartache and had no chance to rectify past mistakes. Letty was gone. He had to live with his choices for the rest of his life.

Allison readied their coffee, thankful she at least knew how to do that much. Seated once again, Clyde accepted his with a grave nod.

His gaze met hers across the table. "You're from Virginia?"

"Yes. Norfolk."

"Guess you got a fancy house."

"It's true that I have the financial means to provide Izzy and Charlie with a comfortable life."

"I've been dirt poor my whole life," he mused, work-worn hands molded around the cup. "Don't see that changing."

"In my mind, love, guidance and emotional security are of far greater value."

Clyde studied her with open curiosity. "Why do you want to be their mother?"

"They've become precious to me." Allison had difficulty forming the right words, knowing he would weigh them, dissect her reasons. He hadn't made a decision yet, that much was obvious. "I've wanted a family…children… for many years. I've never been married, you see, so when I met those sweet babies in desperate need of a mother, I began to imagine myself in that role. As the days passed, they formed an attachment to me and I to them."

Blinking away the gathering tears, she angled her face away and plucked at the ends of her sleeves. Beyond the glass, dawn crept across the blue-black sky. Her entire body felt on edge, nerves stretched to their breaking point.

"Tell me about your life in Virginia."

Allison told him about her parents and George, her childhood and about Shane entering their world. She told him about her church, her friends, her charity work. She talked about her niece and nephews, too, hoping he'd see what a good life Izzy and Charlie could have.

Clyde quietly sipped his coffee, and she longed to read his mind.

"Letty would want her babies to grow up in a good home."

Her pulse skipped. Meeting his gaze once more, she soaked in his sorrow and the wish for a different outcome.

"You can provide that for them," he said gruffly. "But I can't let you take them away. I need to be a part of their life. For their momma's sake, I gotta be sure they're okay."

Her throat started to close up. "What are you saying?"

"You can raise them if you stay here."

Allison rose and, blindly dumping her mug's contents in the discard pail, gripped the counter's edge.

"You have a problem with that?"

"Not me." She envisioned Shane's reaction. How could they possibly coexist in this small town without making each other miserable? "I like Gatlinburg. I've made friends here."

"It's the sheriff, ain't it?" The chair legs scraped against the wood. He joined her at the counter. "I've seen you together. You don't think he'd like it if you stuck around?"

Unwilling to discuss Shane with him, she said, "If I stay, what role do you intend to play in their lives?"

"You wouldn't have to worry I'd take 'em back someday. I'll sign papers." His eyes darkened to midnight. Scraping his hand along his jaw, he said, "I can't give them the kind of life they deserve. Trust me, they don't want the Whitaker legacy. I just wanna know them, and I want them to know me."

"If someday I met someone I wished to marry, you'd have no say in my choice." While that was not likely, she had to make it clear he couldn't control her life.

His nostrils flared. "As long as the man you choose treats my kids right, I'm fine with that."

Allison touched his sleeve. "Spend the day with us."

"Huh?"

"I need time to consider everything. Besides, today is Christmas Eve. Do you have special plans?"

Anticipation flashed over his features. "What about Fenton?"

"He's a good man, Clyde. Give him a chance to get to know you."

He looked doubtful. "All right. I'll stay."

He'd rather be anywhere else but here.

The merry atmosphere inside the church clashed with his black mood. Adults talked and laughed together along the wooden pews. Near the front, Megan was attempting to corral the rambunctious children, while Lucian and their older kids were busy arranging the pageant props.

He'd never attended the Christmas Eve service before, and he wouldn't be here now if not for the reverend and Claude's insistence. What he wanted to do was hole up in his cabin and hibernate the whole winter long. If only he could sleep for months and wake up free of this constant, all-consuming pain and desolation, not to mention the burning anger he felt for himself, his faceless, coward of a father and his pathetic excuse for a mother.

He'd done the unthinkable. Instead of keeping his distance, he'd fallen in love with Allison. And, just as he'd feared, he'd wounded her. The memory of their last kiss and the destruction afterward kept him up nights. He was so sleep-deprived, he walked around town in a fog, his eyes gritty, his head pounding and his chest one huge, numb hole.

His gaze lit on the rough-hewn cradle filled with straw. This year, Christ's birth held a special significance. Jesus hadn't come to earth for everyone else *except* him. Shane was included in the ones He loved and wanted for His own.

I'm sorry, Lord. I realize my attitude isn't what it should

*be. Help me focus on You and Your priceless gift. And I
beg You, please prevent me from hurting Allison further.*

"Good-sized crowd tonight." Ben had moseyed over
to the far right corner where Shane stood alone, trying to
blend in with the shadows. Sconces lining the space's outer
walls provided the only light. "I don't see Allison, though.
She is coming, isn't she?"

Readjusting his gun belt to set lower on his hips, he bit
out, "I have no idea."

Ben's hearty chuckle sparked Shane's annoyance. "This
has been a satisfying holiday season, I must say."

He ran a finger around the inside of his shirt collar. His
suit coat wouldn't sit right on his shoulders. His waistband
felt awry. Shane was uncomfortable in his own skin.

"Aren't you going to ask why?" His deputy had dressed
up for the service, his unruly hair tamed into submission.

"Nope."

Shane focused once more on the rear alcove to his left,
unwillingly searching for Allison. Would she show? Or
would she stay away because she dreaded seeing him? He'd
feel even guiltier if he caused her to miss the highlight of
the season.

"I haven't had the opportunity to see you like this before." His green eyes danced. "For a while there, I suspected you weren't quite human. You were so controlled.
So perfect. Then Allison Ashworth came to town, and suddenly you developed normal emotions. Glad to see you're
like the rest of us common folk."

"Perfect? Me?"

Serious now, he said, "You're the finest lawman I've
ever known."

"I'm only the second one you've worked with."

"No need to compare you to anyone else. I aspire to
reach your standards. If I do, I know I've done my best for
the folks of this town."

Shane looked out over the crowd, not really seeing any one individual as he processed his deputy's praise. He hadn't known Ben saw him as someone to model himself after.

"You do a fine job," he said gruffly. "Proud to work with ya."

Ben's wide grin reappeared. "I appreciate that, boss."

Unused to doling out praise, he pushed off the wall and gestured to the exit. "I'm going to take a walk around outside."

"I'll keep an eye on things in here."

Shane strode to the alcove. Rounding the corner, he almost collided with Allison, who had Izzy in her arms.

"Sorry," he rushed out, steadying her with a hand at her elbow. Her light, tantalizing scent washed over him, making him ache clear down to his boot soles. Her hair was a shining braid-halo about her head, and she was wearing that cranberry outfit that made him think of snowy mornings and hot cocoa and marital bliss. "Wasn't watching where I was going…" He trailed off as his gaze intercepted the young man behind her. "Allison?"

"Clyde's here at my request," she said stiffly. "Be nice."

Clyde met Shane's glower with an unflinching perusal of his own. He looked too natural carrying Charlie. Didn't they look like the proper family?

"Let's find a seat, shall we?" Allison directed over her shoulder. Her wide green eyes swerved to him. "Would you mind, Sheriff?"

He realized he was blocking their way and had caused a line to form behind them. Stung by her distant manner, he edged back. *You brought this on yourself, Timmons.*

They walked past him. A small, mitten-encased hand slipped into his. Matilda smiled tentatively up at him. "It's Christmas Eve, Sheriff."

"That it is." He tapped her nose. "You must be getting anxious to open your gifts."

"There are four with my name on them!" Her eyes shone.

Allison had bought her another dress, he noted. This one was crafted of floaty, pristine white fabric and accented with a bright red sash about her waist. Her short hair had been combed to a high shine and adorned with a matching ribbon. She was flourishing in Allison's household.

"Any guesses what they might be?"

Her brow wrinkled. "I'm not sure. Maybe a new scarf or hat. Miss Allison likes pretty things."

His gaze involuntarily slid to the last pew nearest them. She and Clyde were engaged in what looked to be a serious discussion. Concern warred with the need to act. But she didn't seem to require his interference. Her lovely countenance exuded determination.

"Sheriff?"

"Hmm?"

"Know what I want most for Christmas?"

The hope in Matilda's eyes socked him in the gut. He'd failed her, just like he'd failed Allison. He'd allowed his worries over Allison and the twins to eclipse this little girl's very real and urgent need.

Tugging her aside, he crouched to her level. "I think I have an idea."

"I want to live with Allison and the twins."

Lord, give me wisdom. Gingerly smoothing a hank of hair behind her ear, he strove to reason with her. "Sweetheart, we've talked about this before."

She bounced with excitement. "Miss Allison's not going back to Virginia. She's gonna live right here. Mr. Whitaker asked her to stay in town, and she said yes."

His breath froze in his lungs. "Are you certain?"

"I overheard them talking this afternoon. Isn't it wonderful?"

Chapter Twenty-Six

Surely Matilda had misheard. As the congregation's voices lifted to the rafters in a reverent rendition of "Silent Night," Shane wasn't singing. His attention was on Allison and Clyde. Standing side by side, the babies in their arms, they appeared at ease in each other's company. A telling clue. They must've come to an agreement. Could it be marriage?

A roar of protest built inside him. He thrust his fingers through his hair, tugging at the ends. Allison was meant to marry for love. But if Clyde had issued an ultimatum, she wouldn't hesitate. She'd do it for Izzy and Charlie.

Shucking his suit jacket, he draped it over the hard-backed chair shoved against the back wall. It was roasting in the church's confines. He could find relief outside, but something kept him here. A penchant for torment, he supposed.

On Allison's other side, Matilda sang along, occasionally twisting around to look at him. Fenton was on the end, dapper in his black pants, white shirt and a bow tie that had to be a gift from Allison. Like Shane, the old man wasn't singing, but he looked content for someone who eschewed town life.

That was Allison's doing. The woman possessed an incredible ability to draw others in, to care and nurture and offer her whole self without asking for anything in return. In a few short weeks, she'd created a ragtag family, one he'd give anything to be a part of. *He* was supposed to be by her side, supporting her, loving her. Not Clyde. Not some faceless Norfolk businessman. Him.

The song ended, and the people resumed their seats. Clyde murmured something, and Allison smiled.

That smile pierced Shane's heart. How was he supposed to stand by and watch her hand her life and love over to another man? And if Matilda was mistaken, and Allison was planning to leave Tennessee, how could he survive her absence? Everything in him rebelled. He couldn't go back to his former way of living. Couldn't face that bleak existence.

He loved her. More than that, he needed her in his life. But after everything that had happened between them, would Allison be willing to give him a chance to show her how he felt?

Megan directed the children to take their places. As scores of other children had before them, they portrayed Mary and Joseph's welcoming of the Christ child, events that changed the course of mankind. His thoughts shifted to Jesus's purpose, His plan and, ultimately, His forgiveness.

Shane's father and mother had acted despicably. They hadn't sought forgiveness from their only child. But by withholding it, the only person he was harming was himself. What had a lifetime of resentment gained him? Fear and bitterness, that's what. The good people of Gatlinburg thought he was courageous, when, in fact, he was afraid of a lot of things. Not the usual things, like outlaws and violence, but things common to everyone—love, family, relationships.

I need Your help, Father. I want to let go of the past, but I can't do it alone.

He was still pacing and praying when the program

ended. Those in attendance started gathering their things, and he noticed Matilda had fallen asleep. Threading through those already making their way to the exit, he greeted Fenton and, ignoring Clyde, sought Allison's gaze.

The moment she saw him, her features grew guarded. Sadness filled him. He could only blame himself.

"Want me to carry her to the wagon?"

Shifting Izzy to her other shoulder, she glanced at the sleeping girl. "Yes, please."

While she and Clyde took the lead, Shane hung back with Fenton. Matilda was a slight weight in his arms.

He sensed Fenton's perusal as they traversed the grassy churchyard. "What's on your mind, son?"

His gaze glued to the couple yards ahead of them, he said, "Why didn't you send for me when Whitaker showed up?"

"He was there when I went down for breakfast this morning. She had it handled."

"She doesn't need me," he murmured without thinking.

"Allison is a strong woman, that's true. She can do a lot of things on her own. Still needs you, though."

Shane was accustomed to helping people in tangible ways—rebuilding after a fire, searching for lost possessions, getting injured folks to the doctor. While he was confident in his abilities as a lawman, this thing with Allison was different. He didn't know how to go about being one half of a relationship, whether it be as a suitor or fiancé or husband.

"Are they getting married?"

"Is that why you're walking around like a coonhound without his mate?" His eyes reflected amused shock. "The boy's nine years younger than her."

"He's a man, not a boy, and you know it. Plenty old enough to marry."

His amusement faded, and Shane knew he was thinking of his granddaughter. "As far as I know, he's given her permission to raise the twins. But she has to live here. I ain't heard no talk of marriage."

Shane fell silent as they neared the wagon, waiting until the babies were situated before settling Matilda in the back. Allison thanked him but offered nothing more.

Shane touched her arm. "We need to talk."

"You're right, we do. About Matilda's future."

"Among other things," he said. "Can I come over tomorrow?"

She hesitated. "Tomorrow's Christmas."

That she didn't wish to spend her most favorite day with him hurt. "The day after, then."

Her eyes went soft. "Do you have someone to spend Christmas with?"

"The O'Malleys."

"Good. I'm glad you won't be alone." Sincerity rang from her voice. "Good night, Shane."

Watching her climb onto the seat and ride off with her makeshift family, he felt like the loneliest man in the world.

"Merry Christmas, Allie."

"Thanks for including me, Allison."

Midafternoon on Christmas Day, hat in hand, Clyde's gaze swept the room a final time. The woolen scarf she'd given him—yet another gift meant for a friend in Norfolk and needed here instead—was wound about his neck. His humble surprise and gratitude over the simple gesture had brought tears to her eyes. He hadn't received much in the way of kindness in his home, she'd surmised. The decision to stay in Gatlinburg was the right one. Clyde's affection for his children was undeniable. After spending the past two days in his company, she had no doubt the twins would benefit from knowing their father.

After he'd gone, she began to pick up discarded ribbons

and strips of plain brown wrapping paper. The twins were asleep upstairs, worn out after a full day of being entertained by Clyde and Matilda. Matilda was in her room, likely enjoying the book Allison had bought her. While her reading proficiency needed improving, she seemed content to pore over the many drawings until Allison or Fenton had time to read the story to her.

Allison paused before the tree and fingered a popcorn strand, remembering the brief bursts of happiness she'd experienced with Shane. Making snow angels. Crafting paper ornaments. Sharing dessert and cocoa on a deserted mountainside.

They could have tons more moments together, if only...

She lowered her hand, despondency dimming the joy of the day. Allison had played the *if only* game most of her life, ever since a fourteen-year-old boy had arrived and stolen her heart. It had to stop. She had to accept what was and forget dreaming about a reality that wasn't going to materialize.

God had granted her dearest wish—a family of her own. That Shane wasn't included caused her great sorrow. It was something she was going to have learn to live with. Perhaps someday in the distant future she'd be able to walk down Main Street and greet him without her heart splintering into pieces.

Taking the stack of paper and ribbons into the dining room, she deposited everything in the corner and turned to the table laden with leftovers. Without Fenton, they would've feasted on bread and cheese for Christmas dinner.

Through the windows, she heard male voices. Thinking Clyde had lingered to speak to Fenton, she didn't bother to investigate. She had carried a stack of dishes into the kitchen when she heard a rap on the main door.

Hurrying through to the living room, she swung it open. "Did you forget something?"

"Hi, Allie." His husky voice washed over like warm caramel.

"Shane."

His tall frame filled her vision. Dressed more formally than usual, he had on his cream-colored Stetson, camel-hued suit coat and a navy vest and shirt that molded to his broad chest.

"I know you preferred that I wait until tomorrow, but I have gifts to deliver." He indicated the bulging pillowcase thrown over his shoulder.

"The shops aren't open today."

His mouth curved into a tentative smile. "I did my shopping early."

Flustered, she retreated. He entered, his gaze lingering but a moment before sliding away. His presence seemed to shrink the room as he lined the paper-wrapped gifts on the coffee table. She studied his suntanned, capable-looking hands and wished she could latch on and not let go.

She smoothed her hair and hoped there weren't bits of mashed potatoes in the strands. "Izzy and Charlie are asleep, but I can get Matilda for you. Fenton's in the barn."

"How about I go and get him while you find Matilda?"

There was an earnestness about him that threw her off-kilter. Allison couldn't pinpoint what exactly was different. His mouth was softer, the lines of tension that usually bracketed it gone, and his eyes were brighter.

She gave her head a little shake. *You're being fanciful. Perhaps he's merely had a good day visiting with his friends. It is Christmas, after all. No doubt it's one of the most relaxing days of the year for a lawman. Folks were busy feasting and celebrating.*

"All right. I'll meet you back here."

With a half grin, he nodded and let himself out. Why was he so lighthearted all of the sudden?

When Matilda saw Shane, she threw herself in his arms. "Merry Christmas, Sheriff!"

His face relaxed further into full-blown affection. Ruffling her hair, he murmured, "Merry Christmas, Matilda."

Allison fought off the emotions threatening to overwhelm her. Shane handed out the gifts. Matilda didn't hesitate to tear into hers. Fenton sat on the sofa, watching with obvious pleasure. Like the other adults, he'd grown fond of the little girl.

"Look what I got!" she exclaimed, showing off her assortment of peppermint sticks, hair ribbons and a set of marbles and jacks.

When he came to stand before Allison, he shot her a mock grimace. "What do you get the woman who has everything?"

Not everything, she wanted to protest. Opening the box, she gasped at the delicate garnet brooch nestled in creamy fabric.

"Do you like it?" he said, a furrow between his brows. "I couldn't decide between one that matched your eyes and this one. The red color put me in mind of Christmas, and I know how much you adore this time of year."

"It's exquisite." She removed it to get a closer look. "I'll treasure it. Thank you, Shane."

With a grave nod, he slipped his hands in his pockets, watching closely as she pinned it to her bodice.

"How does it look?"

"Perfect." But he wasn't looking at the jewelry. He was looking at *her*.

"Oh, I almost forgot." Allison brushed past him and retrieved those packages remaining beneath the tree. "These are for you," she told him.

Matilda crowded close as he opened them. He seemed pleased by the gifts—new gloves and a shaving set—and touched that they'd thought of him.

When he saw what was inside the box from her, his smile widened in surprise. "These are great, Allie."

"When I saw your journal collection, I sent George a letter and asked him to bring the latest editions."

She'd also tasked her brother with choosing a leather wallet for Shane and engraving his initials on it. He took his time inspecting it, his blunt fingers running along the smooth leather. His azure gaze brushed hers. "Thank you."

"I'll pass your thanks on to George. He picked it out."

"I have another gift for you, but I'm afraid I left it at home." He spoke with his gaze downcast, his long lashes obscuring her view.

"Another one? The brooch is more than enough." And no doubt had cost him many weeks' earnings.

Neatly laying his gifts aside, he stood and addressed her, the teeniest bit of stiffness entering his tone. "Will you come with me to get it?"

"Now?"

"Yes. Please."

"I don't know...the twins will wake up soon—"

"I'll see to Izzy and Charlie." Fenton waved off her objection. "You don't wanna disappoint the sheriff on a day like today, do you?"

Having no choice but to agree, she went to gather her bonnet and cloak. Shane had her horse saddled by the time she went outside. He exuded a familiar tension, and she wondered at his strange mood. Perhaps this was a mistake. Spending time alone with him would only serve to intensify her misery.

She wouldn't address the matter today, but tomorrow they would have a serious discussion about how they would navigate life together in this small town.

The ride to his house was blessedly brief. Shane wasn't inclined to converse, and he seemed lost in a world she couldn't access. In the blustery December afternoon, his cabin struck her as isolated and sad.

The inside was unchanged. No decorations, not a single piece of greenery to denote the season. She tried to ignore the melancholy that arrowed through her.

Standing uncertainly in the middle of the chilly room, she waited as he tossed his gloves and hat on his bed. "Um, make yourself comfortable. You can hang your bonnet here." He indicated a single hook by the door. "Your cloak, too, if you'd like."

As she removed her bonnet and gloves, Shane went to the single hutch in the corner and riffled through the contents. Finally, he closed the cabinet doors and turned to her. She couldn't see what he held in his hand.

His chest expanded in a ragged sigh. "I'm not sure how to do this." Beneath his tan, he looked pale. "I don't know what to say. Or how to say it."

"You're making me nervous, Shane."

"Right. Sorry." Hurrying over, he took her hand and guided her to the lone cushioned chair. "How about you have a seat."

Bewildered, she sat and arranged her skirts and waited.

"I knew you were special the moment I met you. We were both very young, but I was drawn to you. In my dark, miserable world, you represented joy and light." He began to pace, gesturing as he spoke. "I did everything I could think of to push you away. And I succeeded."

"That didn't stop me from caring."

"I know," he said softly, his eyes in turmoil. "I regret every moment of pain I've ever caused you."

She bowed her head. Was this an elaborate attempt at an apology? "I think I should go."

"No!" His vehemence brought her gaze up. "Please stay, Allie. Hear me out."

Lips pressed together, she nodded and told herself that

all she needed to do was stay strong for the next few minutes and then make her escape.

His throat worked. "When I learned you were coming, I arrogantly thought I'd do what I'd done in the past. It worked then. Surely it would work again." His mouth curved into a self-deprecating smile. "I've been a first-rate idiot. It's a wonder you've put up with me."

Allison wanted to tell him none of that mattered. That the pain was worth it if it meant they could be together. More than anything, she wanted to tell him she loved him.

She didn't dare.

"Many others would've given up. They would've told me off. Refused to spare me a moment of their time." He went on his knees before her, drawing a gasp. "But not you. You're an amazing woman, Allie. I've never met anyone who could hold a candle to you."

Shane's gaze warm with ardent admiration, he took her hand and pressed something hard and cold into her palm. "I know I'm confusing you. Maybe this will explain my feelings."

Allison's breath caught. The plain gold circle was polished to a high shine. Not a single nick or scratch marred its surface. "It's a wedding band."

"Quinn wasn't thrilled that I interrupted his breakfast this morning, but when I explained my reasons, he graciously opened the store so I could pick this out."

Hope unfurled in her chest, but she needed to be sure. Needed to hear him voice his intentions. "This is the gift you couldn't wait to give me?"

"This has to be the worst marriage proposal in history." With a groan, he bent his head, his forehead resting against her knee.

She gingerly smoothed his hair, relishing the blondish-brown strands' silken softness. "Talk to me, Shane."

Straightening, he stared deep into her eyes, hiding nothing of what he was feeling. "It's hard to put this into words, but here it goes… I know that I admire your compassion and determination. I adore your smile. Your laughter makes my petty problems fade into the background, and your zest for life makes me realize I've been far too serious for too long. I need to learn to have fun, and you can teach me that." Reaching out, he reverently traced her cheek. "I know that I don't want to live another day without you. I want you to be my wife."

Her eyes filled with tears. "I never thought I'd hear you say those words."

He cupped her cheek. "Ah, sweetheart, I forgot to say the most important ones. I love you, Allison. I've loved you for a while… I just didn't know how to recognize it. If you'll let me, I'll spend the rest of our lives making up for the tears I've caused you. I'll spend my days finding ways to make you smile. What do you say?"

"I love you. I think I've loved you since that first day. But I have to be sure this is what you want. You won't be taking on a wife, but an entire family. Izzy and Charlie. Matilda. Life with us won't be easy. It'll be messy and demanding. I have to know you won't shut me out again. I couldn't take that."

His expression turned grave. "I don't know how to be a husband or father, but with God's help and yours, I'll give it everything I have. I'll need you to be honest with me and tell me if you sense that I'm withdrawing. I'm not adept at expressing my feelings, as you've seen, but I give you my solemn promise that I won't shut you out again."

Overwhelmed, feeling as if a lifetime of impossible wishes were being granted her, she laid her hand against his cheek. "Surely this is a dream."

"If you say yes, it'll be a dream come true."

"Yes! Yes, I'll marry you."

"Yes?" His clear blue eyes lit with happiness, and his

smile dispersed any lingering doubts. "Can I kiss you now?"

At her nod, he framed her face and kissed her with a tenderness that made her heart sing. The past no longer lingered between them. There were no questions, no reservations. Shane *loved* her. Holding him closer, she basked in his affection, amazed that he was hers.

He raised his head far sooner than she wanted. Grinning lazily, he made up for that by brushing sweet kisses along her cheek, temple and forehead.

"You're right," he murmured, his breath fanning her eyebrows. "This does feel like a dream."

"I always thought I'd have a spring wedding," she mused.

Lifting her hand, he kissed her knuckles. "I'd wait a lifetime for you, Allie."

"I've waited for you since I was twelve. Spring seems very far off." She brushed a stray lock of hair off his forehead. "Do you think we could find a place to live by February?"

"Sweetheart, if that's all that's holding us up, I'll find a place before the new year."

"I like the way you think." Allison laughed and pulled him close again.

Epilogue

One year later

Shane let himself into the farmhouse, sacks of roasted chestnuts warming his pockets. He hung up his Stetson and shrugged out of his coat. The place was quiet. It shouldn't be at this time of day, not with eighteen-month-old twins and a gregarious twelve-year-old around.

"Hello? Where is everybody?" he called, unfastening his gun belt. "I've got a treat to share."

The patter of little feet echoed along the upstairs hallway.

"Sheriff's home!" Matilda assisted her siblings down the stairs, her face bright with excitement. After a year of living with them, she still called him by his title. She treated him as if he were her pa, though, and that made him happy.

Giving her long braid a gentle tug, he chucked her chin. "How was your day?"

"Allison taught me how to make gingerbread," she announced proudly, eyes dancing.

"Did she now? I thought I smelled molasses when I walked in."

Not satisfied with the basics Fenton had passed on in

the early days of their marriage, his wife had appealed to the O'Malley women for further instruction. He had zero complaints about her cooking skills these days.

"Papa." Izzy and Charlie tugged on his pant legs, impatient for their daily greeting. One by one, he swung them up for hugs and sloppy kisses. Their giggles tickled his ears.

He'd never tire of this...being these kids' father and Allison's husband. Not every day was picture-perfect, but whose life was? Their home—the cozy white farmhouse with green trim in the shadow of the Smoky Mountains, the house where he'd fallen in love with Allie and the one he'd purchased from the Wattses—was marked with love and understanding and patience.

Fenton was a treasured part of their family and a regular visitor. His health had stabilized since he'd started getting more rest. The farmhand that Shane had hired went a long way in easing Fenton's burdens.

Clyde's visits were far less frequent. Unable to reconcile with his father, he'd worked odd jobs across the state of North Carolina, unable or unwilling to settle down. He'd kept his word, though. He'd given his permission for Shane and Allison to adopt the twins and was content to be known as a favorite, albeit distant, uncle.

Glancing toward the dining room, he wondered what was keeping Allison. It was her habit to welcome him along with the kids, and he was eager to see her.

"I got something for you." He placed the sacks in her hands.

"Chestnuts!" She inhaled deeply. "Thanks, Sheriff."

The twins crowded her in efforts to peer inside.

"Can I share with them?"

"Of course. You'll have to shell them, though. And make sure the children stay seated while they eat. No running around."

"Yes, sir."

He leaned down to ruffle Izzy's wild curls and tap Charlie on his button nose before they joined Matilda at the coffee table.

Whistling a favorite Christmas carol, he laid his sheriff's badge on the side table and walked to the foot of the stairs. "Allie?"

"I think she's in the kitchen," Matilda told him.

Passing the dining table decorated with a red-and-ivory cloth and topped with greenery and candles in shining holders, he entered the sweet-smelling kitchen. Trays of gingerbread men covered the work surface in the middle of the room. His wife was at the other counter drying dishes.

"Hello, beautiful." Putting a hand on her shoulder, he bent to kiss her cheek. The wetness there surprised him. "Hey." Tipping her chin up, he inspected her tearstained features with concern. She'd been distracted the past few weeks, which was unlike her. "What's the matter?" Another thought hit him. "George and Clarissa are still coming next month, right?"

"As far as I know, they are."

He exhaled. Allison was looking forward to seeing her family, especially her niece and nephews.

"Then why are you crying?"

"Don't mind me." Averting her face, she reached for a spoon to dry. "How was your day?" She dashed the moisture away, not meeting his gaze.

"Other than the fact Ben has broken another young lady's heart, and my lunch was interrupted by her tirade, it was rather uneventful."

"Hmm."

Shane's gaze widened. Allison shared his opinion about his deputy's disregard for the local ladies' finer feelings, and normally she would've demanded more information.

Gently taking the towel and spoon from her hands and laying them aside, he said, "Let's sit." Guiding her to the small table, he sat and pulled her down beside him, curving his arm around her shoulders. "Talk to me, Allie."

"I can't."

Something inside him froze. "You haven't had a problem telling me what's on your mind before." This past year of marriage had taught him so much. Together, they'd worked hard to be open and honest with each other. He trusted his wife as he'd trusted no one else.

"I'm afraid you're not going to be pleased with what I have to tell you." When she finally turned her face up to his, her green eyes shimmered and her lips trembled. "Our house is full. Our days are busy. The twins are into every-thing and only going to need more attention in the com-ing year. Matilda will need help with school reports and navigating friendships—"

"Allie." Cupping her cheek, he peered deep in her eyes. "I love you. I like that our life is messy and chaotic, because it means I'm not across town, alone in that cabin where the quiet was deafening. I chose this life with you, remember?"

The love she held for him surged in her eyes, and as always, it humbled him. Each and every day, he thanked God for giving him a second chance with this woman. He'd been blessed with what he'd always wanted—a fam-ily of his own.

"I love you, too. I—I don't know if you're ready, though... I mean, I know we talked about more kids, but—"

"More kids?" His heartbeat hammered in his ears.

Her gaze wide and hopeful, she bit her lower lip and nodded. "I've been tired lately. And sick to my stomach. I went to see the doctor today. He told me that I'm about eight weeks along."

Easing back, he examined her middle, stunned that his and Allie's baby was nestled there. "You don't look any different."

Her laugh was shaky. "That's all you have to say?"

Framing her face with his hands, he kissed her for long moments, emotion rising up within him. His eyes grew wet as he gently rubbed her middle. "This baby is as precious to me as you are."

Happiness wreathed her face. "Truly? You're fine with this?"

"Oh, sweetheart, I'm not fine. I'm awestruck. Over the moon. Pleased as punch." Kissing her again, he whispered, "And very, very blessed."

Circling her arms around his neck, Allison smiled, at last free of worry. "Wouldn't it be funny if we had twins?"

He shot her a look of mock horror. "If that's the case, Fenton is moving in with us."

She laughed, and Shane joined her. He was confident that whatever the future might bring, they'd walk through it together.

* * * * *

If you enjoyed THE SHERIFF'S CHRISTMAS TWINS, don't miss the rest of the SMOKY MOUNTAIN MATCHES *series.*

THE RELUCTANT OUTLAW
THE BRIDAL SWAP
THE GIFT OF FAMILY
"SMOKY MOUNTAIN CHRISTMAS"
HIS MOUNTAIN MISS
THE HUSBAND HUNT
MARRIED BY CHRISTMAS
FROM BOSS TO BRIDEGROOM
THE BACHELOR'S HOMECOMING
RECLAIMING HIS PAST
THE SHERIFF'S CHRISTMAS TWINS

Dear Reader,

I hope you enjoyed Shane's story. As the good sheriff has appeared in nearly all of my *Smoky Mountain Matches* books, I've lived with this character for several years. It's about time he got his own happy ending!

This was my first time writing about a hero with major doubts regarding God's love. While it's easy for Shane to believe in a divine Creator, he struggles to accept that God could truly care about him. His spiritual journey was a challenge to portray, and I pray I succeeded in meshing it seamlessly with his flourishing relationship with Allison.

For information about my other books, please visit my website www.karenkirst.com. You can find me on Facebook and on Twitter @KarenKirst. If you'd like to email me, my address is karenkirst@live.com. I'd love to hear from you!

Merry Christmas,
Karen Kirst

"There's the land office," Simon said, nodding to a whitewashed building ahead. He strode to it, shifted Nora's case under one arm and held the door open for her, then followed her inside with his brothers in his wake.

The long, narrow office was bisected by a counter. Chairs against the white-paneled walls told of lengthy waits, but today the only person in the room was a slender man behind the counter. He was shrugging into a coat as if getting ready to close up for the day.

Handing Nora's case to his brother John, Simon hurried forward. "I need to file a claim."

The fellow paused, eyed him and then glanced at Nora, who came to stand beside Simon. The clerk smoothed down his lank brown hair and stepped up to the counter. "Do you have the necessary application and fee?"

Simon drew out the ten-dollar fee, then pulled the papers from his coat and laid them on the counter. The clerk took his time reading them, glancing now and then at Nora, who bowed her head as if looking at the shoes peeping out from under her scalloped hem.

"And this is your wife?" he asked at last.

Simon nodded. "I brought witnesses to the fact, as required."

John and Levi stepped closer. The clerk's gaze returned to Nora. "Are you Mrs. Wallin?"

She glanced at Simon as if wondering the same thing, and for a moment he thought they were all doomed. Had she decided he wasn't the man she'd thought him? Had he married for nothing?

Nora turned and held out her hand to the clerk. "Yes, I'm Mrs. Simon Wallin. No need to wish me happy, for I find I have happiness to spare."

The clerk's smile appeared, brightening his lean face. "Mr. Wallin is one fortunate fellow." He turned to pull a heavy leather-bound book from his desk, thumped it down on the counter and opened it to a page to begin recording the claim.

Simon knew he ought to feel blessed indeed as he accepted the receipt from the clerk. He had just earned his family the farmland they so badly needed. The acreage would serve the Wallins for years to come and support the town that had been his father's dream. Yet something nagged at him, warned him that he had miscalculated.

He never miscalculated.

Don't miss
CONVENIENT CHRISTMAS WEDDING
by Regina Scott, available November 2016 wherever
Love Inspired® Historical books and ebooks are sold.

www.LoveInspired.com

LIHEXP1016